MAGDEBURG NOIR

By David Carrico

Magdeburg Noir Copyright © 2020 by David Carrico. All Rights Reserved.

All rights reserved. No part of this book may be reproduced in any form or by any electronic or mechanical means including information storage and retrieval systems, without permission in writing from the author. The only exception is by a reviewer, who may quote short excerpts in a review.

1632, Inc. and Eric Flint's Ring of Fire Press handles Digital Rights Management simply. We trust the **honor** of our readers.

Cover designed by Laura Givins

This book is a work of fiction. Names, characters, places, and incidents either are products of the author's imagination or are used fictitiously. Any resemblance to actual persons, living or dead, events, or locales is entirely coincidental.

David Carrico
Visit my website at https://davidcarricofiction.com/

Printed in the United States of America

First Printing: Jan 2020
1632, Inc. Eric Flint's Ring of Fire Press

ebook ISBN-13 978-1-948818-66-7
Trade paperback ISBN-13 978-1-948818-67-4

Prior Publication History

An earlier version of Lex Talionis appeared in The Grantville Gazette #75, copyright 2018

An earlier version of Apostate was serialized in The Grantville Gazette in Issues #83 and 84, copyright 2019

This is the first publication of If the Shoe Fits . . . .

DEDICATION

To Bjorn Hasseler

*Good friend, sterling editor, forthright critic and alpha reader, and all around great guy,
whose late-night message conversations had a great deal to do with the creation of these stories.
Thanks for years of friendship, and here's to many more.*

CONTENTS

LEX TALIONIS 1
Apostate 37
   Afterword 135
If the Shoe Fits 136
Chapter 1 137
Chapter 2 151
Chapter 3 167
Chapter 4 177
Chapter 5 187
Chapter 6 197
Chapter 7 205
Chapter 8 217
Chapter 9 225
Chapter 10 233
Chapter 11 241
Chapter 12 249
Chapter 13 259
Chapter 14 267
Chapter 15 273
Chapter 16 281
DRAMATIS PERSONAE 285

By David Carrico

LEX TALIONIS

Magdeburg
Early March, 1636

Marla Linder stopped. "What's that?" Her head tilted to one side.

"What?" her husband Franz Sylwester asked. He moved a couple of steps past her in the snow, then stopped and looked back. "What?"

Marla turned slowly, head still tilted, almost as if she was hunting something. After a few moments, she stopped. "That," she said, pointing toward a nearby door.

Franz gave her an 'are you jesting' look. "That's Walcha's Coffee Shop."

"Not that." She looked at him from under lowered eyebrows. "The music."

That caused Franz to close his mouth on the statement that was about to come out of it, and listen. After a moment, he could hear what Marla had evidently heard with no problem—a faint sound of guitar or lute music, apparently wafting out of Walcha's Coffee Shop. At that exact moment, the door opened for a patron of the shop to exit, and the music became louder. He still couldn't tell if it was guitar or lute, but whatever it was, it was being played by someone with at least some level of skill.

"I think I hear a cup of chocolate calling my name," Franz said with a grin.

"Ditto for a cup of coffee." Marla shivered. "C'mon."

Franz opened the door and ducked through the doorway after Marla entered. Walcha's was about half-full: not unusual for early afternoon. Anna, the server, waved at them after she set an order on a table, and Georg looked over his shoulder and grinned at them as he poured water into a coffee maker.

Franz waved back, but his attention was immediately drawn to the side of the room. Marla was drifting in that direction, and he followed. They settled at a table for two near where a man's head was bent over a down-time vihuela as he played it. At least, Franz assumed it was a man; legs were clad in trousers, shoulder-length disheveled hair hung about his downturned face, and large knobby-knuckled hands stuck out beyond short cuffs and moved so smoothly as to almost be caressing the instrument. Franz didn't recognize the music, but he did recognize the talent and craft. This was no tyro. For a street musician, this was rare skill.

Marla was focused on the performer with her usual intensity, so when Anna came by, Franz just murmured, "The usual." Anna responded by mouthing "Coffee and chocolate?" That got a nod from Franz before he turned his own attention back to the music.

The music didn't sound much like a structured piece. But about the time their drinks arrived, Franz decided it wasn't just idle doodling, either. So he sat and sipped his chocolate, listening to the musician but watching his wife. Marla was leaning forward a bit in her chair, eyes focused on the player, head slightly tilted to one side. Franz recognized this; this was her "acquisitive" mode, where something attracted her attention and she studied it intensively. He'd seen it before, especially with music. And he was glad to see it now, as it was one more sign that she was getting over and moving beyond the trauma and loss of the miscarriage of their daughter Alison back in October.

The music shifted, and Franz realized that what he was hearing was an improvisation, an extended variation on a theme. His own interest rose, and he became as focused as Marla, setting his cup down and resting his arms on the table.

The player's fingers began to move faster, bringing forth ripples of melody, of moving lines and parallel sounds, of brightness, evoking images of flowing water. Fingers danced, notes followed, up and down the neck of the vihuela, until a final ripple flowed up the neck to end with a single clear high tone singing from the last plucked string.

Still almost crouched over the vihuela, the player sat motionless for a long moment, until the last resonance of that last note faded from the air. Then the tension fled his body, and he slumped to the extent that it looked for a moment as if he would slide out of the chair. But then he took a deep breath, rested the butt end of the vihuela on his left thigh, leaned the neck of it against his shoulder, and wiped his hair out of his face with his right hand. A couple of the patrons tossed coins into a hat on the table as they walked out.

Marla started clapping. The performer's head jerked around toward her, eyes widened, obviously startled, maybe even a bit alarmed. Franz felt that was a bit odd. Most performers welcomed applause. But there, the man was relaxing, so maybe it was just surprise.

Now that he had a clear look at the man, Franz found himself a bit startled. The visage facing him was heavily lined, with a network of wrinkles, for all that the hair surrounding the face was uniformly dark. This was not a young man, not by anyone's standards, which might explain the skill that had been demonstrated.

Marla stopped her applause. The player embraced his instrument and inclined head and shoulders toward her. "My thanks, Frau . . ."

"I'm Marla Linder, and this is my husband, Franz Sylwester."

Franz's mouth quirked as the player's eyes got very wide and round again. "Not . . . *the* Marla Linder?"

Marla's eyebrows rose, and she looked over at Franz. "Is there another Marla Linder in Magdeburg?"

Franz grinned. "I believe you're the only one, dear heart."

She looked back at the player, and Franz could hear the laughter in her voice as she said, "Well, if I'm not *the* Marla Linder, I'm as good as you're going to get here in Magdeburg. There doesn't seem to be another one around. And you are . . ."

Franz couldn't see how the man's eyes could have gotten any wider, but it seemed to happen nonetheless. "I . . . uh . . . my name is Karl." He swallowed. "Karl Tralles."

Anna came by, and Franz pointed to their near-empty cups and at Karl. She nodded and moved on.

"Well, Karl," Marla continued, "you play a mean guitar."

Franz had to chuckle at the expression that came on Karl's face. "She's an up-timer," he interjected. "They have some unusual figures of speech. She means you play your instrument very well. Where are you from?"

"Ha . . . Hamburg," Karl replied, still hugging his vihuela.

"Cool." Marla beamed at Karl. "I don't think we've got anyone from Hamburg in our group, do we?" She looked at Franz.

He shook his head. "A couple from Hannover, but no one from Hamburg."

Anna arrived with their drinks, which paused the conversation for a moment. Tralles started to push his cup away, but before he could say anything, Franz said, "I'm buying. Drink up." He smiled, which seemed to put the other man more at ease, as he relaxed his stranglehold on his vihuela and lifted his cup to his lips. When he lowered it, Franz almost laughed at the sight of a bit of chocolate foam on his upper lip.

After burying his laugh in his own mug of chocolate, Franz picked up the thread of conversation. "That was a nice piece you just played. Yours or someone else's?"

"Oh, I didn't write that," Karl protested. "That started as a violin solo piece by Master Johann Schop, the best composer in Hamburg." His eyebrows lowered for a moment, as if thinking, then went back to normal. "In that part of the Germanies, for that matter."

"Schop, Schop," Marla repeated. "Don't think I've heard of him. We need to see if Master Schütz knows him."

"I heard of him when I was in Mainz," Franz replied. "We never played anything by him, though."

"He does very nice work for strings," Tralles said. "Anyway, I learned the piece while I was a violinist in the city players, then started trying to adapt it for the vihuela."

"You play violin?" Marla said, then snorted. "That was silly of me. You just said you did. I think what I meant to say was, are you as good with the violin as you are with that?" She pointed at the vihuela.

"I used to be better," Tralles said. "Somewhat out of practice now. But I love the vihuela more."

"Why?" Franz asked.

"I can get more voices than I can with a violin, even with a slack bow, never mind an Italian-style bow. The most I can get on a violin is three. I can get four or more on the vihuela, so it makes more complex music, more voices, more layers and complexity." A grin appeared on his face that lit it up. "I love that."

"True," Franz said with a nod, "but if that's your desire, why not an organ, or even a clavier?"

"Or piano," Marla added.

"Hard to carry on your back," Tralles' grin reappeared.

"Also true." Franz responded in kind. "So why are you here in Magdeburg?"

Tralles grimaced. "Hamburg got a new Kappellmeister, and . . ." He said nothing more, but Franz could read the rest of the story in his face. The new music leader had booted Tralles from the band of musicians for whatever reason—maybe his age—and he was left with no place, and being a musician, doubtless had little money.

"And so you came here?" Marla asked quietly.

Tralles nodded. After a moment, he found his voice again. "And so I came to Magdeburg. After hearing the stories of the music, after hearing the Trommler record of Do You Hear the People Sing, where else would I go?" He looked at Marla. "But I didn't expect to meet you . . . or at least, not like this."

"What did you expect?" Marla grinned at him.

"To see you in palaces, in mansions, in fancy carriages driving by. Not walking the streets or sitting in . . ." He looked around. ". . . coffee shops."

Marla laughed, silver voice flashing above the background noise of mingled conversations around them. "Oh, Karl, you set too high a standard for me. I'm just another musician. I walk in the same mud and slush and snow and dirt you walk in. I eat the same food and drink the same wine as you do. I have to please patrons just like you do."

Franz's eyebrows twitched for a moment as he saw Tralles waver in his chair. It dawned on him it was quite possible that the man hadn't eaten well in a long time. He looked around, saw Anna by Georg's counter, stood and made his way there.

"You need something, Franz?" Georg asked.

"You have any soup today, and some plain bread?"

"Ja, some cabbage soup and both wheat and barley rolls."

"Three bowls of the soup, then, and three wheat rolls. Our friend hasn't eaten in a while."

"Ah. Say no more."

Franz returned to the table and listened as Marla and Tralles discussed the stringing and tuning of the vihuela. As he suspected, four courses of paired octave strings, common enough in the down-time. Luthiers had yet to standardize on the six-string guitar model, although Franz suspected that the samples of up-time instruments that came back through the Ring of Fire would speed that process up. He listened, sipping on his cooling chocolate, as they talked about that very thing. Marla's brother had played guitar, so she was more than familiar with the history of the instrument.

"You need to go to Grantville," she said, as Anna appeared with a tray, "and spend some time with Atwood Cochran. He'll show you the modern designs and teach you the techniques to play them." Anna started setting bowls of soup out and small plates with rolls. Tralles looked confused and started to push his away.

"Eat it," Franz said, picking up his spoon. "You need it."

"I can't pay for it."

"I'm buying. Eat it."

Now Tralles looked distressed. "I can't pay you back."

"You don't have to. And before you tell me that you can't take it, the up-timers have this concept called paying it forward, where if you get help from someone today but can't pay them back right away, you just give similar help to someone who needs it in the future. There were those who fed me in my poorest days. I'm paying it forward today. You'll do it for someone else before long." Marla nodded as she took her spoon in hand.

Tralles didn't look convinced but took up his spoon and began eating. It took some little while, as he spooned the soup up slowly and with care, pausing to take small bites of the roll which he chewed thoroughly. That spoke of previous experience with being undernourished. On the one hand, Franz was glad to see him not gorge himself to the point of triggering the inevitable vomiting. On the other hand, he was sorry that Tralles had had the experiences that had taught him that self-control. It was no fun to be brought to that point of hunger.

"So where are you staying tonight, Karl?" Marla asked.

He ducked his head for a moment. "They said I could sleep here tonight if I played for the patrons this evening."

"Take them up on it," Franz advised. "They're good people, and they'll let you stay a night or two. But you'll have to develop some other places to play as well."

"Try The Green Horse Tavern," Marla said. "It's just down the street here. Tell Ernst, the owner, that I sent you. He should give you at least a couple of nights to perform, and maybe let you sleep in the common room after everyone leaves at night."

Tralles nodded. "Thank you, Frau Linder."

"Call me Marla," she said with a smile. She pushed back her sleeve and looked at her watch. "We need to be someplace else."

Franz stood. "Leave word here where you will be," he said to Tralles. "We'll catch up with you."

"Good luck," Marla said. She patted Tralles on the shoulder, then led the way out. Franz lifted a hand in farewell and followed his wife. He could hear the music again as he stepped through the door.

Half a block down the street, Marla muttered, "I really don't care for cabbage soup."

Franz chuckled. "It's good for you, and it was all they had. And if we were going to get him to eat it . . ."

"We had to eat it with him. Got it." A few steps farther on, she said, "We need to keep track of Karl. I don't want to lose him. He's too good to let drift away. I want him to go to Grantville and study with Atwood like that Italian guy did. We need a really good guitarist here in Magdeburg."

"And for that matter, I want to hear what music he knows. And maybe get a connection to Master Schop. It would be good to have someone in that part of the Germanies to correspond with and send news and music both ways."

"Yep. Remind me to check with Master Heinrich to see if he's corresponded with the man. That would make it easier."

"Right. Now, we're almost late to the Academy."

"Step it up, then," she said with a grin. "You're the one doing all the talking."

And Franz found he had to step it up indeed to keep up with her as she headed toward the Royal Academy of Music.

❇ ❇ ❇

Over the next week or so, Marla shepherded Karl's career in Magdeburg, guiding him from taverns to restaurants to inns. The pinnacle of the experience was the evening she had him sit in with her friends when she sang at The Green Horse Tavern. Her friends were great to play with. They'd feed him the key for each song and let him just play chords and support the music. As the night went along, he got the feel for the music and began to elaborate more, adding obbligatos to later verses and somewhat flashy runs to choruses. He caught grins and nods from some of the other musicians, especially Franz and his close friend Isaac.

The highlight of the evening came when Marla offered Karl an opportunity to perform a song of his own. He hadn't known she was going to do that, but he was an experienced performer so he had a song tucked away in the back of his mind. Shaking his right hand to limber it up a bit, he stepped forward and, without saying a word, started playing a sprightly dance tune. It was in a triplet meter and literally seemed to bounce. He saw smiles around the room and heads bobbing and hands waving as he played it through three times, ending with a flourish after repeating the chorus.

The rest of the evening passed in a blur—song after song after song. He was caught up in the rush of the music; caught up in the heat of it, playing with fervor, smiling and laughing, shaking the sweat-soaked hair out of his eyes. For a brief moment a thought crossed his mind that this was the most he had enjoyed himself in months, maybe years. Definitely since before he had left Hamburg. And everyone around him seemed to see that, as he got smile after smile from them all, especially Marla.

The evening drew to a close with a rambunctious version of Tim Finnegan's Wake, which left them all limp and laughing when it was done—all but Marla, that is. From what Karl could see, she was ready for another round. She looked around at the rest of them, though, and obviously decided to have mercy on them, for she waved her hand over her head and called out, "Good night! See you next time!"

Karl was almost panting, and it took him a long moment to get his vihuela put back in its bag. Just as he got it slung over his shoulder, Franz walked over and passed him some USE dollars folded over. "Your share."

"Thanks," Karl responded as he riffled the money with recently acquired expertise, and felt his eyebrows rise at the amount contained in the bundle.

"Ernst the owner threw in a little extra at the end of the night," Franz said with a grin. "Even with Marla leading we don't ordinarily pull in that much."

"Thanks," Karl repeated.

"You remember you're staying with us tonight?"

"Ja."

"You ready to leave?"

Karl shook his head. "I want to have a mug of beer and let my mind slow down first."

"Okay. You remember how to get there?"

"Ja."

"Don't take too long. Word is the weather is looking nasty outside."

"How can you tell?" Karl asked. "It's pitch dark out."

Franz laughed. "Some of the latest customers say they've been seeing a few snowflakes."

Karl shivered. "Right. That qualifies as nasty. I won't be long."

Franz clapped him on the shoulder, then joined Marla by the door. She waved at Karl. He waved back and watched as they left.

Karl slumped at a table and lifted a hand as a server went by. A few moments later a mug of beer landed in front of him, and he passed over a couple of pfennigs. And for the next little while, he took slow sips of the beer while he simply basked in what had happened earlier that night. It had been a long time since he had been able to play with other musicians just for the joy of it. And never had he been able to play with a group like the players who surrounded Marla Linder. He was as close to heaven in the afterglow of the night as he had ever been or likely ever would be while he walked the earth.

Karl reached the bottom of the mug at last, looked around, and realized he was one of the last three customers. Ernst was there that night behind the bar counter. He looked at Karl, didn't say anything, didn't change his expression, but Karl could tell he wasn't getting another beer that night. So he stood, waved a hand at Ernst and the two servers, and left the tavern, still feeling the warmth of the evening.

By David Carrico

That lasted for about one breath after he closed the door behind himself. It was an early March night in one of the coldest years in recent memory, and the snow had thickened from the few desultory particles reported earlier in the evening to a steady fall of thick flakes. The street lamp not far away from the tavern's door was partially obscured. Karl shivered, pulled his collar up around his neck, stuck his hands in his pockets, and started trudging through the accumulating snow.

After some time, Karl shook off the cold and realized that nothing around him looked familiar. Somehow he must have missed the turn-off of the street that would have taken him into the Neustadt. And now that he thought about it, he kind of remembered crossing the Big Ditch, which would mean he was in the Altstadt part of Magdeburg. But where?

The snow was getting thicker. Karl turned around in a full circle. He couldn't see much at all. And he had no idea where he was. But there . . . there was a light visible through the snowfall. He headed that direction. It resolved into a torch starting to gutter beside a low door. It must be a tavern, Karl decided. He pulled the door open and ducked in.

Karl shook his head to dislodge some of the snow that had settled on his hat and hair. Afterward, he looked up to see every eye in the tavern staring at him. The warmth in those gazes was on a level with the temperature of the air outside the door.

"Um-mm," he stuttered, "I . . . I lost my way in the snow. I need to get to the Neustadt. Can anyone here help me?"

The man behind the bare board counter snorted, then growled, "Go out the door, turn left, next street go left, go to the big street before the wall. That's Gustavstrasse. Turn right. Once you're across the bridge, you're in the Neustadt."

And from what Karl remembered, that would be by the Royal Opera Hall and the Royal Academy Music. He thought he could find Franz and Marla's house from there. "Um, thanks."

The guy behind the counter turned away. Everyone else still stared at Karl, cold-eyed. He suppressed a shiver and ducked back through the door.

Once outside, he followed the directions and started slogging back the way he'd come—he hoped. The snow fall was still thick. He could make out the nearest buildings, but not much beyond that in the blurry darkness. There was the corner, so he took the turn. Karl could see his earlier footprints in the snow, so that helped him make sure he was at least retracing his steps . . . although, as thick and as rapidly as the snow was falling, he wasn't sure how long he would be able to make them out.

Karl shivered, fisting his hands inside his pockets. It was cold and felt like it was getting colder. His feet were so cold they hurt. Cold, dark, trudging through the snow, he really hoped he could find Franz and Marla's house before too long.

"Hey!"

Karl's head jerked around at the call from behind him, but he kept moving.

"Hey! Wait for me, man! I can help you." At that, Karl slowed down. A dimly seen, almost just sensed, bulk began to manifest through the snow, until a broad-shouldered man came up beside him. "I'm glad I caught up to you. I was back in the Chain . . ."

"The Chain?" Karl asked.

"The tavern back there. I was there when you came in, but you left before I could get up and speak to you." The man's voice was a nasal tenor, penetrating, that in other circumstances would have grated horribly on Karl's ear. At the moment, maybe because he was so cold, Karl didn't care. "I was ready to leave anyway, so I can help you get where you want to go, and if you want to give me the price of a mug of beer, I'd be thankful for it."

"Do you know where Frau Marla Linder and Franz Sylwester live?"

The man snorted. Karl couldn't see his face, but he had the impression that the man was grinning. "Everyone knows where Frau Marla lives. That where you need to go?"

"Yes, please. And I'll give you a beer's price when I'm there."

"Done and done," the other man said. "So, keep heading the way you were heading." They faced up the street and started walking again. After a few steps, the other man said, "You from around here?"

"No," Karl said. "I'm from Hamburg."

"Figured that," the other replied. "You don't sound like Magdeburg, and most folks here don't come to the Chain unless they have business there or they don't have any place else to go."

The other man's tone had gone flat, so Karl didn't think it was wise to say anything in response. He just kept putting one foot in front of another in the deepening snow.

"So, you're going to Frau Linder's house. You a musician, too?"

The other man's voice sounded back to normal, so Karl coughed to clear his throat, then said, "Ja."

"You been in town long?"

Karl started wondering at all the questions. Maybe the guy was just trying to be sociable, but it was starting to feel a bit odd. "Couple of weeks, maybe."

Two steps farther he felt the other man's hand on his arm. "Come on, let's go this way. It's a shortcut that will save you almost a quarter of a mile."

The sudden yank on his arm took Karl by surprise and left him so off-balance that he had no choice but to follow the other man's lead for a few steps. Once he regained his balance, he planted both feet.

"Wait a *hunh* . . ."

A fist like a mace buried itself in Karl's stomach, producing a sudden compression of his diaphragm which forced all the air from his lungs and left him both dizzy and nauseated. In that condition he was unable to resist the grip on his arm which slung him around in a semi-circle until his back slammed against a stone wall, punctuated by the thunk of his head making contact with that same wall. His hat provided a minimal amount of cushion for the blow before it fell off, but it still hurt.

Head spinning, groaning with pain, Karl groped for his buttons to try to free his vihuela from where he was carrying it inside his coat. Rough hands knocked his out of the way and ripped the coat open, then spun him around and yanked it off his shoulders and down his arms, leaving him exposed to the bitter cold. He heard, "Aha!" just before the bag containing his vihuela was stripped from him.

"No!" he groaned, turning and reaching for the bag.

The mace slammed into the back of Karl's skull, which propelled him face-first into the stone wall. He felt his nose break, and his teeth mangled the insides of his lips. Everything started going dark as blood began flowing from his nose and mouth, but he tried one more time to turn, only to be rammed back against the wall again. That final thump of his head against the stone finished him off. He felt one of those rough hands press against his chest to hold him up long enough for the other hand to search for pockets and pouches. His fading hearing heard the exclamation as the hands found the parcel of bills that Franz had given him. As his vision totally faded to black, he felt the hand release him, and he slid down the wall to collapse into the darkness like an abandoned marionette. He never felt the kicks that added to his body's abuse.

Karl couldn't see the other pick up his coat and the vihuela in its bag and walk away, chuckling. In moments the night was dark and quiet, the only noise the susurrus of an eastern wind, the only motion the continuing fall of fat snowflakes. After some time, the snow began to stick to Karl, and before long there was a mound covering him where he slumped against the stone wall.

By David Carrico

✳ ✳ ✳

Pastor Gruber looked around as he trudged through the snow. The unseasonable blizzard had lasted a day and a half and had left the streets of Magdeburg, both the old city and the new, covered with snow. Even though it was the afternoon of the day after, there were only paths cleared on the main streets, mostly from horses forcing their way through the drifts and mounds. Apprentices and journeymen were out in places with shovels and boards, trying to broaden and extend the paths.

Fortunately for the pastor, the street on which St. Jacob's Church sat was one of the major streets in the Altstadt part of Old Magdeburg, so there was already a path made that ran in front of the church. He only had to break through the snowdrifts that mounded before the front of the building in order to reach the doors.

Pastor Gruber was breathing quite heavily by the time he had waded through the deep snow to set foot on the first step leading to the doors. He paused to breathe, wanting his racing heart to slow down. As he took deep steady breaths of the cold air, his attention was caught by something to the side of the church building. He considered it, then pulled his foot down and slowly made his way through the snow toward the object of his attention. Once he was near it, he stopped again to breathe.

"Dear God," he said, once his breathing had settled again, "let this not be what I fear it is."

With that, the pastor bent over and reached out a hand to touch the top of the mound of snow before him. Snow dislodged and fell away, revealing brown disheveled hair. He brushed snow away from the head and face beneath the hair, revealing a visage partially covered with frozen blood.

Pastor Gruber took off one of his mittens, leaned forward, and touched the figure's forehead. Ice cold. Dead. No question of it. He put the mitten back on, then rested a hand on top of the body's head. His lips moved soundlessly for several moments before he straightened, crossed himself, and murmured, "In Nomine Patris, et Filii, et Spiritus Sancti. Amen."

✳ ✳ ✳

"Byron, I'm telling you that I've got a missing friend."

That voice carried down the hallway into the detectives' office. The ones who were there all looked up.

"Uh oh," Gotthilf muttered. "That's Marla Linder. If she's got a problem, she's going to be all over the lieutenant, since he's her brother-in-law."

"Right." Karl Honister spoke out of the corner of his mouth. "She's the one Byron said was made of sword steel, right."

"Ja. And every word true, from what I've seen of her."

"Marla, I can't help that." That was Byron Chieske, the lieutenant that Inspector Hoch reported to, up-timer, and until recently Hoch's senior partner as an investigator. "We've got a dozen known dead found in the last four days after the storm, and we're still finding more. Unless you want to go to the morgue and examine bodies, I don't have anything else to show you." Byron was sounding long-suffering. It also sounded like he was heading this way.

"I'm telling you he's missing, and you need to be looking for him."

Byron came through the door into the investigations office, followed by a very determined-looking Marla Linder and her husband Franz.

"Guys, listen up," Byron said. That attracted the attention of Gotthilf and the two sergeants in the room, Karl Honister and Kaspar Peltzer. "Frau Linder here has a friend that may be missing. Marla, describe him."

"Short," she began, holding a hand above the floor to mark a height that was still taller than Gotthilf. "Straight brown hair about shoulder-length, brown eyes, no obvious scars on his face, but old enough that his face is very wrinkled. From Hamburg, so he has that northwest accent. Last seen in a bluish-gray coat. He'd have a vihuela or guitar with him."

Byron looked at the detectives and raised his eyebrows. Honister and Peltzer shook their heads. Gotthilf thought for a moment, then reached over and opened a file which had been delivered from the coroner that afternoon. There was a photo on top of the papers in the file. He picked it up, looked at it for a moment, then turned it around to display to Byron and his sister-in-law.

"Is this him?"

Marla took two steps forward and bent to look at the picture. Gotthilf could see the recognition dawn in her eyes before they closed. She lowered her head, and stood in that bowed position for a long moment. Then she straightened, and when her eyes opened Gotthilf almost flinched. The steel in her almost shone from them.

"That's him," she said in a very hard tone. "That's Karl Tralles. Dead? Why didn't you know about this before now?" Her voice had a very accusatory tone as she looked at Byron.

Gotthilf put the picture down and made a note of the name. "Because the coroner hadn't made his report yet."

"Coroner?" Marla almost spun to face Gotthilf. "If he froze to death in the storm, why would the coroner be involved?"

"Because." Gotthilf picked up the report from the folder and summarized it. "It appears he was assaulted. Multiple bruises to the face and head, broken nose, probable cracked skull, at least one fractured rib, and severe contusions to the abdomen and right leg." He flipped through the rest of the report. "No coat, no vihuela." He looked up. "Apparently robbed, beaten, and left to die in the storm . . . which the storm accomplished." He put the papers back into the folder, placed the picture back on top and closed the folder. "We received the coroner's report two hours ago."

Marla's hands fisted at her sides, and her head slowly turned toward Byron.

"He was a stranger here—an unknown." Her voice shook slightly. "He had no enemies. He was a good man and a great musician. And somebody killed him for a coat and a guitar. Some scum of the earth killed him . . . for nothing. For next to nothing. I want that person found. I want him held accountable. I want him punished for taking the life of Karl Tralles."

"We'll do the best we can, Marla," Byron said in a quiet tone. "But we have nothing to go on here. The storm basically wiped out any evidence at the scene, so we really don't have anything to go on."

"You can look for his vihuela." Her voice was sharp and hot.

"Right. Look for a guitar in a city of 100,000 people, many of whom are musicians or wannabe musicians. We'll look, but unless you can identify and prove that a specific instrument was his, we're not going to have much luck."

"Byron, please!" There was raw naked pleading in Marla's voice, but still hot tones. "You can't let this go. Karl deserves to know that his killer was caught." After a moment, she repeated in a softer tone, "Please."

Byron sighed. "We'll do our best, Marla. We don't want someone like that running around free if we can help it. But we have no evidence, so even if we develop a suspect, it will be hard to bring charges. We can only do so much."

Marla gave a sharp nod, then turned and left. Franz lingered long enough to say, "I gave Karl thirty dollars after we played at The Green Horse the night the storm began. He was supposed to come to our house that night. He never made it." Then he followed Marla.

Byron looked at Gotthilf. Gotthilf looked back and said, "We'll check into it, but it's like you said . . ."

Byron nodded. "I know. But ever since Marla's baby was stillborn back in October, she's been really moody and temperamental . . . almost as bad as she was right after the Ring of Fire happened, which is pretty bad. This isn't good. So do what you can, okay?"

❋ ❋ ❋

"We're at a dead end, Marla." Byron's voice was solemn, and he had his hands clasped in front of him on his desk. "The storm basically wiped out any physical evidence we might have found otherwise. The body and the environment was covered with snow. There was no way to remove the snow without destroying any evidence that was there, and when the snow melted, it basically destroyed what hadn't been disrupted when they removed the body. We have nothing to go on from the scene."

"Well, can't you ask around?" Marla's face was grim, her voice was hard, and her posture in one of Byron's visitor's chairs was rigidly upright. Waves of wrath almost seemed to be rolling off of her. Gotthilf leaned away from where he was sitting in the other chair.

"We did," Gotthilf said. "We took his picture up and down every street and alley between The Green Horse and the riverbank. And the only thing we found was that he apparently stumbled into The Chain in the middle of the evening."

"The Chain?" Marla's control broke for a moment to show puzzlement. "What was he doing in that place?"

"The only thing we can figure is that he got turned around in the snow. It was coming down heavy enough by mid-evening that that would certainly have been possible, especially since he was new to town."

"So what did you get out of them?" Marla's hard exterior was back.

"Nothing," Gotthilf replied, fervently wishing he had something else to report. "The tavern keeper admitted that he came in for a moment, asked for directions back to the main road into the Neustadt, and then he left." He shrugged. "That's his story, and he's not wavering from it."

"What about anyone else in the bar?"

"He won't tell us who else was there. Says he doesn't remember."

"And you can't force it out of him?" Marla's tone verged on bitter.

"We know who many of the regulars are," Gotthilf concluded. "We questioned them anyway. No one admits to seeing him. They all claim they were home the night of the storm. After we sent a squad into the tavern to break up that big fight a few months ago where a couple of people got killed, they won't talk to us about anything. Not even things that would help them."

"Somebody's lying. You need to come down hard on them."

Byron sighed. "Marla, we're the good guys. We have to operate within the law. The third degree isn't an option here and now."

"Well, maybe it ought to be," she muttered.

"Marla." Byron didn't say anything else, but his voice was very cold. Gotthilf had only heard that tone from his former partner once before, really early in their partnership. He was not glad to be hearing it now, although he understood why. Hopefully it wouldn't need to be repeated any time soon.

"Sorry," Marla said quietly after a moment. Her tone, while still angry, did express some regret. Her body, however, showed no flexing, no bending, only rigid uprightness.

"We have no witnesses and no evidence other than a snow- and water-soaked frozen body," Gotthilf said with care. "We have nothing to go on. It will take a miracle to give us a suspect. And God hasn't delivered many of those lately. We've got two dozen unsolved anonymous suspicious death case files on my desk right now. I hate to say it, but this looks to be just one more in that growing list."

Marla stood suddenly. "Keep looking." Her voice rivaled the blizzard for coldness. "There's got to be something out there." She swept out the door, with Franz right behind her.

Byron and Gotthilf looked at each other. Byron shook his head. "That was as bad as anything I saw after the Ring of Fire fell."

"Ja," Gotthilf said. "After that, I'm worried she may do something."

"What could she do if we can't find anything?"

"She knows Achterhof."

The two men stared at each other with glances that bordered on horrified.

"Crap," Byron said after that sank in.

"Indeed."

❋ ❋ ❋

The door into The Green Horse Tavern opened. Gunther Achterhof looked up as Marla Linder entered, shadowed as usual by her husband Franz. He straightened as she stalked over to the table where he sat with some of the local leaders of the Committees of Correspondence.

"We need to talk," she said in a tight voice.

✼ ✼ ✼

Wilhelm Schneider looked up at the sound of the bell on his door ringing. Two people entered his shop. His face tightened at the sight of the second man—Gunther Achterhof. That meant the other man was probably also one of the CoC. They lined up at the counter. Gunther looked at his man, who pointed at a vihuela hanging on the wall behind the counter.

"That one. That's new."

Gunther looked at Wilhelm and raised his eyebrows. Wilhelm took a deep breath, but said nothing as he lifted the instrument from the hook it hung from and passed it to Gunther.

He lifted it in both hands, looking at it carefully, turning it to and through the light and examining it with care. He paused for a moment and fixed Schneider with a stare. "You oiled a varnished instrument?"

"Ja," Wilhelm replied. "It was dirty, so I cleaned it and oiled it to make it shine."

"Idiot," Gunther muttered, and returned to his examination.

Wilhelm schooled his expression to blandness, and folded his hands together behind his back. He wasn't sure what was going on, but he had a feeling he wouldn't like it.

Gunther set the vihuela on the counter, pulled a device from his pocket, and started squeezing a handle. Bright light shone from one end. Wilhelm swallowed. That had to be an up-time flashlight, which were incredibly rare and impossible to acquire. That meant Gunther was playing with the up-timers, which meant Wilhelm was now playing in a game that was well above his usual level. He swallowed again.

Gunther shone the light into the sound openings of the instrument and moved it around. After a moment, he stopped motionless, then with deliberation turned the flashlight off and returned it to his pocket. The gaze he directed to Wilhelm should by rights have turned him to stone.

"There's a label from a Hamburg luthier glued to the back," Gunther said to his man. "You're sure this is a new item in here?"

"Ja. Wasn't here last week," the nameless CoC man said. "You can tell, there's no dust on it."

Gunther looked at the vihuela, ran a finger along the top edge, and displayed the clean digit to Wilhelm. "You see, Master Schneider, I have reason to suspect that this vihuela was stolen from a friend of Frau Marla Linder's, one Master Karl Tralles, from Hamburg."

There was a sardonic grin on Gunther's face as he made that statement, and Wilhelm's heart sank even lower. Oh, God—Frau Linder had access to the Emperor. If she had cause against him, he needed to start running a week ago. He mustered his nerve and retorted with, "I have no knowledge of that, and unless you have proof, you should be careful making such allegations."

"Of course you are totally innocent, Master Schneider. No one would suspect you of receiving stolen property." Gunther's voice dripped sarcasm, but Wilhelm said nothing. He had learned long ago that the less he said to anyone, the more trouble he stayed out of. But he was also sure there was more to come. He was right.

"What you don't know, Master Schneider," Gunther's voice switched to a cold hard tone, "was that the theft was accomplished by the murder of the friend in question."

That jolted Wilhelm, and his eyes widened despite himself. "I know nothing of that!"

"I believe you," Gunther said, still in that hard tone, "because I know you don't have the courage to take the risks involved in fencing property associated with a murder. I absolutely believe that whoever you bought the vihuela from didn't reveal that to you. It is, nonetheless, true."

Gunther's hard eyes still speared Wilhelm. "What did you pay for this instrument, Master Schneider?"

"Eight guilders," Wilhelm replied, his mouth moving before his brain could catch up with it.

Gunther turned the instrument over to reveal the scrap of cheap paper glued to the back of the instrument with a number written on it. "Yet you are only asking ten guilders for it. So based on your usual practices, that means you really only paid maybe five guilders for it, maybe as little as four. Right?"

"Five," Wilhelm snarled. Gunther had him caught. His business methods were well-known. "And not a pfennig less."

Gunther looked at Wilhelm without expression for a long moment. When he spoke, his tone was level. "I will give you six guilders to redeem this instrument: five to recoup your investment, and one to give you enough of a profit to make the deal fair and remove any possible cause of action later."

Wilhelm's mouth twisted, but he gave a short nod of his head. Gustav's companion stepped up to the counter, pulled several coins out of a pocket, and counted out six guilders onto the countertop. When the sixth hit the wood, Wilhelm scooped them up and pushed the vihuela toward Gunther. He started to turn away but stopped as Gunther laid a hand on his arm.

"A receipt, if you please." Gunther's focus returned to Wilhelm. "Marked paid in full."

Caught in that gaze, Wilhelm had no choice. He pulled out a piece of paper, opened an inkwell, dipped a pen, wrote out a receipt, and signed it. Gunther examined it, then tucked it into a pocket. "Something to take this label off?" He pointed at the paper.

Wilhelm rummaged around, found a rag that he dipped into a nearby bucket and wrung out before rubbing the paper with the wetness of it.

The cheap paper immediately crumbled upon being soaked and then rubbed by his calloused fingertips. He finished with a wipe of his sleeve and handed it back to Gunther.

"Give me that rag." Gunther proceeded to wipe the vihuela down all over. "Too much oil. Shouldn't have been oiled at all. Idiot."

He shoved the rag back at Wilhelm, and the two of them left the shop with no further words. Wilhelm dropped the rag in the bucket, sat down, and put his head in his hands. He needed beer.

* * *

"Where did you get this?" Marla asked, eyes gleaming with unshed tears as she turned the vihuela in her hands.

"Is that your friend's instrument?" Gunther's voice was calm. He wanted this to be a low-key discussion, although he wasn't certain that would be possible.

"I think so," Marla said. She looked over at Franz, who nodded. "It looks like it." She plucked a string and winced at the tuning, but continued with, "Sounds like it." Her gaze returned to Gunther. "Where did you get this?"

"I'm not going to tell you." Still in the calm tone.

Marla's gaze darkened, and she lowered her eyebrows in a harsh frown. "Why not?

"Because you don't need to know. Because the person we got this from could not have been the person who assaulted your friend. He is totally incapable of doing that."

"But if he had this, he must know who did it." Marla's tone was harsh and cold. "Tell the police. Take this to Byron—they can check it for fingerprints."

"It won't do any good, Marla," Gunther said. "The guy wiped it down with oil to clean it and make it shine. The only fingerprints will be his and mine. And this guy will never admit anything to anyone. We were lucky that someone noticed this." He reached out to touch the vihuela.

"I want the killer," Marla snarled. "I want him to pay for what he did to Karl."

"Marla, leave it to the police." Gunther made a calming gesture.

"No! If they can't find him, I want you to find him! I want him to pay for what he did!" She sat back in her seat, breathing heavily.

"Marla, leave it to the police," Gunther tried again.

"No!" She leaned forward, eyes narrowed, and slammed a fist down on the table between them. "No! If they can't do it, if you can't do it, I'll do it!"

Gunther felt his mouth twitch and took a deep breath. He really had hoped it wouldn't come to this.

"Marla, you don't want to do that." She opened her mouth, but before words came out he pointed a finger at her and barked in his commander's voice, "Listen to me!" Her eyes got round, she paled, her mouth closed, and she sat back in her chair again.

"You will listen to me now," Gunther continued. "I promised you and Franz three years ago that I would protect you to the best of my ability. And I've kept that promise. But I never expected that I would have to protect you from yourself."

Marla blinked, and she still looked angry, but a look of confusion was slowly forcing the anger down.

"You don't want justice," Gunther said in a slightly less intense tone. "You want revenge. And I understand that. Trust me, if anyone in Magdeburg can understand that, it's me." He jerked a thumb into his chest as he said that.

Gunther watched as the thoughts of his reputation crossed her mind, as she lifted her head and took a deep breath of her own. Before she could muster words, he continued with, "I don't think you could find and identify the man who killed Herr Tralles. But even the hunt would be bad. Marla, that kind of anger, that kind of rage and implacability, will poison you. It will change you in ways you don't even realize. It will change the way you relate to people. It can't help but do that, because you will become harder and darker." His thumb hit his chest again. His own mood was growing darker and his tone was hard, as the conversation was taking him back into his own memory.

He leaned forward and tapped the tabletop with a calloused finger. "It will change the way you relate to your friends." Tap. "It will change the way you relate to your students." Tap. "It will change the way you relate to Franz." Tap. He saw out of the corner of his eye that Franz was sitting very still.

"It will change the way you relate to your children." Tap-tap. Marla jerked at that one, and shook her head hard. The reference to children got through a major chink in her armor from the death of her child. "Yes, it will. I know." God, did he know.

Tap . . . tap . . . tap.

"And perhaps worst of all, it will change the music. You won't be able to find the joy in it anymore."

Tap.

There was a moment of silence as that most telling of points was made.

"So tell me, Marla, is it worth that price? Is it worth destroying everything you have?"

Her face was stricken. One lone tear edged out from her right eye, and slowly rolled down her cheek. Franz stood and stepped behind her, bending to wrap his arms around her and place his head next to hers. "He's right, Marla," he murmured. "He's right. Please don't go there."

"'How many barrels will thy vengeance yield thee even if thou gettest it . . .'" Gunther quoted. It surprised a short laugh out of Marla.

"*Moby Dick*?" she said. She wiped her face with both hands. "Really?"

Gunther shrugged. "It's better than *Atlas Shrugged*."

"Oh, God," Marla replied with a pained expression. "Reading the dictionary would be better than *Atlas Shrugged*." She reached a hand up to palm Franz's cheek for a moment as the other grasped the arms that encircled her, then joined them before her on the table.

"Now I want to be mad at you," she looked at Gunther from under lowered eyebrows. "I was really working myself up to be a nemesis. I really wanted to be that. But you had to go and talk to me about the cost, didn't you?" She took a deep breath. "So now I can't go there."

"No, you can't," Franz said. He had straightened, and his hands rested on her shoulders. "You can't trade yourself for destruction, not of yourself, not of someone else."

"I'm surrounded by wisdom here." Marla's mouth quirked. "So if I can't hunt this guy down and skin him for my new boots, what do I do? Hmm?"

"Embrace the grief, cherish the memories of your friend, and move on." Gunther's voice was quiet, giving her the advice that some days he wished he had been given years ago. "Be yourself. You have some experience with that, I think."

Tears glistened in Marla's eyes again. She wiped at them again, and looked up. "Yes . . . yes, I do. I got through that. I'll get through this. But damn, it hurts." That last was almost whispered, and she looked down at where her hands were clasped together again, white-knuckled.

Gunther leaned forward and placed his hand on top of hers. "Yes, it does. But you'll get through it." And his voice was rock solid certain.

After a moment, he stood and gestured to his companion who had stood all this time against the wall. "I've got to be someplace else in a few minutes. Let the boys know if you need to talk to me again."

Franz looked at him over Marla's head and mouthed, "Thanks."

❊ ❊ ❊

There was silence in the room after Gunther closed the door. Marla considered her hands, feeling the tension and pressure as they clung to each other as if they had lives of their own. Finally she made them release and unwind from their intertwined position. She took a deep breath, placed her hands on the table, and pushed herself to her feet.

"Are you all right?" Franz murmured from behind her. Marla said nothing, simply stepped to the corner cabinet and lifted the decanter to pour herself a glass of wine. She took a sip, then turned to face him, holding the glass in both hands.

"No, but I will be. It will take some time, though."

Marla drained the glass and set it back on the cabinet tray, then crossed to stand before her husband. Reaching out, she took his crippled left hand in both hers. She traced the lines of his frozen fingers, gentlest of touches.

"I feel like this looks inside right now," she said quietly. "First Alison, now Karl. It hurts, Franz." The tears began to drip from her face to his hand. "It hurts so much." She rubbed the tears with her fingertips like lotion, then just held the palm of his hand against her face. "It hurts," she whispered.

Franz said nothing, simply opened his arms to gather her in. Turning, Marla snuggled into his chest and brought his left hand up to cup her right cheek. She stood in the shelter of his strength as she released her grief and wept.

* * *

A few minutes later, Gunther's companion said, "So, are we done with this then? Not going to follow it up?"

"No."

* * *

Wilhelm Schneider stiffened in dismay when the shop door opened and Gunther Achterhof and his man came in. "What do you want now?" he snarled. "Haven't you done enough harm?"

"Simple," the CoC leader said. "I want the name of the man you bought that vihuela from."

"No," Wilhelm bit off. "You know I can't do that, Achterhof. My clients rely on me keeping their identities secret."

"Now what we have here," Gunther mused, "is what the up-timers would call a failure to communicate. Let me be perfectly clear, Schneider. I don't care about what you normally do, and I don't care a donkey's fig about your clients and their wishes and identities, secret or not. But this man killed one of Frau Marla's friends by beating him up and leaving him to freeze to death in the blizzard."

Wilhelm swallowed at that.

"You can tell me what I want to know this one time, Schneider, or I will park Heinz here," he jerked his thumb at his companion, "and his brother Fritz outside the door to your shop, where they will explain to all who pass by that your shop no longer has the confidence of the

Committees of Correspondence and that we do not recommend patronizing you."

Gunther said nothing more. He didn't have to. Wilhelm could see that this would destroy him in a very short period of time.

"That's . . . that's uncalled for. It's illegal. It's immoral. It's . . ."

Gunther held up a hand, and Wilhelm sputtered to a halt. "Spare me the irony of you protesting legality and morality, Schneider. It is almost enough to make me laugh. Regardless, it will happen if you don't give me what I want. And don't think to protest to the Polizei. We are acquainted, and instead of defending you, they are much more likely to wonder what we know and begin investigating you . . . in depth."

And that, Wilhelm knew, was nothing less than utter truth. And that would also ruin him. He slumped and put his head in his hands. "What do you want?"

"The name, Schneider. Give me the name, and we are gone as if we had never been."

Wilhelm didn't raise his head. "Make him go away." He watched out of the corner of his eye as Gunther jerked his thumb at the door, and Heinz left.

"The name." Gunther's voice was colder than it had yet been.

Wilhelm straightened. "Matthias Ackermann," he whispered. "And if you tell the Polizei, or anyone, I'll deny it."

"Matthias Ackermann," the CoC leader repeated.

Wilhelm nodded. In response, Achterhof turned and left the shop without another word.

Wilhelm placed his head back in his hands. His head hurt. He needed beer. He needed a lot of beer.

❧ ❧ ❧

"So are we done now? Are you giving up?" Heinz sounded a bit disbelieving.

Gunther snorted as they rounded the corner headed for the Magdeburg Golden Arches. "Of course not."

"But didn't you tell Frau Marla to leave it to the police?"

"Yes, because she should."

"And haven't you been telling us to let the police be the police?"

"Yes." Gunther stopped, and motioned Heinz and Fritz closer. "But there are two additional considerations here. First," he held up an index finger, "the Polizei won't be able to solve this without cracking either Schneider or Ackermann. Schneider will never talk, because he'd be a dead man if he did. Ackermann is just smart enough to keep his mouth shut. So they'll never be able to map that situation out."

The name of Matthias Ackermann hadn't surprised Gunther when he heard it. He was a reputed bully and strong-arm type in the city, who was known to have spent much time in The Chain. The CoC were aware of Ackermann. He wasn't from Magdeburg originally, although his accent wasn't far different from the regional norm. He was one of the earliest folks who had come to Magdeburg after the emperor had named it the new capital.

Ackermann had almost received a visit from CoC men at least once in those earlier days due to his bullying of children and women. He was smart enough, though, to first figure out that there was a line, and second figure out where that line was and to not quite cross it. He had, however, been observed frequently dancing along the edge of it. So yes, the CoC were very aware of Ackermann.

For the reasons he had given them, Gunther was going to keep this matter contained within the very small circle of himself and the two brothers. No one else was to know of it.

"What's the second thing?" Fritz growled.

Gunther held up the middle finger alongside the index finger. "I'm taking this personally. I promised Frau Marla and Franz years ago that we would protect them and theirs, and we should have protected Tralles. We didn't, and that's our fault. If I thought the Polizei had a good chance to bring Ackermann in, I'd let it go. But they won't be able to do it playing by their rules. So this once, this once we will play by the old rules."

❈ ❈ ❈

And so Gunther found himself in a boat on the Elbe River in the middle of the night with Heinz and Fritz Beierschmitt, two of his hardest CoC hands, men who had seen and done everything to survive in the years that had passed. They were also the only other men beside himself who knew of the connection of Ackermann to Tralles.

The boat neared the middle of the stream, and Gunther's musings stopped. "Okay, stop," he whispered. Sound carried extremely well over the water, and even in the middle of the night they didn't want to be heard.

The moon hadn't risen yet, so it was dark where they were. "Pull the oars in," was his next order. The two men on the thwarts ahead of him pulled their oars out of the locks and laid them inside the western gunwale of the boat. "Okay, move him. Carefully," he stressed, still in a whisper. "We don't want a huge splash."

Heinz and Fritz bent and pulled and rolled the unconscious Ackermann up to the gunwale of the boat. Moving the limp weight took some doing. Gunther leaned to the west to try to balance the load as they rolled him over the east side gunwale as gently as they could. There was an inevitable splash as his bulk hit the water. They all froze for a long moment, but there was no call from the bridge behind them or the banks on either side. After a long held breath, Gunther whispered, "Right. Back to shore."

As the brothers pulled the oars to turn the boat and return to the western bank, Gunther contemplated what they had just done.

Fritz had actually known Ackermann, at least enough to use his first name, so he was able to encounter Ackermann one night and get him good and drunk, and had gotten enough out of him to pretty much establish that he had beaten Tralles the night of the storm and stolen the vihuela. They had no factual evidence, only word of mouth, but Gunther was at that point absolutely certain that Ackermann had told the truth in his cups.

In the end, Gunther had decided on a case of biblical-level justice, and knowing what they knew, Heinz and Fritz were in agreement. They also understood the need to keep it quiet.

The three of them had taken Ackermann tonight. It was a few days after the evening carouse. There was no connection with Fritz or the rest of them. There were no witnesses. They just applied a sock full of sand to the back of his head as he headed down an alley and then carried him away like he was a drunken friend.

They had taken him to one of the nooks in the northeast corner of the Altstadt, the poorest part of Old Magdeburg. He roused once they doused him with cold water, then they had beaten him, much as he had beaten Tralles into insensibility. Shouts and sounds of fights were not uncommon in that part of Magdeburg, and the Polizei patrollers moved with care in that district, especially at night. With three of them, it didn't take long, and they were gone with the evidence before anyone came to investigate.

Which brought them to the river. They didn't have a blizzard available to balance the conditions when Tralles had been assaulted, but they did have the Elbe River, which at the moment was almost liquid ice. So they had just left the unconscious Ackermann to the mercies of the frigid river, much as he had left the unconscious Tralles to the mercies of the freezing storm. Ackermann had been shown equal mercy to what he had shown his victim and was now in the hands of God, or of fate, whichever you wanted to believe in. He could survive. It was about as likely as Tralles surviving in the storm, but it was possible. Gunther was at peace with that.

The body of a badly-beaten man in rough clothing might be found floating in the Elbe from any point from the Navy yards to hundreds of miles downstream. By the time he was found he would hopefully be unrecognizable. But even if someone downstream could identify him as one Matthias Ackermann, late of Magdeburg, what would they connect him to, and why? The odds were great that it would simply be assumed that this was another result of another argument among the growing underworld in Magdeburg. And ironically, Ackermann was exactly the kind of man who would likely have ended up that way anyway. This happened almost once a week, and most of the case folders about such in the Polizei file cabinets were marked closed but not solved. No reason why this wouldn't be treated as another, as long as the three of them never brought it up.

Which they wouldn't.

"Easy, lads," he whispered. "There's the wharf."

APOSTATE

Grantville
May, 1634

Caspar Bauhof sat in his room, meditating . . . or at least attempting to meditate. Not the silliness that the up-timers called meditation, of course. The idea of trying to empty his mind and find peace therein was ludicrous. How could emptiness be anything but waste?

No, he was attempting to meditate scripturally, taking a verse or passage from Scripture and considering it carefully, turning it around and around in his mind until he felt he had drawn every bit of meaning and wisdom out of it, and then applying it to his world and his life. Except that today, every time he began with his chosen passage, his mind very quickly wandered away from it. It was beginning to frustrate him.

Caspar closed his Bible and pushed it away to rest his chin on his fisted hands. He thought he knew why he couldn't focus. He needed to make a decision, and his conscience was not going to allow him to avoid it any longer. It was a dangerous decision, though—dangerous to him personally, dangerous to those who would follow him, and ultimately, dangerous to the rest of the world. That was one reason why he had put off dealing with it for so long. But he couldn't avoid it any longer. The time was now. The circumstances were in place.

Fine. He was ready . . . he thought.

He sat up straight in his chair. Marcion was right. There. Decision made. Even though Marcion had been considered a heretic during his life in the second century AD and for the over 1400 years since then, the books that had appeared with Grantville more than proved to Caspar's satisfaction that the being named God in the Old Testament was not the same being named God in the New Testament, which was the core tenet of the so-called Marcionite heresy. The Old Testament God was at best a demiurge, and at worst was more than likely the same being called Satan in the New Testament. If he had created the world, then the world was undoubtedly evil, and all that it contained. And that, Caspar decided, had major implications for Europe—indeed, for all of Christendom.

Caspar's religious background was . . . different. His family heritage had been Anabaptist at one time. His great-grandfather had, in fact, been involved in the Münster Rebellion carried out by radical Anabaptists in 1534. When the city fell to the troops of the archbishop in 1535, the family had escaped to Holland, where they remained for the next few generations. His grandfather had turned Calvinist in reaction and followed a particularly harsh branch of that sect. Caspar himself had attended a Calvinist school in Switzerland until a few years ago, when he had broken with them over doctrinal differences and become an itinerant Arminian pastor and preacher.

Marcion was neither the first to espouse those teachings, nor the last. Caspar was very aware of that from his studies in school before the Ring of Fire. In point of fact, southern Europe still echoed from four hundred years of struggles between the Catholic Church on one hand and the Cathars, Albigensians, Bogomils, and others who had held similar beliefs. None of them had ended well, either. The Inquisition had been founded to combat them, after all, and mention of the Albigensian Crusade would still raise hackles in certain parts of France, Spain, and Bavaria. Every teacher of the truth had ended poorly. The reactions of so-called orthodox Christianity had seen to that. The last of those struggles had barely settled when Luther nailed his theses to the Wittenberg cathedral door and began an even more intense struggle, the Reformation, which was still ongoing.

No, Marcion had not been the only teacher of those truths. He had, however, been the best—the purest. The others had all been tainted by the evil world they had professed to reject. The scraps that had survived to the future, only to be brought back in the miracle of the Ring of Fire, proved that. But what did that all mean? What did it portend?

Was Caspar the only down-timer to find those scraps, those precious truths? He seriously doubted it. The God he served would not be so niggardly as to allow only one man to receive this revelation, this enlightenment. So . . .

He considered Marcion's teachings. He agreed with Marcion's rejection of the Old Testament. But he thought that Marcion's selected canon from the New Testament, limited to the Gospel of Luke and only some of Paul's epistles, was perhaps too narrow. The Ring of Fire event made it clear that the teachings of the end times in other volumes would be needed. So, he needed to think on that.

Caspar's mind drifted to Luke chapter 8 and the parable that began in verse 4. Of course! The seed would be broadly sown, but only a small amount of it would fall on the equally small amount of available fertile soil. He nodded. As the Saviour Himself said, "He who has ears, let him hear."

God would make available to all, but only a few—perhaps a very few—would respond.

God would not find Caspar wanting. But at the same time, it would not serve God well if Caspar were to make the same mistakes as those who had gone before him. It would not serve God for Caspar to build a house of straw upon a foundation of sand. He must build a base, a foundation, of committed believers of the truth. Then he could build the New Jerusalem, the new kingdom of God in this world, that only the true believers would be a part of, and when that was done, even the Pope and the Lutherans and the Calvinists would have to step back in awe.

God would not find Caspar wanting.

Chin back on his fists, Caspar began to plan. He laid his thoughts out one by one, building the structure of the future, secure in the knowledge that he was God's chosen, that his will was God's will.

Grantville
May, 1636

Marike Gendt looked up at her brother Dirck as the SRG wagon pulled to a stop at the bus stop. He looked down at her and smiled. "Do good at school today, eh? I'll see you tonight."

She nodded, not saying anything. He patted her shoulder in encouragement and climbed up onto the wagon, settling into the seat beside the driver, who flicked his reins and clucked to the horse. Dirck looked back over his shoulder and smiled as the wagon started rolling.

Marike wrapped her arms tighter around her binder. She hoped the school bus got there soon. It was chilly out this morning. For all that she loved her brother dearly, she sometimes wished he wasn't quite so . . . protective was the right word, she thought. He was actually her half-brother, but he had always treated her as if they were full-blood kin. There were eight years between them, so he had been an adult figure in her life for almost half of it. But she was sixteen now, and he still treated her like she was eight most days. But considering everything they had been through recently, she guessed that shouldn't be too surprising.

They were the sole survivors of their family and had only recently arrived in the Grantville area after a long journey fraught with more risk than they had expected. They had left the town of Alkmaar in Holland some six months ago. Walking across the Rhineland and through much of Franconia had taken longer than they had hoped, especially after Marike had fallen and badly sprained her ankle. It had taken a couple of weeks for her to recover enough to be able to walk for very long or very far, and even now it twinged her occasionally.

There had been a couple of scary moments as well, when outsiders approached them in menacing manners. Fortunately, Dirck's pocket pistol had been enough to warn them off. He'd been a journeyman gunsmith in Alkmaar, and his master had allowed him to make a pistol for himself. He'd had to pay for the materials, of course, and it wasn't a work of art to match those his master had produced, but it worked reliably. Staring down the big bore of it had caused more than one thief to leave its vicinity rapidly.

That pistol had also provided a job for Dirck not long after they arrived in Grantville. When he approached the masters at Struve Reardon Gunworks and showed them the pistol when they asked for a sample of his work, they had hired him immediately. And that had given them the stability they had needed ever since Marike's parents had died. They had rooms in a rooming house outside the circle of the Ring of Fire along the road to Rudolstadt. And for the first time in a long time, Marike had enough food to eat.

Many of the workers in the businesses and manufactories of Grantville lived out that way. And Marike took some comfort that some of the people were Anabaptists. She and Dirck hadn't approached any of them yet, but they needed to. They needed to find fellow believers to worship with. Marike brushed her hand down the front of her worn skirt. She needed better clothes. So did Dirck. What little they had had survived their travels and was now not fit for much more than selling to the rag pickers for the paper makers. Maybe now that they were safe and Dirck was working again he would agree. She didn't want to appear at worship dressed so poorly. It would be . . . disrespectful.

The big yellow and black school bus rumbled up and halted at the bus stop. The doors swung open. Marike gathered her courage and stepped up into the bus. Another day at the school. It was so different.

※ ※ ※

Marike settled at the table in the far corner of the school's lunch room. It still seemed strange to her to have such a large room just for the purpose of gathering the students to eat. In her previous schools, when she had been able to attend, students and teachers alike had eaten in whatever room they were in when it was noon. But then those schools had been much smaller, with only ten or twenty or so students, as opposed to the hundreds that attended Grantville High School.

She took her lunch out of her pocket, unfolding the napkin to reveal the slice of bread. She wasn't the only student who brought food from home. Dirck had said they couldn't afford the fees for the lunches provided by the school, and after looking at them, she wasn't sure she wanted to eat them anyway. Just looking at the mixture of up-time and down-time dishes sometimes made her stomach do flip-flops.

Marike sighed as she tore the corner off the piece of bread and put it in her mouth. Grantville was so strange, she thought as she chewed. The town might be a miracle from God, but it certainly wasn't Heaven. So many things were different from Alkmaar, and things like the buses were only the beginning . . . the mixture of clothing, the mixture of languages and dialects and accents, e-lec-tri-ci-ty—she sounded the word out carefully—how spread out the homes were. The up-timers kept calling Grantville a town, but it was larger than any city she had ever seen, even if it didn't have a wall around it.

And the libraries—sweet Jesu, the libraries! Even the fabled library of Alexandria must have paled in comparison. She had never seen so many books, about so many things. Even books that contained just made-up stories, for no other purpose than to treat the mind to wordplay and frothy ideas. Surely even the pope's library in far-off Rome would not have the like, much less the sheer mass of them. She thought there was surely more knowledge in Grantville than anywhere else in the world.

What was Marike, a small town girl from Holland, supposed to make of all this? She was sure she and Dirck were there for a reason, but for what? That thought rolled around and around in her mind as she mechanically chewed and swallowed her bread.

As she finished the last bit, a nearby conversation intruded in Marike's thinking.

"The Latin is *Ecce Homo*," a girl's voice said.

"Yes, it is, but that's not a primary text. We work from the Greek primary texts, right?" That was another girl. "That's *Ide ho Anthropos*."

"I know, but it's a useful touch point. It seems to support the English translators more than it would Martin Luther," the first girl replied.

Marike's ears perked up. What were they talking about?

"I just can't figure out how or why Luther translated that verse as 'Behold what a man this is!' That sense just isn't in the original texts, Barbara."

"I know, Kat. You've explained that to me before."

Barbara and Kat. Those names rang bells in Marike's mind. She didn't think she had any classes with them, but she thought she had seen them around. She glanced over her shoulder. Yes, she did know them—Barbara Kellarmännin and Katharina Meisnerin. She'd seen them around the halls of the school, and in assemblies. She didn't have any classes with either of them, though. At least, not yet. Every time she saw them, they were animated—eyes wide open, talking to each other or their other friends, smiling frequently.

Marike thought she'd been told they were both Anabaptist. She hoped so. It would be nice to know some other girls close to her age that she could also see at worship.

Katharina was a short girl, even for a down-timer, albeit a bit taller than Marike. Katharina's hair—or what Marike could see of it under her cap—was dark and thick. Certainly her eyebrows were. Her features were pleasant, although not striking, and for a down-timer her teeth weren't bad.

Barbara was a little taller than her friend, and somewhat stockier with dark blonde hair. Both girls wore plain conservative clothing, somewhat different from Marike's, but similar in color and general shape: ankle-length skirts in dark colors and undyed shirts under vests or short jackets.

"Gospel of John, chapter nineteen, verse five?" Marike said. The girls turned to look at her, and her hand flew to her mouth as she realized she'd spoken out loud.

Katharina grinned at her. "Yes. You know it?"

"My grandfather was an Anabaptist pastor," Marike managed to reply, lowering her hand, "and the Gospel of John was his favorite of all. He used to read me to sleep with it." She dropped her eyes. "I miss him."

Katharina moved closer and touched her shoulder. "Sorry. I know that feeling. You're Marike Gendt, aren't you?"

Before Marike could reply, Barbara said, "Marike Gendt, Anabaptist, new to Grantville, traveled quite a distance to get here, um, from the

Netherlands, maybe near Amsterdam from your accent." She smiled shyly. "Did I get it right?"

"Uh, yes, I guess so," Marike replied. "But why . . . how . . . ?"

Katharina laughed. "Oh, Barbara tries to learn everything she can about people. She can tell a lot about folks just from looking at them." She thumped her companion on the shoulder. "Of course, to use the up-time phrase, she sometimes drives us nuts with it."

Marike looked to Barbara. "How . . .?"

Barbara held up a hand and started ticking off fingers. "First, you're new to Grantville because you haven't been attending school here very long. Second, you're Anabaptist because your clothing styles and colors match those of Anabaptists from the west. Third, from the Netherlands, again from your clothing styles and from your accent. Your Hochdeutsch is good—better than mine when I got here, actually—but you still sound like a Hollander. Fourth, you traveled a long way—partly because you're from the Netherlands, yes, but also because," she leaned forward and dropped her voice, "truthfully, your clothes and your shoes are worn." Marike flushed and started to look away, but both the other girls reached out to her. "We understand," Barbara said. "It's nothing to be ashamed for. My clothes were more mends and darns than woven material when my family arrived here."

"Mine as well," Katharina added. "My family had been running for so long that we only had what was on our backs, and none of it was in good shape. Once we were able to get new clothes, most of what we had went to the rag buyers. They didn't even make good cleaning rags."

"Really, you're doing better than most of the Anabaptists were when they got here," Barbara concluded. "With a little time and patience, you'll be able to improve your family's situation."

Marike looked down at where her hands rested on the table. She said nothing. After a moment, Katharina sat down beside her, followed by

Barbara on the other side. "Look," Katharina said, "Barbara didn't mean anything by that. But she notices things about people. It's almost a gift. She does it with everybody now. She wasn't picking on you."

Barbara nodded. She didn't say anything, but she had the most plaintive look on her face.

Marike looked at them through slightly watery eyes, and nodded.

"Look, you'll be all right," Katharina said. She laid her hand atop Marike's. "Honestly. You're safe here in Grantville."

"I want to believe that," Marike whispered, "but it's hard."

"You'll be all right," Katharina said, patting Marike's hand. Marike turned her hand up, and Katharina grasped it firmly. "Honest."

After a moment, Marike looked up with a tremulous smile. "Do I really sound like a Hollander?"

Both girls smiled. "Yes," Barbara said. "It's a distinctive accent—it sounds a lot like a Plattdeutsch speaker, but a little different. Nothing wrong with that, of course." She giggled. "Not like some of the up-timers trying to speak Hochdeutsch. Some of them sound like they're trying to swallow their words, and some sound like they're gargling."

"Be fair," Kat said, even though she was smiling. "How well would you have done if you were pushed back to four hundred years ago Persia?"

"Oh, I know," said Barbara with another giggle. "But for all the tragedy and heartache it's caused them, it's still a bit funny."

Marike smiled back at them. She thought of a few of the up-timers she'd heard, and agreed with Barbara.

✿ ✿ ✿

It was three days later that Dirck came home from work with good news. "Marike!" he called out as he entered their rooms. "Marike!"

"I'm right here," she said, as she came out of her room.

"I met someone at work today who has clothes to give us," Dirck said with a broad smile.

Now Marike was confused. The day of her conversation with Katharina and Barbara, she had told Dirck in no uncertain terms that he needed to either get them some clothing or at least some new cloth for her to sew new clothes. She couldn't face going to worship in their worn clothing, she insisted. It was disrespectful to God and to the congregation. He hadn't acted happy about that, muttering that he didn't know where the money was going to come from. But now he seemed almost excited about it.

"But how . . . why . . . ?" she started.

"He belongs to a group that tries to help people who are newly come to Grantville," Dirck explained with a bit of impatience. "Especially those like us who don't have much when they get here. He told me he'd meet us at their storeroom in half an hour. Get your coat on, we need to go if we're not going to be really late."

"But . . ." Marike still wasn't sure she understood.

"Come on!" Dirck said, frowning at her.

Marike stopped talking, got her coat, and walked through the open door where Dirck was waiting impatiently. She gave a small headshake, followed by a deep breath. Dirck had always been a bit impetuous.

Her brother led Marike at a fast walk to the building where the storeroom was, always two or three steps ahead of her and not heeding her calls for him to wait for her. It was growing chilly in the gloom of evening, and she shivered a bit.

Dirck pulled to a stop by a side door of a two-story building just as another man turned the corner at the other end of the building. "Ho,

Dirck," the stranger called out. "You beat me here. You must have been running all the way."

"*Nein*, Johann," Dirck replied. "We just got here ourselves."

"Well, what matters is you're here. Let's go see what we can do to help you." He pulled open the door and waved them both inside.

Marike entered last and closed the door behind them. She looked around. The room was lined with shelves, some of which were laden with tools and hardware, some of which were holding sacks and boxes of what looked like grain and beans, and some of which had piles of cloth on them.

There was a man across the room from them moving some of the cloth on one of the shelves. He looked over his shoulder. "Ah, Brother Johann. It is good to see you."

"And it is good to see you, Brother Matthäus. This is Brother Dirck Gendt and his sister Marike, who are newly arrived in Grantville. He works with me at the gunworks. They arrived with not much more than you see with them, and I brought them to see if we had any clothing that might do."

"Of course, of course. Scripture says that we are to tend to the needs of the brothers and bear one another's burdens, after all." Matthäus looked Dirck up and down. "I feel certain we have something that can help you, Brother Dirck. I'm not so certain," he added with a glance at Marike, "about you, young Marike. We don't have much women's or girls' clothing at the moment. But let us see what we can see."

It didn't take very long. They found three shirts and two pairs of trousers that fit Dirck well enough. For Marike they only found one shirt. She suspected it was actually for a youth rather than a young woman, but she was small enough that it worked. There was one skirt, which was definitely made for someone who was both taller than Marike and broader as well, but she thought she could alter it to fit—or at least fit better. She dithered about it, but ultimately ended up taking it.

"So," Brother Matthäus said, as they bundled everything into an old sack, "it is good that we can help you. Will you be able to worship with us this Sunday?"

"Yes," Dirck replied. "I'd like that."

"Good. Brother Johann will be able to tell you where we meet." With that, the older man turned back to the shelves and began rearranging things that had gotten disrupted during their search.

Johann was standing by the door, so Marike headed that direction as Dirck swung the sack up on his shoulder. They exited together.

"I am glad that we were able to find some things for you," Johann said. "Oh, and the meeting house is over there." He pointed to a building visible down the cross street.

"Indeed," Dirck responded. "Our thanks."

"See you tomorrow, then." Johann waved and turned away. Dirck headed toward their rooming house, and Marike scurried to catch up to him.

Neither one of them said anything as they walked back in the dark. Marike suppressed both a frown and a sigh, but felt her forehead crease as her brows drew down. The whole evening had been strange. But after a few more steps, she shrugged. They had a few more clothes, at any rate. And she had her mother's needles, so she should be able to adapt the skirt to fit her. That was good.

✳ ✳ ✳

The next Sunday Marike followed Dirck to worship with Johann and Matthäus. She wasn't too surprised when they ended up at a building that wasn't built like a regular church. All too often the persecution of Anabaptists had forced them to meet in out of the way places or buildings that weren't obvious places of worship. Even in Holland their worship had been done mostly in houses.

They were among the last to arrive. Johann had been waiting for them at the door, and he ushered them right inside. The room they found themselves in wasn't large, and there were several people already in it, but Dirck was able to find a spot for them to stand where they could see the front of the room. Brother Matthäus was standing there beside another man that Marike had never seen before.

Marike didn't see any kind of a signal, but suddenly one of the men at the front began singing a hymn. The others mostly joined in, although she saw one or two of them not singing. It wasn't a hymn that she knew, either the music or the words, so she listened with her head bowed. By the third verse, she could follow the melody well enough that she hummed it softly. When that hymn was over, another of the men began a different hymn, this time one that she knew. She sang along with it, but again softly. She was the only woman in the room. from what she could see. She didn't want to draw attention to herself.

After that came a time of prayer, where various of the men in the room alternated in praying aloud. Then, after a moment of silence, Brother Matthäus took a step forward. "Today's Scripture reading is from the Gospel of Matthew," he said, "chapter twenty-four, beginning with verse fifteen.

"When ye therefore shall see the abomination of desolation, spoken of by Daniel the prophet, stand in the holy place,
(whoso readeth, let him understand:)

Then let them which be in Judaea flee into the mountains:
Let him which is on the housetop not come down to take anything out of his house:
Neither let him which is in the field return back to take his cloak.
And woe unto them that are with child, and to them that give suck in those days!
But pray ye that your flight be not in the winter, neither on the Sabbath day:
For then shall be great tribulation, such as was not since the beginning of the world to this time, no, nor ever shall be.
And except those days should be shortened, there should no flesh be saved; but for the elect's sake those days shall be shortened.

Marike didn't quite frown, but her eyebrows did lower. That was a dark passage—not one that was often preached by Anabaptist pastors. She wondered what his homily would be for that passage.

"And now Brother Caspar will instruct us."

Matthäus took a step back, and the older man that stood beside him began to speak.

"Our Blessed Savior gave us this warning when He walked the face of the earth and wrestled with Satan. I come to you today to tell you that we are in these last days, that we are in the days where we must flee, leaving behind coats and friends and families to reach the safety of the hills of God. So many of you have already had to flee, and I sorrow for that necessity. Yet the times are growing even more dire."

This Brother Caspar was nothing special to look at, Marike thought. Not very tall, not very large, certainly not handsome with his bulbous nose and thinning hair. Yet his voice made you forget that.

By David Carrico

When Caspar spoke, it was with a rich warm voice that filled the room with resonance and melody. It was a voice that drew a hearer in, that invited and enticed one to be part of its whole. It was mesmerizing. It made Marike feel like she was the only one in the room with Caspar, that they were having an intimate tête-à-tête, and that he was talking only to her. By the end of the first sentence she was drawn in, despite her initial reaction to his opening words. By the end of the second, she was awash in emotion, hanging on his every word, leaning forward slightly as if to hear his words even faster. Marike had heard many good pastors before, not least of which had been her grandfather, but this Brother Caspar was like no one she had ever heard. She managed to look over to Dirck once, to see him nodding in agreement, but then Caspar's voice caught her up again.

Afterward, Marike didn't remember everything Caspar said that morning. But she did remember feeling accepted, being drawn into the group, feeling warm inside for the first time in a long time. That remained with her for a long time after the meeting was over and she and Dirck returned to their rooms.

※ ※ ※

Brother Caspar remained at the front of the room and watched as those who had come to the worship left. "The tall one, that is the Hollander?" he murmured to Matthäus.

"Ja."

"Is he Sword or Staff? *Schwertler Täufer* or *Stäbler Täufer*?" In other words, would he fight if necessary?

"He's a gunsmith," Matthäus replied, "so he almost certainly is Sword. He works for Struve-Reardon Gunworks."

"Ah. As you say, then, almost certainly Sword. Keep track of him. He may be useful."

Caspar watched as the Hollander left, followed by . . .

"Was that his wife or his sister?"

"Younger sister is what he told us."

"She seemed . . . appropriate. Well-mannered." Caspar paused for a moment as the last of the men left. "Keep track of her as well."

Grantville
June, 1636

"Hi, Marike."

Marike looked up to see Katharina's smile as she dropped into a chair beside her in the lunchroom. "Hello," she responded.

"I haven't seen you the last few days," Katharina said. "I was starting to get worried you were sick or something."

Marike frowned a little. "No, I've been here at school every day except Saturday and the Sabbath."

Katharina shrugged, still smiling. "I must have just missed you when I came in, then. Anyway, I wanted to see if you would be interested in coming to a women's Bible study."

A women's Bible study? Marike hadn't heard of such a thing. She felt her frown deepen a little. "What would that be like?"

"It's led by one of the up-timer women, Frau Kathy Sue Burroughs. We meet at her house once a week. She teaches a lesson, and then we talk about it. It's fun, but I've learned a lot from her, too."

"So . . ." Marike was still trying to understand what Katharina was talking about. ". . . is this a church just for women? Like a convent, or something?"

Katharina laughed. Marike liked the sound of her laugh. It was almost like a silver bell ringing.

"No," Katharina said. "We're not a church. In fact, we come from several churches. Nona and I go to Mountain Top Baptist, Barbara Kellarmännin and Marta Engelsbergin go to the Stäbler congregation, and the other girls go to other churches. Reed and Kathy Sue Burroughs do host a church in their house on Sunday mornings, and sometimes some of us will visit that, but the Bible study is held on Sunday afternoons, and you don't have to go to the church to go to the Bible study."

Now Marike was very confused. "I thought you were Anabaptist, but you go to these other churches?"

"No, no," Katharina exclaimed. "I am Anabaptist, and so are Barbara and Marta and some of the others. Most of us were going to the First Baptist Church in downtown Grantville. We went there because they practice adult baptism."

Marike nodded at that. Any church that did that would attract Anabaptist attention. But . . . "You say 'were going.' You're not now?"

"No. Many of us really liked the pastor, Dr. Al Green. He's a really well-educated man, and he knows more about the Bible than just about anybody. And he's a good pastor, too. But some of the deacons of the church—who are really elders, not like deacons as we think of them—got upset with him, and they eventually convinced enough of the church members to side with them and forced him to leave."

"They can do that?" Marike was stunned.

Katharina nodded, a most sober expression on her face. "They call it 'congregational governance.' The up-time Baptist churches didn't have bishops or governors. Each church decided who would be their pastors and leaders, and that included deciding that someone they had brought in would have to leave. So they told Brother Green that he would have to leave."

"But why did you leave?"

"Because one of the reasons they forced him to leave was because he was reaching out to the down-timers around them. Some of the deacons didn't like that, and they're just going to hold services in English now. So most of the Anabaptists who had been going there left with Brother Green. Some of us followed him to form this new Mountain Top Baptist Church, and some went to either the Stäbler or the Schwertler Anabaptist groups, who were happy to receive them, of course."

Marike shook her head. "It sounds like the up-timers aren't any better than our own neighbors."

"Oh, they are and they aren't," Katharina said with a bit of a smile. "They will all stand up and defend their ideal of 'freedom of religion,' even if they all have a slightly different idea of exactly what that means. But they are all men and women just like we are, and they have their own ideas of how things should be done, even at church. Up-timers in positions of leadership and authority can act just as badly as down-timers. As Marta's brother Joseph says, that's both disappointing and comforting."

"How does he mean that?" Marike asked.

"Disappointing because apparently in almost 400 years mankind hadn't significantly improved in some very basic ways, but comforting in that they still, for the most part, recognize that they need God just as much as we do."

Marike thought about that for a moment, then nodded. "I think I understand that."

"So, have you found a group to worship with yet? If you haven't, please come to Mountain Top, or try Reed and Kathy Sue's house church. I think you'd like either one."

"Umm," Marike said slowly, "Dirck has been taking me to a group that helped us when we first got here with clothes and stuff." She was hesitant to say more.

"Which group was that?" Katharina said, just as the bell for the end of the lunch period rang. She sprang to her feet. "Oh, I've got to run. I have science class next. I'll catch up with you later, okay?"

"Okay." Marike intoned the still unfamiliar up-time word as Katharina spun and dashed out the nearest door.

✸ ✸ ✸

Marike set the last stitch and tied off the knot, then used her small penknife to cut the thread. "Finally," she said, holding the completed vest up before her. It looked good, she thought.

When Dirck had given her some money to buy cloth with, she hadn't expected to find anything like this dark green at a price she could think about. But the cloth seller told her that the up-timers had revolutionized the dye and cloth industries by producing deep rich hues from chemicals at a fraction of the price that the traditional plant-based dyes would have commanded. "And they wear well, too," she'd insisted.

This finally gave her a set of clothes for Sabbath worship that was . . . presentable, she thought. No one had said anything when they came to worship with Brother Caspar's followers, but she could tell that even for workmen's families she had been shabbily dressed, and that had bothered her. She knew that to God it wasn't important, but she wanted to be respectful of God, of the other people around her, and of her family, even though that was only Dirck at the moment, and he didn't care. Respectful and respectable, that was what she wanted. And that was hard enough to do and be when you were an Anabaptist in the Germanies, much less a fugitive from Holland.

Marike laid the vest on the table top and smoothed it out to give it one last scrutiny. She checked the seams—they were all straight. The toggle buttons were all sewn on straight. Even the button holes, always her worst details, were sewn well and tightly. So it was good. And the rich green would go well with the dark brown skirt, she thought with satisfaction. Just in time to wear it tomorrow.

And wear it Marike did. It was Sunday—the Sabbath. She laid out Dirck's best clothes early in the morning, then spent some time making sure that her hair was coiled neatly and tightly. She took some pride in her hair. Oh, she knew it was vain of her, but even the Apostle Paul had said that long hair was a woman's glory, and hers was long indeed, and thick and shiny compared to most other women's hair. So she took some little time to brush it out and then coil it before dressing.

Once Marike had finished dressing by donning her new vest, she smoothed her hands down her front, feeling the nap of the rich fabric crossing her palms as her hands moved. It was smooth . . . perhaps the smoothest fabric she'd ever felt. She began to understand why wealthy people could fixate on having rich clothes, if they felt that good or better all the time.

"Marike! Time to go!" Dirck called out from the front room. She grabbed her coat from the peg on the wall and swung it on as she stepped through the door into the front room. Dirck had the front door open already, so she just kept walking and led the way into the hall. In a matter of moments, they were outside.

Her brother was funny sometimes, Marike thought as they walked down the road. On the way to worship, he never talked. Any other day of the week, he'd be chattering away, telling her about the work that he was doing or what his plans for the future were, but not on Sunday. On

Sunday, he might have been a dumb mute once they left their rooms. Not a word—not a syllable—would pass his lips until they arrived at the meeting place, no matter what she said to him. He'd always been that way, and she'd eventually given up trying to start a conversation. She had to admit that it wasn't necessarily bad. It wasn't like he ignored her most of the time, and having the time to think and consider without interruption anything that was weighing on her mind, or matters of the Gospel, was actually kind of nice.

They arrived at the meeting place with a bit of time to spare. This was the third Sunday they would worship with the church that had helped them. Dirck found them a place to stand that was a little farther forward than where they had stood the first Sunday, nodding to the men who were already there. Marike stood beside him, hands folded before her. Others entered through the door behind them. She was able to see them if she turned her head a bit. She smiled a bit when an older couple came through the door with two children—a girl and a boy—who were close to her age, she thought. At least she wasn't the only female at the service this time. Maybe they could talk a bit after the service.

The worship followed this group's usual pattern: various men led the singing, seemingly choosing hymns and songs at random, some of which she didn't know and some of which she did. Although the older woman and the girl who was probably her daughter both sang out, Marike still sang softly when she knew a hymn well enough to join in.

The singing ended when Brother Matthäus stepped forward. She still hadn't figured out how he knew to do that, because every time they'd come the number of hymns they'd sung had been different.

"Today's reading is from the Apostle Paul's Second Epistle to the Thessalonians, chapter two, verses three through twelve.

> *"Let no man deceive you by any means: for that day shall not come, except there come a falling away first, and that man of sin be revealed, the son of perdition; who opposeth and exalteth himself above all that is called God, or that is worshipped; so that he as God sitteth in the temple of God, showing himself that he is God. Remember ye not, that, when I was yet with you, I told you these things? And now ye know what restraineth that he might be revealed in his time. For the mystery of wickedness doth already work: only he that now restraineth will do so, until he be taken out of the way. And then shall that wicked man be revealed, whom the Lord shall consume with the spirit of his mouth, and shall destroy with the brightness of his coming: whose coming is after the working of Satan with all power and signs and lying wonders, and with all deceivableness of unrighteousness in them that perish; because they received not the love of the truth, that they might be saved. And for this cause God shall send them strong delusion, that they should believe a lie: that they all might be damned who believed not the truth, but had pleasure in unrighteousness."*

Brother Matthäus closed his Bible. "And now Brother Caspar will instruct us."

Marike managed to not shake her head. Another dark passage, another reading with portentousness. This was not what she was used to hearing in Anabaptist meetings. Their pastors, like her grandfather before he died, mostly preached from the Gospels. This, while she knew it was in the Bible, did not lend itself to the kind of messages her grandfather had preached.

Brother Caspar stepped forward. "A hard saying," he began. "A hard saying, indeed, for a dark time." Marike felt his voice sink into her, seeming to flow in and nestle against her bones. It was so odd, but after the barest of moments seemed so natural. "But we live in a dark time, brothers, do we not?"

There were murmurs of agreement and nods all around the room. Dirck shifted his feet, which caused Marike to glance up at him out of the corner of her eye to see his mouth working. Caspar was affecting even him, who had been immune to pastors in the past.

"A dark time," Caspar repeated, his warm voice filling the room with waves of tenor and timbre. "A saying that is a challenge to understand, for it prophesies the future, and how can a man understand the future?" Marike drifted on his voice. "But the Apostle Paul was given a revelation, and he had so told the Thessalonians. And today, in the shadow of Grantville and the Ring of Fire, we have our revelation, and I can reveal to you the mysteries that Paul spoke of. First and foremost, that we are living in the times Paul spoke of, and that the man of iniquity that he described walks the streets of Europe today, nay, the streets of Magdeburg..."

Brother Caspar continued in that vein for some time. Marike gradually began to understand that he was linking Emperor Gustavus to the man of iniquity set forth in the passage, but those words didn't make much sense to her. The men in the room continued to nod their heads and murmur affirmations. She simply rode the waves of his voice.

The worship ended with a concluding song, by the end of which Marike had settled into herself again. Afterward, the others began filing out, but for some reason Dirck lingered, so Marike was forced to wait on him. She began to be a bit uncertain when Brother Caspar began moving toward them. "Brother Dirck Gendt, is it?" he asked, approaching Dirck directly.

"Yes." Marike looked up at Dirck in surprise. His voice was strained and hoarse, a tone she'd never heard from him before.

"I hear good things about you, young man," Brother Caspar said. His rich voice seemed to just flow over them, and brought a shiver to Marike's spine. She froze as the pastor's gaze moved to her. "And who is this?"

"My sister," Dirck replied, his tone smoothing a bit, "Marike Gendt."

Caspar clasped his hands behind his back and slowly walked around the two of them. Marike stood still, but she could feel his gaze on her back.

"Brother Dirck," the pastor said when he had finished his circuit, "I have heard good things about you. God has a plan for you, I believe, and once it is clear to us Brother Matthäus will undoubtedly call upon you."

The last of the other worshippers were gone. Marike and Dirck were alone in the room with the two elders. She swallowed as Brother Caspar's gaze focused on her again. "And you, young woman, are a credit to your family. You should be your parents' jewel, and their parents as well." Marike started. Caspar's eyes caught the slight movement. "Did I say something amiss?"

"No . . . no . . ." Marike stammered. "It's just that . . . that was my grandfather's pet name for me."

"A man of discernment, rare perception, and deep wisdom, then."

If possible, Caspar's voice became even warmer, and Marike just wanted to melt into it. "He was an Anabaptist pastor."

Caspar's eyebrows raised. "A paragon, indeed." He moved a bit closer. "So, a granddaughter of a pastor. Perhaps the daughter of one as well?"

Marike shook her head. "*Grootpapa* was my mother's father. My father was a weaver."

"Ah." Caspar almost seemed disappointed for a moment. "Still, a distinguished lineage, and one to whom you bring honor." He clasped his hands behind his back again. "Will you favor us by taking off your bonnet?"

Marike had been lulled by Caspar's voice. By the time the inappropriateness of the request penetrated her mind, she had untied the bonnet and was removing it from her head. She brought it down to her chest and clutched it in both hands, elbows tight to her sides. She wasn't sure, but it looked as if Caspar's eyes had widened a bit as her dark hair was revealed rolled and pinned on the back of her head.

The room was silent. No one spoke. Marike could barely breathe. Finally, Caspar broke the silence.

"Please," his tone was lowered, rich and dark, "would you loosen your hair?"

Marike flinched. She didn't think what he was asking was right, but he was a pastor. She looked up at Dirck. After a moment, he gave a single sharp nod. Marike sighed, reached up with both hands, and pulled out the two wooden pins that constrained her hair. As the weight of it fell free down her back and shoulders, she shook her head from side to side before bringing her hands back together before her chest.

Everyone in the room seemed to freeze in place, except Caspar. He stepped forward to face Marike, staring into her eyes. He raised one hand and reached toward her hair. She closed her eyes.

Caspar didn't touch her, but she could sense his hand hovering over the top of her head, then slowly moving to his right, her left. She could hear the rustle of his clothing as his hand passed down the side of her head, causing some of the freed hair strands to move about, then across her shoulder and down her arm. He never touched her, and after a long moment she sensed that he had dropped his hand. She opened her eyes when she heard him step away.

She was watching Caspar's back as he exited the room by the inner door. Brother Matthäus cleared his throat. "Brother Dirck, I will call upon you before long." He hesitated a moment, then added, "Your sister is a remarkable young woman—a commendable young woman." Then he turned and followed the pastor through the inner door.

Marike released her pent-up breath. They were alone. She stripped her coat off and thrust it and her bonnet at Dirck, then put the hair pins in her mouth and reached back to grab her hair and roll it into a rough ball and plunge the hair pins into it before cramming the bonnet back on her head and grabbing her coat back. She wrestled into it as she walked out the outside door.

Marike led the way home, setting a pace that Dirck had trouble keeping.

Nothing had happened. Nothing. But if that was true, why were her eyes burning and her stomach trying to climb out her mouth?

✱ ✱ ✱

Caspar looked up from where he sat at a table reading his Bible. "The work at Angelroda preparing the New Jerusalem progresses well," he said. Matthäus entered the room and closed the door behind him. "The village there in the west is ours. The folk have embraced the cause. I assume it does so here also?"

Matthäus nodded. "We have recruited as many Mighty Men as we had hoped for, and there are a few others beyond that count who could be brought into the fold."

"Good. If they are at all suitable, bring them in. We will need as many stalwarts as we can find. And the goods? I will be glad when we move everyone to Angelroda. The three days to travel there grow wearisome."

"Our men at the gunworks managed to bring another five rifles to us. But they say that will be the last for a long time. The owners are very concerned about how many shipments have been shorted and how many rifles have gone missing. They've changed their procedures, and it will be a lot harder to 'misdirect' rifles in the future."

Caspar nodded. "We could only hope for this primary phase to work for a short time, but that gives us, what, forty rifles now? It is enough to begin with. Do we have contacts in the army for the second phase?"

Matthäus smiled. "We do. Not brothers, not true believers, but there are some that worship gold who will help our cause with gunpowder and more rifles for their own reasons."

"Always the weakness of others will serve us," Caspar said. "Pay them well, but when we are done, remember who they are. They will receive their just reward then."

He waved a wand in dismissal, but Matthäus stood in place and said nothing, simply looked at him with one raised eyebrow. After a moment, Caspar nodded and said, "I find Sister Marike . . . suitable. She is quiet, modest, not given to unseemly talking . . . "

"Devout . . ." Matthäus added.

"Devout," Caspar agreed with a nod, "and of a good family, it appears." He was silent in an apparent moment of introspection, finger smoothing his wispy mustache as he did so. "See that she and Brother Dirck have what they need."

Matthäus nodded. Caspar looked back to his Bible as his associate left the room.

✻ ✻ ✻

"Hi, Marike!"

Marike didn't look up as Katharina plopped down on the chair beside her in the lunchroom. She was sure from the sound of the other girl's voice that there was a big smile on her face. Today that didn't get through to her, though. Today she just stared at her hands holding her unwrapped lunch.

"Marike?" Now Katharina's voice didn't sound like a smile. Soft, tentative, almost as delicate as the touch of her hand on Marike's left wrist. "Are you ill?"

"No," Marike whispered after a long silence. "Not ill. Just . . ." She couldn't continue.

Katharina waited, then finally said, "Just . . . what? Is something wrong?"

"I don't know," Marike continued in a whisper. "Just . . . "

"Has someone hurt you?" Katharina's tone remained low, but became more urgent. "Are you or your brother in trouble?"

"Hurt? No. Trouble?" Marike's whisper wavered, and she bit her lip.

"What is it?" Katharina's urgency increased.

"I . . . can't talk about it. Nothing has happened. Just . . . "

"Are you afraid of something?"

"Something?" Marike's voice was a bit stronger. "No."

"Someone, then?"

Another long silence. "Maybe." Marike's voice had returned to its whisper.

"Tell me what's happened." Katharina's tone had dropped to her own whisper, but it was intense enough to cut. "Please. I want to help. I can help. Please."

The depth of imploring in Katharina's voice almost broke Marike's control, but not quite. She wouldn't involve her friends in her situation. They couldn't help, and could end up in trouble of their own. She raised her eyes to look at Katharina.

"Nothing's happened," Marike said in as close to a normal tone as she could manage. "Nothing's going to happen. I've just had some bad dreams, is all. But don't tell anyone, especially the teachers." If word got back to Brother Caspar . . .

Katharina still looked disturbed, but Marike kept her own gaze steady, and the other girl finally leaned back. "Well, if you're sure . . . "

"I am."

"Okay." She leaned forward again. "But if something happens or you need anything, even if it's just to talk, you find me, all right?"

"Yes."

The end of period bell rang.

"Rats!" from Katharina. That startled Marike, and she looked at her friend with furrowed brow. "What?" Katharina responded. "Oh, you mean rats. The apostles tell us not to be vulgar, but we still need words to release tension. I heard Dr. Green say that one day, and after I quit laughing at it, I decided to use it myself. Now I've got to run to science. You remember what I said, and find me or send for me if you need me, right?"

Marike nodded.

* * *

Katharina usually lingered while taking her shower after last period gym class, enjoying the warm water sluicing over her body. It was such a contrast to the tepid baths she had at home. Today, however, she rushed through the experience because she wanted to be first out of the locker room so she could catch her friends. She achieved that goal, but then had to stand and wait for the others. At last Barbara appeared. Kat waved and beckoned her over, and just as she arrived Marta Engelsbergin appeared in the doorway, to likewise be flagged down. Katharina began talking as soon as Marta was close enough to hear her.

"Do either of you have a class with Marike Gendt?" Receiving headshakes from both of them, Kat frowned. "Rats. Do you know if anyone in our group does?"

"Amalia Ramsenthalerin might," Marta said. "Why?"

"I think she's either in trouble or got trouble." She gave them a rundown on her lunch conversation, concluding with, "I know she's quiet, but I've never seen her act like that before. She wouldn't say anything more than that. I think we need to try and watch over her, see if we can figure out what's really happening and if we can help."

"We can do that at school," Barbara said, "but none of us live near her, and I don't know where she's going to worship. Do you?"

"No," from Marta.

Kat shook her head, and said, "We've got to get her to come to the Bible study. Kathy Sue might be able to figure it out."

"We can't drag her," Marta said.

Kat shook her head again. "Maybe not, but there has to be something we can do. I'm sure she's scared, and I'm scared for her."

✳ ✳ ✳

Marike looked up as Dirck came in the door.

"Good, you're here," he said. Before she could ask why, he continued, "I was told today that Brother Matthäus would be stopping by tonight, and that he wanted to see both of us."

Marike's heart sank. She clasped her hands in her apron. "Wh . . . why?" she stammered.

"I don't know, but it must be pretty important for him to come here instead of making us come to him. So straighten things up and get yourself in order. I need to wash."

Marike looked around. There wasn't much out. She hadn't started their supper yet. She threw a towel over the bread and the cutting knives, straightened out the cushions on the chairs, and ran the broom around the front room and swept the sweepings into her sleeping room. She'd clear them away later. She closed her sleeping room door and swiftly unbuttoned her vest, throwing it on a wall peg and pulling down her good green one. It went okay with the skirt she was wearing, which she didn't have time to change. Just as she finished the last button on the vest, she heard a knock on their room door. She straightened her cap and ran her fingers through the loose wisps of hair, trying to tuck them behind her ears.

"Marike!" Dirck hissed outside her door. She opened it and stepped through. Dirck said nothing more, just stepped to the main door and opened it. She saw a drop of water fall from his hair, so he must have had a hurried wash.

"Brother Matthäus," Dirck said. "Please, come in." He pulled the door wide and stepped aside.

Matthäus entered the room, nodding to them both. "Peace to you, Brother Dirck, and to you, Sister Marike."

"Peace," they responded in unison, Dirck's voice louder than Marike's. She fought to keep her hands from instinctively clenching, instead pressing them flat on the front of her thighs. She felt the rough weave of the fabric against her cold palms.

Another man followed Matthäus into their room, carrying a couple of large packages. He said nothing, simply stepped to one side. Matthäus motioned to Dirck to close the door.

"Brother Dirck," Matthäus began, "I am here in Brother Caspar's place. He is aware of your faithfulness, and of your stern resolve, and he has accordingly sent me to ask you to join his band of Mighty Men."

"Mighty Men?" Dirck asked in a wondering tone.

"Yes. They are named after the Mighty Men named in 2 Samuel chapter 23, who stood with King David in defense of his throne and God's Ark."

"And what will Brother Caspar's Mighty Men do?" Dirck asked.

"Stand to defend Brother Caspar and the truth," Matthäus replied.

Marike's stomach was in knots. She wasn't sure she liked where this was going. Her right hand was clenched in the fabric of her skirt, but she managed to keep her face calm.

"Am I not too young, or too new, to be considered for such an honor?" Dirck asked.

Matthäus shook his head. "Brother Caspar knows that, but feels that you are worthy. Will you accept his wisdom and judgment?"

Dirck bowed his head. Marike prayed that he would refuse, but her heart fell when her brother looked up again and said, "I will."

Matthäus smiled and took one of the packages from his companion, removing from it a coat. "Then accept this coat of the Mighty Men, so that all may know you are a part of them. All of the Mighty Men have received these recently." He held it up and open, inviting Dirck to put it on. Dirck put one arm down a sleeve, then the other, shrugging the shoulders on. Matthäus turned him around and fastened the buttons, then turned him again to face Marike. "There. Does Brother Dirck not look worthy, Sister Marike?"

She had to admit that the black frock coat with the dark gray facings looked well on her brother. And she could see from the smile on his face that he was pleased with what had happened. So she mustered a smile and said, "Yes, he does." The others didn't seem to notice that her smile faded quickly and the tone of her voice was thin and thready.

Matthäus turned Dirck a quarter turn, and said, "You should wear this to worship, Brother Dirck, and you must wear it whenever you are called out to face our foes."

"I will," Dirck replied in a determined tone.

Matthäus' gaze moved to Marike, and her heart sank even more. He smiled, a smile that for all that Marike was sure he thought was warm and friendly, looked to her to be assured and calculating. "And Brother Caspar has not forgotten you, Sister Marike. In honor of your brother's attainment, he has sent this for you as well."

The still unnamed companion held out the other package. Matthäus drew out first a skirt of deepest blue, which he draped across the back of one of the chairs, followed by a matching jacket with silver embroidery and button froggings across the breast of it which he laid atop the skirt.

"These are for you, Sister Marike," Matthäus said. "In honor of your brother, and in honor of your family and your faithfulness. Please accept them, so that I can report to Brother Caspar that his gifts found favor in your sight."

Marike swallowed. She didn't really want to do this, but she saw the pride and pleasure on Dirck's face as he nodded at her. She couldn't disappoint him. She stepped forward and ran her hand down the front of the jacket. The fabric was fine—the finest she had ever touched. And the blue was so beautiful. She had never seen a hue so rich. Not even on the few trips to Amsterdam she had taken when younger.

She sighed, her hand still resting on the jacket, and looked up at Brother Matthäus. "Please tell Brother Caspar thank you for his gift."

The smile appeared on Matthäus' face again, a bit sharper this time. "The only thanks he needs is to see you wearing his gift to worship."

Marike gulped again and nodded.

❈ ❈ ❈

The next several days were frustrating to Katharina. She and her friends were able to keep an eye on Marike at school and even on the school bus, as one of the girls lived out the same road as Marike. But so far nothing had become apparent to them as a cause for Marike's fear. Katharina was getting worried, because Marike was still in her very withdrawn mode, not talking any more than necessary in class and not at all in the halls or the lunch room.

It wasn't until the next Monday that they got their first clue as to what might be going on. Marta came up to her that morning dragging Amalia Ramsenthalerin by the arm.

"Kat!" Marta exclaimed. "Amalia has news for us."

Katharina turned to the other girl. "Amalia?"

Amalia shook her head a bit. "I don't know if it's important or not, but yesterday I saw—I thought I saw—Marike Gendt with her brother going into the place where those men of Brother Caspar's worship. I thought it was her, but I couldn't tell for sure. Whoever it was was wearing nice clothes, though . . . nicer than anything I've seen Marike wear. So it may not have been her."

"Oh." Katharina was taken aback by that thought. "I never would have guessed that. I mean, they're Anabaptists. Why would they go there?"

"They're new, Kat," Marta said. "They wouldn't have found out where else they could go unless they joined one of our groups. If they connected with the Casparites first, they could be drawn in. But maybe she's seen or heard something . . ."

"We have got to get her to come to the Bible study so Kathy Sue can talk to her," Katharina said firmly.

The others nodded in agreement.

By David Carrico

✳ ✳ ✳

The Bibelgesellschaft meeting came to its usual conclusion, and Katharina, Barbara, and Marta lingered as the others all gathered their stuff and left. Dr. Green looked up from where he was sitting and raised his eyebrows in surprise to see them gathering in front of him. "What's up, girls?"

"You've talked before that Brother Caspar is probably forming a cult," Katharina said. "Can you tell us more what to look for to know if we're talking to someone who might be involved in one?"

The pastor leaned back in his chair and laced his fingers across his middle. "Why? You all think you know someone who's getting mixed up in it? Someone besides the ones we've seen already?" All three girls nodded, and his expression turned grim.

Dr. Green said nothing for a moment, then sighed and began with, "There are some theological distinctives of most cults, and some social distinctives as well. All cults will show some of them. Contrariwise, if a group shows more than one or two of them, there's a high probability they're a cult, even if they seem to be good people doing good work.

"Theologically, every cult that I know of both historically and in the up-time always disagreed with orthodox doctrine in at least one of two ways. The first way is they either disputed the nature of God, usually in denying some aspect of the Trinity, but sometimes also in denying the common identity of God the Father between the Old Testament and the New Testament."

"Is that last one the so-called Marcionite heresy?" Barbara asked. "The one that said that the God of the Old Testament was a demon and the Old Testament itself was full of lies?"

"Yes, although he was not the only one to teach that. But most cults attack the divinity of Jesus. He's an easier target, you might say."

Dr. Green paused again, apparently gathering his thoughts. After a moment, he said, "Socially, the issues are a little more nebulous, but there are some common patterns. One is they tend to try and involve people who are new to a community, who are lonely, who don't fit in, or who want or need authority—someone who wants someone to tell them what to do." The girls looked at each other. He caught that, and his brows lowered. "Does that fit with what you're seeing?"

"Kind of," Katharina said. "She's new to Grantville, and they don't know many people yet."

Green nodded. "A real candidate, then. Another common problem is they try to isolate their people from the rest of society, dictating who they work for, where they shop, and what schools they attend. They will eventually try to take over their finances, getting them to give all their money to the cult and then turning around and giving some of it back, which weirdly enough has the effect of making the person grateful to the cult, even though they're only getting back a fraction of the money they gave. In really bad cases, the cult will make them move to a new town or a new country just to increase their control, and in some extreme cases the cult led them to drink poison on command, just to demonstrate their control."

The girls shared horrified looks. Green continued, "You said 'she.' Is it a girl you're concerned about?"

"Yes," Katharina said. "She and her older brother are Dutch Anabaptists who arrived here a few weeks ago. They have no family, but I think that he is working for Struve-Reardon Gunworks. She is in school with us."

"Do I know her?"

"I don't think so. They haven't been here long."

"*Schwertler Täufer*, then," the pastor said. "What did she say?"

"Only that she was afraid, that she had bad dreams, and that she didn't want us to tell anyone," Katharina said.

"Okay, I won't pry any further, but stay close to her," Green said. "Try to get her to come worship with you or to your Bible study."

"We've tried."

"Keep on trying. It's important."

Grantville
July, 1636

Kathy Sue Burroughs opened her front door to see Press Richards, Grantville's police chief, standing on her front porch. She opened the screen door. "Come on in, Press," she said. "Brother Al is already here."

"Thanks, Kathy Sue." Press took off his cap and stepped through the doorway.

Kathy Sue closed the door and led the way to the living room. "You want something to drink? I think I may still have some instant coffee in the cabinet."

"Just some water would be fine," Press responded, knowing she probably didn't have any coffee and didn't need to waste it on him if she did. "I've had my morning cup of coffee already. Morning, Brother Al." Press nodded to his pastor where he sat on the sofa before he settled into an easy chair set at right angles to the sofa.

"Good morning, Chief." Al Green smiled and nodded in return.

Kathy Sue came out of the kitchen with a glass of ice water, which she handed to Press before she resumed her seat at the other end of the sofa. Press took a drink, savoring the chill. Even sitting in Germany in 1636, Grantville in July was warm enough to appreciate a cool drink. He lowered the glass and looked at the pastor.

"You called this meeting, Brother Al. What's up?"

The pastor took another sip of his own water, then set his cup on the coffee table and sighed. "You remember that conversation you and I had some time back about how Brother Caspar and his followers are a cult, and might be a dangerous one?"

Press grimaced. "Yeah. So far I haven't seen anything since that first couple rounds of guys wanting to rough up folks who didn't agree with Caspar."

"Me, neither," Kathy Sue said. "And I've been keeping my eyes open, for sure."

"I don't blame you," Al Green said. "And for that matter, so have I. But until recently, I hadn't seen or heard anything else."

"Recently?" Press said. "So something has come up?"

"Maybe. I'm getting this third-hand, and it doesn't sound like anything definitive has occurred, but what I've heard hints at some serious trouble."

Press frowned. "So what have you heard?"

Green leaned forward, putting his elbows on his knees and letting his hands dangle between them. "Have you heard of child grooming?"

Press frowned and nodded, while Kathy Sue looked confused and shook her head. Press said, "Yes, I was briefed on that in one of the FBI classes I took." He looked at Kathy Sue. "That's a term that came into use several years before we came back in the ROF. It refers to children, usually girls, being trained to be sex objects. It happens a lot in international settings, and it happens more often than you would have wanted to know in religious settings, both non-Christian and Christian."

"Yuck!" Kathy Sue said with a frown of her own. "I never heard about anything like that."

"That's because in backwater Grantville the worst we saw was two teenagers in the back seat of a '79 Chevy, and the girl getting pregnant."

Press looked back to Al Green. "So you think it's possible that's happening here?"

"Possible, yes. Probable?" The pastor shook his head. "I just don't know. Like I said, I heard this third-hand, so I may be reading things into what I heard that won't prove to be there, but enough signs are there that it's possible."

"So what have you heard?" Press asked.

"Three of the girls in the Bibelgesellschaft are concerned about one of their school classmates who may have gotten involved in Brother Caspar's organization. She reportedly said he approached her, complimented her, didn't touch her, but now she's scared. They said she was always quiet, but now she says nothing. And he may have given her new clothes."

"Shit!" Press said. A moment later, "Sorry."

"I've heard the word before," Green replied with a small smile. "And I agree that strong language may be justified just now."

"Okay, tell me what that means," Kathy Sue interjected, "because I don't get it."

Press grimaced. "First of all, a significant behavior change, especially withdrawing from people, is a common symptom of being groomed or being taken advantage of sexually. Second, gifts, especially expensive ones, are a way of making the person feel connected and obligated to the giver. Together, that's the beginning of a strong circumstantial case that there's something going on. How old is this girl? And who told you about this, anyway?"

"Katharina Meisnerin, Barbara Kellarmännin, and Marta Engelsbergin. They wouldn't tell me her name, but she's close to their age."

"So that's going to make her in the sixteen to eighteen age bracket," Kathy Sue said. "And they're all in my Sunday Bible study and come to our house church sometimes, so that's why you wanted me here. I was wondering."

"Right," Green said. "They all agreed that the girl said nothing had happened, but they also said they think she's definitely scared. They said they're going to watch over her at school, but they want to know if something can be done when she's not at school."

"In the absence of criminal evidence, probably not." Press' tone was sour. "The most we could do is send a patroller by their residence periodically, depending on where they live. If they live far enough out, we couldn't even do that."

Green's face was as sour as Press' voice. "I was afraid of that. Until she says something more, there's nothing you can do. And that's a pretty common problem with these cases, I understand."

"Yep."

The pastor sighed. "I was trying to keep the sexual angle muted from the other girls, but that's probably a forlorn hope."

Press quirked his mouth. "Did you say Barbara Kellarmännin is involved in this?"

"Yes."

Press shook his head. "She's studying to be a profiler, so she's read most of the Crime Classification Manual. She's probably already figured that out, and if she has . . ."

"The other girls will know it," Kathy Sue said.

"Yep."

Green sighed again. "Definitely a forlorn hope." He looked over at Kathy Sue. "This may come up in your Bible study, so I wanted you to be prepared if it does. And they say they've been trying to get the girl to come to the Bible study."

Kathy Sue took a deep breath. "Right. I'll deal with it."

Press looked first at Green and then at Kathy Sue. "Both of you, stress to those girls that people who do these kinds of things are not normal, even if they are religious, and they are not at all averse to hurting or killing someone who gets in their way. Tell them to not take any chances. I don't want to have to explain anything to their parents."

※ ※ ※

Marike came out of her room after changing out of what she thought of as "Brother Caspar's worship clothes." This morning was the first time that Brother Caspar had been back in Grantville after a few weeks away. The sermon had been drawn from the book of Jude, and had been more of Brother Caspar's teaching about how they were living in the last times. Those all left Marike feeling uncomfortable, especially when he called the emperor the Antichrist.

Dirck turned toward her, and she saw that he was still wearing his Mighty Men coat. "I have another meeting this afternoon," he said. "I don't know when I'll be home."

"Again?" Marike said. "This is the second Sabbath in a row. I don't like when you leave me here alone."

"I'm sorry," Dirck said, and he did sound regretful. She reminded herself that her brother did love her. "But Brother Caspar has asked to see all of us today. It's the first time he has been back to Grantville in almost a month, and I really need to be there."

"All of you? How many is that?"

Dirck pursed his lips for a moment. "Thirty? Maybe thirty-five? Just here in Grantville, mind you. I think there are some more somewhere else from what they've said."

Marike shook her head. "All right. Go on. I'll find something to do."

Dirck stepped to her and threw an arm around her shoulders. "I'll make it up to you, Marike. Honest."

She leaned into him for a moment, then pushed him away. "Get going, or you'll be late."

Dirck left. Marike turned and picked up her mending box, then sat down in her chair. She found Dirck's sock that she was darning, pulled out the needle from where it had been thrust into the knit weave, and bent over her task. "If he thinks I'm going to sit here every Sabbath while he runs off to his meetings . . ." A thought crossed her mind. "Kat keeps asking me to come to that women's Bible study. Maybe I should."

That thought rolled around and around in her mind as she worked.

❋ ❋ ❋

It was Saturday afternoon. Marike looked at the napkins lying flat on the bread and cheese boards.

"Dirck?"

"Mmm?"

She looked over to where he was running a brush over his boots, trying to clean the mud off of them from where he had walked home after his half work-day. "I need a few dollars. We have no bread, no cheese, no nothing to eat."

He didn't look up, but his brushing got a little more strenuous. "Can't."

"We can't?" Marike wasn't sure she had heard clearly. "Why not? Didn't you get paid yesterday?"

"Yes, but . . ."

"But what?" Marike was confused, but starting to get angry. It wasn't like Dirck to waste his money or to not speak directly.

By David Carrico

The brush stopped, and he looked toward the door, not at her. "I . . . gave the money to Brother Matthäus, to use to help other families in the church."

"You what?" Marike didn't believe what she was hearing. "But what are we supposed to do? What will we eat? How will we pay the rent on the room this week?"

Dirck continued to avoid her gaze. "It . . . is expected of me. The Mighty Men are supposed to be exemplars of charity and ministry."

"Fine." Marike put her hands on her hips. "But did you have to give it all? Now we're going to need charity ourselves."

He finally looked at her. "It . . . is expected. And it's important to me, Mari." His mouth moved for a moment, then he said, "I can borrow some money from friends at work on Monday."

"You just remember that come Monday morning when you're three days without food—you just remember how important this is to you." Marike stomped her foot and went to her bedroom where she threw herself on her bed and stared hot-eyed at the ceiling. She didn't understand what had gotten into Dirck. He had never been less than painfully frugal in the past. How could he have done that? And why would Brother Caspar want these Mighty Men to be giving everything to him? That made no sense. Her grandfather would never have done something like that. But then, her grandfather would never have preached the sermons Brother Caspar was preaching, would he?

Thinking of *Grootpapa* helped Marike relax. She sat up on the edge of the bed and wiped her hands across her face. She stared at the wall as she remembered her grandfather, almost feeling his hand on her shoulder, almost hearing his gravelly voice speaking words of comfort. After a while, she picked up her Bible from the small shelf where it lay and hugged it to her chest. *Grootpapa* had always been her guide in the past. Maybe he would be so in the future.

* * *

The next morning Marike said nothing to Dirck, simply donned her fine clothes and swept out the door when he held it open. She didn't look at him when he walked beside her to the meeting place in his fancy Mighty Men coat. And once there, she stood beside him during the worship, head held high, without a glance in his direction.

Brother Caspar was there that day, and after Brother Matthäus read from Revelation chapter 13, he spoke in his wonderful voice about the lawless man, the Antichrist, and how the end times were upon them. Somehow when he spoke, voice flowing, it all made sense, and Marike found herself again caught up in it.

The attendance was light that day. Most of the Mighty Men Marike had seen before weren't there. She wondered if they had been sent to do some work somewhere; maybe acts of charity or ministry, since that seemed to be such a major issue with them. By the time she finished that thought, the meeting room was almost empty, and Brother Caspar and Brother Matthäus were approaching them.

"Good day to you, Brother Dirck. It is good to see you here at worship. And you, Sister Marike," Brother Caspar's voice in private had even more impact, if that were possible. Marike was drawn to him even more strongly. "It is very good to see you today as well."

Marike's stomach chose that exact moment to emit an almost thunderous growl. As her cheeks heated with embarrassment, Brother Caspar's expression shifted to one of alarm. "Are you ill, Sister Marike? Come, be seated and take a bit of wine."

She found herself being drawn along by Caspar's hand under her elbow, matching the way his voice seemed to hold her mind. Before she could utter a word, she found herself in an inner room, being guided to a chair. "Sit, child, sit," Caspar urged. "Matthäus, wine, now." That short command was not warm. It was hard and carried an edge. The pastor's companion was already at a sideboard pouring from a decanter into a silver cup. A moment later it was in Caspar's hand, and he was holding it to Marike's lips. She took a sip, two, then held her hands up and pushed the cup away gently. She swallowed the wine, then took a deep breath and relaxed against the back of the chair, resting her hands on the arms. Caspar . . . hovered over Marike, was the only way to think of it. "Are you ill, child?"

"No," she said. "Just . . . hungry."

Now Caspar looked confused. "Why?"

She didn't look at Dirck. "My brother gave all his pay to . . ." She waved her hand toward Matthäus. "We have no food, and the rent is due tomorrow."

Caspar straightened, a stern look coming upon his face. "Brother Dirck, while God loves a cheerful giver, he does not expect you to become penurious. The scriptural tithe is thirty percent, no more. You will not give more than that. And Brother Matthäus," he turned to his companion, "whatever Brother Dirck gives will be credited to him for the full offering, but you will return half of it to him immediately. He must see to the care and support of his sister, so we will allow for a reduction of his burden. Is that understood? Both of you?" He looked at both men.

"Yes, Brother Caspar." Matthäus' response was echoed by Dirck.

"When did you last eat, child?" The fulsome warmth returned to Caspar's voice as he turned again to Marike.

"Friday." Her voice trembled a little, which increased her shame.

Caspar passed the cup to Matthäus and went to the sideboard himself, where he picked up a silver plate covered with a napkin and returned to set it before Marike. He whisked the napkin off to reveal a meat pie. "Eat, child. You shall not leave until you've eaten it all. I will not have it said that we allowed one of our own to go hungry." She hesitated, and he nudged the plate toward her. "Eat, child." His voice was softer, and so warm, so soothing . . . she picked up the pie in both hands and bit a corner off it. The gravy and the bits of meat and carrots tasted so good.

Marike tried to not devour the pie, but she was aware that she was eating it pretty quickly. She caught a glimpse of Brother Matthäus passing some silver coins to Dirck, who took them almost with a bow.

It wasn't long before Marike swallowed the last of the pie and sat back with a repleted sigh.

"Do you feel better now, child?"

Brother Caspar wasn't quite hovering, but his expression was still one of concern.

"I do. Please forgive me for my foolishness," she said, her face heating a bit at the memory of what had just happened.

"There is nothing to forgive, Sister Marike," Caspar said with a smile. "And I am glad that we were able to help."

Marike pushed her hands down on the arms of the chair, and stood. "Thank you for your kindness. I'm sure I can make it home, now."

"You are welcome to stay longer," Caspar protested.

"No, we should go home and not take more of your time, Brother Caspar. But . . . thank you."

With those words, Marike led her brother out of the inner room, followed by the two men. She didn't look back as she crossed the meeting room and exited to the street outside. Dirck hastened before her to open the door, and closed it behind them as they left. Because she didn't look behind, she didn't see Brother Caspar turn to look at Matthäus; nor did she see the slow nod Matthäus gave.

✱ ✱ ✱

By David Carrico

It came as no great surprise the next Sunday after worship when Dirck told Marike he had another meeting to attend. She didn't argue with him about it, but once he left, wearing his Mighty Men coat, she looked through her school bag until she found the scrap of paper which had the address for the Bible study group that Katharina had given her. After a moment looking at it, she put on her coat, picked up her grandfather's Bible, and left their room.

As it happened, Marike thought she knew where the street in the address was in Grantville. She was pretty sure her school bus crossed it when taking her to school. So she shouldn't be more than a couple of miles from it, maybe a half more than that. But she had plenty of time to walk that far before three o'clock, and it was a nice day.

It turned out Marike's memory was, if not perfect, at least reasonably accurate, and it was less than an hour before she stood on the front porch of the house number on the address that Katharina had given her. She took a deep breath—this made her a bit nervous—and knocked on the front door. After a moment, she heard the door knob rattle as it was turned, and the door opened, revealing Barbara Kellarmännin in the doorway.

Barbara looked surprised for a moment, then gave a wide smile. "Marike! Come in, please. We weren't expecting you."

"Dirck had a meeting this afternoon, and I'm tired of sitting in our rooms by myself," Marike said as she stepped through the doorway. "Dirck had a meeting this afternoon, and I'm tired of sitting in our rooms by myself. "So I decided to come and see what your Bible study is all about."

"We're so glad you did," Barbara said, closing the door and leading Marike down the hall into a sitting room that, while not overly large, had a sofa, a couple of upholstered chairs, and a couple of wooden chairs from a dining set at the other end of the room—enough seats to hold half a dozen or more people. Most of the seats were filled with young women.

Katharina jumped up from her chair. "Marike! It's so good to see you. You didn't tell us you were coming."

"I didn't know myself until today," Marike said, holding her Bible in front of her. She repeated the same explanation she'd given Barbara: "Dirck had a meeting."

Well, we're glad you came," Katharina replied. "You know the girls, of course." Marike nodded at Marta Engelsbergin and Alicia Rice. "This," Katharina gestured to an older up-timer woman seated in one of the easy chairs, "is Kathy Sue Burroughs, our teacher."

Kathy Sue stood, shifting her Bible to her left hand so she could hold out her right. "I'm very glad to get to meet you, Marike. Thank you for coming today."

Marike bobbed her head as she tentatively shook Kathy Sue's hand. "Thank you for letting me come."

Katharina pointed to two younger women sitting to one side of Kathy Sue. "These are Rosina and Magdalena. They room here with Frau Burroughs. They're Lutheran. And this," Katharina concluded with a smile, "is our friend Astrid Schäubin. She works for Neustatter's European Security Services. Her brother Hjalmar is dating Eva Želivský, who's usually here but couldn't make it today."

Astrid held her hand out as well. Marike took it, while studying her a bit. Her face was thin, her long uncovered hair was blonde, and the hair along with the style of her blouse and skirt were all evidence that this down-time woman had adopted a lot of Grantville's up-time culture.

"Are you at the school?" Marike asked.

"No," Astrid said with a smile. "I work for Neustatter full-time, but I know a lot of the people there."

"So, now that you know everyone, come sit with Barbara and me," Katharina said, pulling Marike over to the sofa and plopping her down between the two girls.

The others resumed their places as well.

"You got here just in time, Marike," Kathy Sue said. "We're just getting started. We're looking at the Gospel of Luke chapter ten, verses thirty-eight through forty-two."

Marike opened her grandfather's Bible and found that passage quickly. She was pretty sure she knew what that story would be, and as soon as her fingers found the page and she found the first verse, she nodded in confirmation to herself.

"Barbara, would you read that, please?"

Barbara lifted her Bible from her lap and held it up so she could read it but speak forward, rather than down.

"Now it came to pass, as they went, that he entered into a certain village: and a certain woman named Martha received him into her house. And she had a sister called Mary, which also sat at Jesus' feet, and heard his word. But Martha was cumbered about much serving, and came to him, and said, "Lord, dost thou not care that my sister hath left me to serve alone? Bid her therefore that she help me." And Jesus answered and said unto her, 'Martha, Martha, thou art careful and troubled about many things: But one thing is needful: and Mary hath chosen that good part, which shall not be taken away from her.'"

"So what do you think is going on here?" Kathy Sue asked.

"Looks like some sister rivalry to me," Alicia said.

"How so?"

"Well, Martha's coming all big sister on Mary because Mary's not in the kitchen helping her."

"How do you know Martha's the older sister?"

"She was the one who invited Jesus to the house," Katharina said. "That would usually be done by the oldest member of the family present."

Kathy Sue pursed her lips, and nodded. "Okay, I can buy that. Is that why she's so upset with Mary, though?"

Marike listened as the others threw out ideas. She remembered her grandfather's teaching on this passage. Her mouth quirked a bit. They were missing the most obvious reason. She must have shaken her head, because Kathy Sue looked at her and said, "Do you have a thought about this, Marike?"

"Well," Marike drew the word out as she gathered her thoughts quickly, "Martha had offered hospitality to Jesus and the others. That meant the family had made a commitment to provide for them. By not helping Martha with the preparations, Mary was not just letting Martha down, she was letting the entire family down. She was about to bring disrespect onto the whole family. Or that's how Martha would have felt, I think."

Kathy Sue nodded after a moment. "I agree. I think it's more than just sibling rivalry here. What else do you all see?"

The rest of the discussion dealt mostly on how Martha was focused on the serving but Mary was wanting to hear Jesus talk, and how so many people could get trapped the first and lose sight of the second. Marike listened, and added a nod or a word of affirmation from time to time.

Kathy Sue brought the discussion to a close after close to an hour. "The big thing to take away from this for me is that it's always best to do the right thing, but sometimes that means you might not be doing what people expect of you, or even what you expect."

Marike felt a chill at that thought, especially since it seemed that Kathy Sue looked directly at her when she said that.

Kathy Sue closed her Bible. "Good time, girls. Thanks for coming. Kat, Marta, when do you all leave for school at Prague?"

The two older girls looked at each other. "Not quite two weeks," Marta replied.

"Are you going together?"

"That's what we're planning," Katharina said.

"Okay. If I don't see you before then, be careful, but have some fun along the way."

With that, the gathering broke up. Everyone stood and gathered their things, Marike included. Kathy Sue approached her as she stood up, holding out her hand again. Marike took it without hesitation this time. Kathy Sue didn't shake it, just held onto it for a long moment as she said, "Thanks for coming, Marike. I hope you enjoyed it."

"I did, Frau Burroughs."

"Good. Feel free to come back or to come over any time. I'll tell you the same thing I tell the other girls: if you want to talk about anything—Bible study, church, school, boyfriends—I'm willing to pour some apple cider or brew up some sassafras tea and provide a listening ear."

Her gaze was direct, but she was smiling, so Marike smiled back. "I'll probably be back for the Bible study, at least."

"Good."

Kathy Sue walked Marike to the door, and patted her on the back as she left. "Have a good evening."

❈ ❈ ❈

"Well, what did you think?" Kathy Sue asked.

"About Marike?" Katharina shrugged. "I'm glad she came. And she didn't seem to be nervous or anything . . . or at least, not more than she normally would have for the first time in a new place."

"She seemed to fit in well," Kathy Sue said. "She said some good things and followed the discussion."

"She really seemed to know her Bible," Barbara added.

"Didn't she tell us her grandfather was an Anabaptist pastor?" Katharina asked.

"I think so," Barbara said. "So that would probably explain it. I wonder if she would like to join the Bibelgesellschaft? We're going to need some new members after you and Marta leave for Prague."

"Couldn't hurt to ask," Kathy Sue said. "Meanwhile, you all keep an eye on her, and if she starts acting nervous or scared again, encourage her to come talk to me."

"Got it," Barbara said.

❋ ❋ ❋

"Where were you?"

Marike was greeted with that question when she walked in the door to their rooms. Dirck was standing in the main room, and he was frowning.

"I have some friends who have a group Bible study on Sunday afternoon. Most of them are Anabaptist, and the teacher is an up-timer woman who is friendly to Anabaptists, so it was safe. They've been inviting me to come to the study for months, now—ever since we got here, in fact. I'm tired of sitting in the rooms by myself when you go to your meetings, so I went to the study. It was good. They looked at a story in the Gospel of Luke today. I liked it."

Marike took her coat off and hung it on a peg by the door, then placed her bonnet next to it. She turned to look at Dirck while putting her indoor cap on and straightening it.

Her brother wasn't frowning, but still didn't look happy. "You should have told me, or left a note, or something. I got home and you weren't here, and I got worried."

"I didn't decide to go until after you left, so I couldn't tell you, but you're right, I should have left a note. I guess I thought I'd be home before you got back, but it took a bit longer to walk to Frau Burroughs' house than I'd thought it would."

"All right." Dirck took off his Mighty Men coat and hung it from its regular peg. He stood still for a moment, looking at where his hand rested on the coat atop its peg. "Marike, don't say anything to Brother Caspar and Brother Matthäus about attending this study. They . . . might not understand."

✻ ✻ ✻

Marike wore the clothes that Brother Caspar had given her to worship the next Sunday. This made the third Sunday in a row that Caspar was in Grantville. That was unusual, because he traveled occasionally to Magdeburg, but more and more to the village of Angelroda, somewhere west of Grantville. He seldom spent more than one Sunday—two at the most—in the Grantville area without moving on. Not even Dirck could tell her why Brother Caspar traveled; only that he did, and it was important.

The meeting room was over half-full when the two of them arrived, but people made way for Dirck in his Mighty Men coat, and Marike trailed along behind him.

When it came time for the teaching, Brother Matthäus stepped forward in his usual way.

"Today we shall read from the Second Epistle of John, the beloved disciple.

'And this is love, that we walk after his commandments. This is the commandment, That, as ye have heard from the beginning, ye should walk in it. For many deceivers are entered into the world, who confess not that Jesus Christ is come in the flesh. This is a deceiver and an antichrist. Look to yourselves, that we lose not those things which we have wrought, but that we receive a full reward. Whosoever transgresseth, and abideth not in the doctrine of Christ, hath not God. He that abideth in the doctrine of Christ, he hath both the Father and the Son. If there come any unto you, and bring not this doctrine, receive him not into your house, neither bid him God speed: for he that biddeth him God speed is partaker of his evil deeds.'

"And now Brother Caspar will instruct us."

Matthäus stepped back and Brother Caspar took his usual step forward and looked around. "The Apostle John lived in times fraught with danger and risk and paganism and apostasy." His rich warm voice contrasted with Matthäus' dark tones. "So do you today. And the beloved disciple's warning about false teachers is perhaps even more urgent today than it was when he wrote his epistle. False teachers are everywhere: in the pulpits of the cathedrals and basilicas and churches. Standing at the front of the meeting houses. Teaching in the schools and universities. The pastors and doyens and bishops teach falsehood. The truth is out there." His voice crescendoed to a peak. "They are antichrists, all! They have heard the truth, but they have willingly and willfully rejected it."

Caspar paused for a long moment. Not a sound was heard in the room . . . not even breathing. Marike was holding her breath for sure.

When he started speaking again, his tone was lower, quieter, but had that velvet warmth that Marike just wanted to sink into. "That is why the truth was revealed to only a few over the centuries. Paul called it a mystery. And that is why even today so very few people know the truth, the truth that we share."

Caspar looked around the room. His gaze seemed to linger on Marike, but moved on before too long. "All of the apostles told us to beware of false teachers, those who provide the tainted milk of apostasy and heresy. Paul told us to not be unequally yoked with those who do not know the truth. Be very careful, my brothers, my sisters," he looked around once more, "be careful who you associate with, and if there are any doubts at all in your mind, consult your elders. Be the holy set apart ones you have been called to be."

Marike lowered her head. It sounded so reasonable when Brother Caspar explained it, but in the back of her mind she knew he was wrong if he thought her *Grootpapa* had been a false teacher. She kept her eyes on the ground as she turned and followed Dirck from the meeting hall.

❈ ❈ ❈

Caspar looked at Matthäus after the last of the worshippers left. Matthäus nodded. "They're responding well," the assistant said. "They should be ready to move soon."

"Sister Marike seemed very intent on the word today," Caspar observed.

"Indeed." Matthäus nodded again, this time with a slight smile.

"We are almost ready for the next step, I think," Caspar said. "I will leave for Angelroda on the morrow. Do you see to it that my next gift for Sister Marike is taken to her. Time for the next step there, as well."

❈ ❈ ❈

"Hi, Marike." Marike swallowed her last bite of bread when Katharina and Barbara dropped into chairs on each side of her in the lunchroom. The Tuesday lunch crowd seemed a bit smaller than usual.

"Hi," she responded. She was, bit by bit, picking up some of the Americanisms so common in Grantville that were beginning to spread elsewhere.

"Did you like the Bible study the other day?" That was Katharina.

"Yes, I did. I learned some things that I hadn't heard before. It was good."

"Great." Katharina's face bloomed with a smile. "Now that you know where it is, you should come to them all. With Marta and I going to Prague soon, Kathy Sue would like to keep the attendance up. Plus she really liked you. She said you made great comments."

"I thought you were still students here in the high school," Marike said. "I was really surprised with Frau Burroughs said you were going to Prague."

"No, Marta and I finished the high school degree requirements back in May," Katharina said. "We're just taking some extra courses to try and get ready for university."

"Like what?"

"Advanced Latin, mostly, with some more intermediate Greek thrown in for me, plus a couple of classes just for fun." Katharina shrugged. "As

Kathy Sue says, 'Can't hurt, might help.' Anything that will help get me started in university is worth doing."

"How about you, Barbara?" Marike turned to the other girl. "Are you going to university also—Prague, or maybe Jena?"

"No." Barbara grinned. "I'm going to stay in Grantville. I've been studying with the police department learning to be a profiler."

"A what?"

"A profiler. That's someone who studies a person, usually a criminal, and figures out what their patterns of behavior are."

Marike could see that Barbara was very serious. "But what good would that do?"

"Sometimes that's how they figure out who the criminal is," Barbara said. "Sometimes, it's to figure out why someone is performing crimes."

"Sounds . . . I don't know . . ." Marike couldn't figure out what to say.

"Sounds yucky to me," Katharina said. "The last thing I want to know is how to think like someone who's not right in the head." She stuck her tongue out at Barbara, who returned the favor. "She's been going on about this for months now and prattling about all the books she's reading."

"Chief Richards thinks I could be good at it," Barbara replied with equanimity.

The bell rang, and all three girls stood.

"Tell Frau Burroughs I'll try to come again soon," Marike offered before turning away.

"She'll be glad to hear that," Katharina responded. "See you."

✷ ✷ ✷

Thursday evening, just a few minutes after Dirck got home, there was a knock at the door of their rooms. Dirck was still washing up, so Marike went to the door.

"Yes? Oh, Brother Matthäus." She was surprised to see the elder standing in the doorway with a bundle.

"Sister Marike," he said with a nod of his head. "May I come in?"

Marike flushed at her lack of courtesy. "Yes, of course. Excuse me, please." She stepped aside, and Matthäus entered the room.

"Brother Dirck," the elder said as her brother turned from the wash basin, wiping his hands and face on a towel.

Dirck gave a nod that was almost a short bow. "Brother Matthäus. Welcome to our home. I did not know you were coming to see us."

"I didn't know myself until a couple of hours ago, but Brother Caspar had asked me to come by, and when it turned out that I had another matter to address in this part of town, it only made sense to meet two obligations in one trip."

"Thank you for visiting, nonetheless," Dirck said. "I'm sorry that we have nothing to offer you to drink. I was about to go get some beer, if you would care to wait."

"No," Matthäus said, with a smile and a gesture of one hand. "I've got to move on. I'm really here just to deliver something for Brother Caspar. First of all, he wants you to know, both of you, how much he appreciates and values your faithfulness in attending worship. Your constant and consistent presence provides both support to him directly and a good example to the others. So he and I both thank you deeply for that."

Marike felt a bit of warmth as she heard the praise, but remained silent. Dirck responded with, "Thank you, Brother Matthäus, but we are only doing what is right."

"That may be so," the elder said, "but would that more did. Just know that you are appreciated and valued. And second," he turned toward

Marike, "Brother Caspar has sent this to you, Sister Marike, as a recognition of your faithfulness and your probity, and to, in some small way, make up for the inconveniences you have suffered of late." He unfolded his bundle and, as she instinctively held out her hands, placed a folded cloth in them.

Marike hesitated. Whatever it was was light. She slowly unfolded the cloth and held it up. In the light of the candle it was revealed to be a shawl woven of fine linen. It was very fine linen, very soft and smooth, and it was dyed a deep burgundy color. Something caught her eye, and she took a corner of the material and brought it closer to her eyes. There were embroidered flowers in the corners. She smiled and checked each corner—flowers in every one. It was very pretty.

Her smile dimmed a little. This was fine work—finer than anything she had ever owned, or her mother had ever owned—finer than even Brother Caspar's previous gift. She lowered the shawl and stared at Brother Matthäus.

"Brother Caspar hopes that this gift will be acceptable to you," the elder said. His eyes seemed to bore into hers. "And if you need anything—anything at all—you need only ask."

Marike swallowed.

✼ ✼ ✼

Grantville
August, 1636

"Hi, Marike." Kathy Sue met her at the door this time. "Come on in. Most of the girls are already here." Marike followed the up-timer back to the living room. "You know most everyone, but for Anna Maria, I think." She pointed to a down-timer sitting next to Magdalena, one of those Marike had met the first time she attended the study. "She was watching my kids last time. Rosina is watching them tonight." Marike nodded to everyone, and settled onto the couch next to Barbara, who smiled and reached out to squeeze her hand.

Kathy Sue settled in her chair and opened her Bible. "Kat and Marta are on the road to Prague. I think it would be good to pray for them before we begin."

Marike bowed her head, and listened as Kathy Sue first prayed for the welfare of their friends as they traveled, then asked for blessings on the study they were about to share. After the concluding "Amen," everyone opened their Bibles.

"Luke chapter eight, verses forty through fifty-six," Kathy Sue said. Everyone paged through their Bibles. "Marike, would you please read the passage for us?"

Marike swallowed, sat up straight, angled her Bible to get the best light on the pages, and began.

"'And it came to pass, that, when Jesus was returned, the people gladly received him: for they were all waiting for him. And, behold, there came a man named Jairus, and he was a ruler of the synagogue: and he fell down at Jesus' feet, and besought him that he would come into his house: for he had only one daughter, about twelve years of age, and she lay dying. But as he went the people thronged him.

And a woman having an issue of blood twelve years, which had spent all her living upon physicians, neither could be healed of any, came behind him, and touched the border of his garment: and immediately her issue of blood stanched. And Jesus said, Who touched me? When all denied, Peter and they that were with him said, Master, the multitude throng thee and press thee, and sayest thou, Who touched me? And Jesus said, Somebody hath touched me: for I perceive that virtue is gone out of me. And when the woman saw that she was not hid, she came trembling, and falling down before him, she declared unto him before all the people for what cause she had touched him, and how she was healed immediately. And he said unto her, Daughter, be of good comfort: thy faith hath made thee whole; go in peace.

While he yet spake, there cometh one from the ruler of the synagogue's house, saying to him, Thy daughter is dead; trouble not the Master. But when Jesus heard it, he answered him, saying, Fear not: believe only, and she shall be made whole. And when he came into the house, he suffered no man to go in, save Peter, and James, and John, and the father and the mother of the maiden. And all wept, and bewailed her: but he said, Weep not; she is not dead, but sleepeth. And they laughed him to scorn, knowing that she was dead. And he put them all out, and took her by the hand, and called, saying, Maid, arise. And her spirit came again, and she arose straightway: and he commanded to give her meat. And her parents were astonished: but he charged them that they should tell no man what was done.'"

"There are two miracles in this passage," Kathy Sue said, "both involving women or girls, one contained within the story of the other. Let's talk about the outer story first. What can you tell about Jairus from this story?"

Marike listened to the others as they listed characteristics of the man: he was an important community leader, he was willing to humble himself by both coming to Jesus and by prostrating himself before Jesus, he cared about his daughter. She didn't have anything to add to any of that, so she kept silent.

"Some teachers and commentators think that this was Jairus' only child," Kathy Sue said, "that that was why he was so concerned about her. I don't know that I can accept that. Scripture is definite that she was his only daughter, but it's silent as to whether or not she had any brothers. I've found that it's wise to be cautious about making assumptions in things where Scripture doesn't speak. It could be that she was his only child. On the other hand, I don't think it would make any real difference to the story if she had any brothers. So let's not spend any more time on that.

"Scripture does tell us, though, that she was twelve years old." Kathy Sue looked around the room. "Why would Luke have made a point of including that in the story? Does it tell us anything about her?"

"She wasn't a little child," Barbara said. "She would have been big enough to do things around the home and help her mother."

Kathy Sue nodded. "Anything else?"

"Would she have started menstruating?" That question from Magdalena rocked Marike a little. She hadn't even thought along those lines.

"Possibly." Kathy Sue nodded. "And that might have some bearing. Most commentators and scholars that I've read say that Jewish customs of the time would have said that a girl was marriageable once she reached puberty, which was often around twelve or twelve and a half. And it was also apparently fairly common for girls to be betrothed earlier than that but for the actual wedding to wait until after that. So, again, I don't want to read something into the passage that isn't there—I don't want to put words in Scripture's mouth, so to speak—but it's quite possible that the girl was betrothed, and might actually have been nearing her marriage time."

Wow. Marike sat back. That thought shed a different light on this passage. She raised a hand, and Kathy Sue nodded at her. "Jairus was an important man in the community. If she was his only child, and was betrothed, that marriage would have been very important for the family, wouldn't it?"

Kathy Sue smiled. "Yes, it would. Even if she had a brother or two, it still could have been very important. And if that was the case, that could put a different emphasis on what's happening here, couldn't it? I'm not saying it is or isn't the case. Scripture doesn't say any more than it does. But what we are told would allow for different factors like that to come into play. And I happen to think that because Luke did tell us she was twelve, something like that must have been there, otherwise, why would he make such a point of it?"

Marike nodded slowly. "And her husband would probably have been an older man."

Kathy Sue shrugged. "Maybe. Maybe not. It's hard to say. For example, tradition says that Joseph was older than Mary, but the Bible doesn't say one way or the other. I confess to getting frustrated sometimes with the details that God leaves out of His Word." She grinned, and most of the girls giggled and nodded.

Marike said nothing more during the lesson, which focused on the miracle itself. But even as she listened to the discussion, she couldn't rid herself of the idea of a young girl marrying an older man.

"We'll pick up from there next week," Kathy Sue said when the clock on the wall chimed the hour. "Go ahead and be thinking about what Luke says about the second miracle."

Marike just sat while the other girls all stood and gathered their things and started leaving. Anna Maria and Magdalena went upstairs, the others moved toward the door, chattering as they did so. After a moment,

Kathy Sue noticed and moved over to sit beside her. "Marike, are you all right?" she asked quietly.

Marike nodded, then after a moment shook her head.

Barbara stopped in the door and looked back. Marike caught Kathy Sue making a motion with a hand out of the corner of her eye. Barbara didn't say anything, just turned and left.

Once the front door closed for the last time, Kathy Sue reached over and patted Marike on the arm a couple of times, then sat back. "Is there something you'd like to talk about?"

After a moment, Marike murmured, "Is it wrong for an older man to want to marry a younger woman?"

Kathy Sue took a deep breath and released it. "That's not one of those questions that has a single definite answer. It depends on their ages, and it depends to some extent on what their society approves of."

Marike looked up at her. "What do you up-timers say?"

"The laws of the State of West Virginia, which is where Grantville was before the Ring of Fire, say that a person must be eighteen years old before he or she can be married of their own free will. If their parents—both of them, if they're alive—approve of it, they can be married at sixteen. Most of the other states in the United States of America had similar laws. Those laws are now part of the laws of Grantville and the County of West Virginia here and now."

"I'm sixteen." Marike placed her Bible on her lap and wrapped her arms around herself.

"Is someone trying to convince you to marry him?" Kathy Sue leaned forward.

"Yes. No. I don't know. He hasn't said anything. He hasn't touched me. But he looks at me. And he keeps giving me things." Marike turned her head away from Kathy Sue. She couldn't stand to see her gaze.

"Who is it?"

There was a long stretch of silence before Marike could make herself say, "Brother Caspar. Our pastor."

Kathy Sue took another deep breath. Marike turned back enough to see her expression out of the corner of her eye. Her face was hard. Her lips were compressed into a thin line. It was another period of silence before she opened her mouth.

"What has he given you?"

Marike shrugged. "Me, he gave a suit of clothes and just the other day a shawl. They are much nicer than anything Mama or Grandmama ever owned. He had some money given to Dirck to take care of me, and he reduced our tithe for the same reason."

"You say he doesn't touch you. That he only looks at you. Has he ever asked anything of you?"

Marike swallowed, and looked away again. "The first time, he asked me to let my hair down. Dirck told me to." She swallowed again. Her voice got thicker. "He didn't touch me, but he held his hand close to my head, and moved it down my arm and back." She looked back at Kathy Sue. Her eyes were wide, and she could feel the tears starting. "He didn't touch me, but I could feel it. I had my eyes closed, and I could feel his hand moving."

Kathy Sue went to her knees beside Marike's chair and wrapped her arms around her. Marike just huddled in that encirclement, as tears slowly moved down her face. After a time, the tears slowed and stopped. She reached up and scrubbed her cheeks.

"Marike," Kathy Sue said. "Has he done anything like that again?"

"No," Marike whispered. "Just that once."

"You said he looks at you?"

"When he's preaching . . . when we're in the same room . . . he looks at me like . . . like . . ."

"Like you're naked?"

"No." Marike bit her lip for a moment. "Like . . . like the breeders look when they see a prize brood mare."

Kathy Sue absorbed that. "So he hasn't said anything to you about marriage?"

"No. But today's lesson made me start wondering." She looked up at Kathy Sue. "Do you know what he's doing?"

Kathy Sue was still for a moment, then looked up. "Maybe." She rose to her feet and walked a few steps back and forth. "We up-timers have a term for what I think is going on."

"Of course you do," Marike said, trying to smile. "You up-timers have words for everything."

Kathy Sue snorted. "Yeah, well, maybe so. But the term for this is 'child grooming,' and it's used to describe what happens where older people, especially ones in authority, start preparing and shaping young people, boys or girls, to be sexual partners."

"So you think he is thinking about marriage?"

"Maybe. Or concubinage. Or just outright bondage. Brother Caspar is not well liked around here outside of his own group. I wouldn't put any of that outside the realm of possibility."

Marike swallowed. "I didn't know."

"You have no reason to know. And I'm not going to spend time talking about the past. But for right now, you need to understand that you have rights under the laws of Grantville. You cannot be forced to marry or submit to anyone against your will."

Marike shook her head. "Dirck is so involved."

Kathy Sue knelt beside her again and looked her directly in the eyes. "Dirck is not your parent. He is not even your legal guardian, since he hasn't been appointed to that by a Grantville or County of West Virginia court. So he cannot legally force you or bind you to do anything you don't want to do. I don't want to split you up, but if things get bad, tell a teacher at school or come here and we'll get you to safety."

Marike looked down. "I don't know."

Kathy Sue lifted her chin up. "If it gets bad, run. Protect yourself. Okay?"

Marike took a deep breath, and nodded.

※ ※ ※

The man who was loitering by a tree on the corner froze as he heard a sound behind him.

"You know," came the sound of an amused soprano voice, "if you're going to keep watch on a place, you should at least try not to be obvious about it, and you really shouldn't let people sneak up on you."

He turned around slowly to see a tall blonde woman standing a couple of yards down the sidewalk from him. "What do you mean?"

"Don't play stupid," she said, her tone becoming rather cool as the amusement faded. "I saw you there watching the Burroughs house from across the street when I arrived, and you're still here when I left. I walked around the block, and you're still here. It's not hard to figure out what you're doing. I'm Astrid Schäubin, a team leader in Neustatter's European Security Service, by the way, so I do have a professional interest in this. What's your name?"

"Johann Eschbach," he replied after a moment. "Not that it's any business of yours."

"Oh, I can make it my business, and I will if I see you or anyone else here again. Do you understand me?" She brushed the edge of her coat back, and he saw the pistol holstered on her hip.

He nodded.

"Good. Now, leave, and tell whoever you're working for that the Burroughs and their friends are off-limits. You understand what that means?"

He nodded again.

"Move."

Eschbach turned and walked away. Astrid watched until he was at least three blocks down the street. She looked back at Kathy Sue's house. That new girl, Marike, was still inside. She needed to talk to Kathy Sue about what just happened, but she didn't want to interrupt anything. Just as she was about to walk away, the door to the house opened, and Marike stepped out. Astrid stepped closer to the tree, but Marike didn't look around as she walked down and turned the corner going the other direction. Astrid gave her a minute or so, then walked across the street and up the steps to ring the doorbell.

Kathy Sue opened the door almost immediately.

"Astrid?" She stepped back to let the younger woman enter. "What's up?"

"Just wanted to let you know that there was a man across the street this afternoon watching your house. I saw him when I arrived and didn't think anything about it, but when I saw him when I left, that rang an alarm. I confronted him and forced him to leave. I also told him to tell his boss that you and your friends are off-limits, but I don't know if that will make any difference."

Kathy Sue scowled, and she muttered something that Astrid didn't quite catch. The older woman took a deep breath and snorted it out. "Come with me."

They walked into the kitchen together, where Kathy Sue picked up her phone and dialed a number. Astrid could hear the ringing faintly as the call went through. After about four rings, Kathy Sue straightened. "Melanie? This is Kathy Sue Burroughs." She nodded at the response.

"Fine. I'm fine. Kids are doing great. Listen, is Press there? Could I speak to him, please?" She tapped her foot while she waited.

"Press? Kathy Sue here. Listen, I've got some info for you on that matter we discussed with Brother Al here the other day." Her mouth twisted. "Yeah, it's not good, and I'm not happy to have heard it myself, but it's not as bad as it could be. I think there's definitely some grooming going on, but she was pretty firm that there hasn't been any physical contact. The girl is named Marike Gendt, and she's a pretty new arrival from Holland, so she's new and doesn't know many people yet. That fits the pattern. They've been sucked in by Brother Caspar's group." She frowned. "Yeah. And to make it worse, one of the things the girls didn't tell Brother Al is this girl is small—petite, in fact—so she looks younger than she really is. That may be a factor here." She listened for a moment, then nodded. "Yeah, that's kind of what I'm thinking, too. No parents. Just her and her brother, and he hasn't been appointed her legal guardian, so that could give you some leverage if needed." More listening. "Yeah. I'll make some notes, and you can send somebody by for them tomorrow.

"And Press? Astrid Schäubin is here. She said somebody was watching the house today. She ran him off, but that may mean that Brother Caspar's folks are getting ready to escalate things again. Thought you ought to know." More listening, more nodding of the head. "Right. Got it. My Remington .300 is up on a shelf in the living room." More listening. "Yes, I'll call first, but anyone who comes through that door without an invitation is going to get ventilated."

Kathy Sue listened some more. "Right. Got it. Just be sure your dispatcher knows that if I call it's for real. Right. Okay. See you tomorrow. Thanks. Bye."

She hung up the phone and looked at Astrid. "Okay, that's done. Chief Richards says thanks for the heads up."

Astrid nodded. "Glad to be of service. Guess I'll make it a point to be here the next few Sundays, and if I can't, I'll have someone else who's packing come."

Kathy Sue nodded. "I think I'd appreciate that for a while."

❈ ❈ ❈

"Brother Matthäus?"

The elder turned to see a young member of their group approaching him. What was his name? Johann . . . what was it . . . Eschbach. That was it. "Yes, Brother Johann? Is it something important? I need to be at a meeting of some of the Mighty Men in a minute or two."

"It . . . might be important," Eschbach said. "I know you said we were to not go near the house of Frau Burroughs. But I thought it might be useful to know who is going to their house, so I've been spending some of my time watching them."

"And?" Matthäus wasn't happy that his orders had been ignored, but if Eschbach was coming to him, maybe he had seen something.

"I saw someone at their house last Sunday. Someone that I think you and Brother Caspar will want to know about."

Matthäus pointed his finger in the young man's face. "I don't have time for this right now. Brother Caspar will be here in an hour. You say nothing to no one about this until after Brother Caspar has heard about it. Understand?"

"Yes, Brother Matthäus."

"Good. Stand over there out of the way."

Matthäus spun and continued on his way. The chances of Eschbach having anything truly worthy of Brother Caspar's notice were slim, but one could never tell.

From what Eschbach could tell, it was a bit over an hour before an inner door opened and an older man in a Mighty Men coat stepped out. "You Eschbach?"

"Ja."

The man nodded at the door to the inner room. "Brother Caspar and Brother Matthäus are in there. Brother Matthäus said for you to enter."

Johann walked up to the door, reached for the handle, and hesitated. He couldn't bring himself to just march in unannounced. He lifted his hand and knocked twice. There was a muffled response, that he took to be a command to enter. Now he opened the door.

Brother Caspar was sitting in a chair pushed back from a table, legs outstretched before him. His coat was unbuttoned and hanging open, and a shirt that was a little the worse for wear was exposed.

Brother Matthäus was standing to one side of the table near the side wall of the room.

Both men looked at Johann. He closed the door and clasped his hands behind his back. "You instructed me to come tonight, Brother Matthäus."

"And so I did," the elder said taking a step forward. "This, Brother Caspar,"—he waved a hand at Eschbach—"is Johann Eschbach, one of your long-time faithful followers. He tells me he has observed something that might be of interest."

Brother Caspar looked at Johann, smiled, and said, "Tell me what you saw, Brother Johann." The warmth in his voice settled into Johann's mind.

"I, uh . . ." Johann began. "I . . . know that we had some . . . issues . . . with the up-time Burroughs family, and I know we were supposed to leave them alone afterward. But it occurred to me that it might be a good idea to keep an eye on them, so I started watching their house on Sundays, just to see who might be coming to their so-called church. Most

Sundays it was the same group of people we already knew about—a very few up-timers and some down-timers, especially Anabaptists."

"But?" Brother Caspar said.

"But last Sunday, I saw someone from our congregation go there."

Brother Caspar's eyebrows drew down, and Brother Matthäus frowned. "Who?" came from Caspar.

"That new girl . . . the Hollander . . . the one who's Brother Dirck's sister. Sorry, I don't remember her name."

Johann took some pleasure in telling them that. He had been a bit peeved that Brother Dirck had been asked to be one of the Mighty Men so soon after joining the congregation. There were other men who had been faithful longer that he thought should have been considered. His thoughts were interrupted before he could go down that list.

"You mean Sister Marike Gendt?"

"I don't think I knew her name before, but if she's Brother Dirck's sister, then yes."

There was a long moment of silence, then Brother Caspar spoke.

"Ordinarily we would not excuse ignoring or disobeying instructions from the elders. However . . ." Caspar drew his feet in and stood ". . .in this one instance good came of it. Thank you for this information. I suggest, however, that you do not make a practice of this."

"Yes, Brother Caspar. I, ah, was caught by one of the Neustatter operatives. She told me to stay away, that the Burroughs family were . . . how did she say it . . . 'off-limits' to me and anyone working for my leaders."

"Then I suggest you listen to her," Caspar said. He turned away from Eschbach.

Matthäus said, "Thank you, Brother Johann." He motioned at the door, and Johann withdrew.

There was another long moment of silence before Caspar spoke again.

"Summon Brother Dirck." There was no warmth in his voice at all. It was thin, nasal, and icy. He picked up a narrow-bladed dagger and rolled it between his fingers.

※ ※ ※

Marike hummed a little bit as she finished changing her clothes and donned her jacket. She was glad today was Sunday. The week leading up to it had been long, it seemed. School seemed different with Katharina and Marta gone. She still saw Barbara and some of the others fairly frequently in the hallways, but the shift to the autumn class schedule meant that many of them were on a different lunch schedule, so she didn't get to have long conversations with them much.

This morning's sermon from Brother Caspar had not been as good as he usually did, she thought while she put her gift suit on its pegs on the wall. He hadn't seemed as warm as usual. Distracted, maybe. He'd looked at her about as much as he always did, but with no sense of connection, somehow. She shrugged. Whatever it was, she was actually kind of glad of it.

Her stomach growled, and she slapped it lightly. "Hush, you." Dirck had announced last night that they would fast today. He hadn't said why, and she didn't ask. They had started growing apart to some extent lately. She wasn't sure how she felt about that. Some sadness, of course. They'd been close for so long, having only each other after her parents died. She wasn't sure that it wasn't a good thing, though. The more he wore his Mighty Men coat, the more uncomfortable she became around him. She suspected the fasting idea had come from them.

She walked out into the main room, and found Dirck dressed in his Mighty Men coat with his hand on the door knob. "Another meeting?"

she asked. Dirck didn't quite look sheepish, but he nodded his head and left without saying anything.

Marike sighed. She wished they had never gone to Brother Caspar's congregation. She wished Dirck had never accepted the Mighty Men coat. But she couldn't deny that the congregation—actually, she was certain it was Brother Caspar's doing—had been good to them. So what could she do? What should she do?

She looked around aimlessly. Her glance finally fell on her grandfather's Bible sitting in her chair. That made her think of the Bible study, and her resolve stiffened. She walked over and pulled her coat from its peg and put it on, then picked up the Bible. Cradling it in her arms, she felt her resolution increase. She walked out the door, left the rooming house, and began the walk to Frau Burroughs' house with firm steps.

* * *

"Goodbye," Marike said to Kathy Sue as she stepped out the door.

"See you next week, dear," the older woman said before she turned to the next girl about to leave.

Marike started down the sidewalk, Bible cradled to her chest, feeling good. The lesson about the woman with the issue of blood, the second part of last week's lesson, had been good. There had been lots of discussion, and she'd been able to say several things herself. She smiled at that thought. Who would have thought that the stories her grandfather had taught her as a little girl would still be guiding her.

There was a shadow on the sidewalk in front of Marike. She stopped and looked up, experiencing surprise and some shock to see Dirck standing there. He reached to take her by the arm and urged her into motion again. She pulled on her arm, but Dirck's grasp was firm, and he wouldn't release her.

"What are you doing?" Marike said. "Dirck, you're hurting me. Let go."

"Brother Caspar wants to talk to you."

A chill ran through Marike. "I don't want to."

"Brother Caspar told me to bring you to him. He wants to talk to you."

Dirck wasn't looking at her. His gaze was fixed straight ahead, and his stride was strong and rapid. Marike was having trouble keeping up.

"Dirck, let me go."

"No."

✽ ✽ ✽

Marike had quit trying to look back, because whenever she did Dirck yanked on her arm and about pulled her off her feet. Dirck had taken her out of Grantville by a different path than she normally used. It was more circuitous so it took longer to walk, but they did end up on the Rudolstadt road finally. It was Sunday, so there weren't as many travelers on the road as usual. She didn't try to struggle or call out. She wasn't sure it would do any good, and in her heart she still hoped that Dirck would not let anything bad happen to her.

She had quit pulling on her arm. Dirck was not letting go, and she didn't want to cause a public uproar. She just wanted to get whatever this was going to be over with, so she clutched her grandfather's Bible to her chest, stared straight ahead, and walked as fast as she had to to keep up with him.

They were past the area where their rooming house was, and were drawing near to the group of buildings where Brother Caspar's meeting house was. She started taking deep breaths and stiffening her back. Whatever was getting ready to happen, she was pretty sure she wasn't going to enjoy it. She just hoped she could get out of it with nothing more than a lot of shouting and shaking. She could deal with that, she thought. Other possibilities, though . . . kept cropping up at the edge of her mind, and she kept trying to push them away.

It wasn't much longer before Dirck turned off the Rudolstadt road, Marike perforce going with him. When they walked by the meeting house, however, that surprised Marike. She looked up at Dirck, but he stared straight ahead as they walked past two more buildings to a small one that stood behind a larger one. It wasn't much larger than a shed, although it did have a porch the width of the building. There was another man in a Mighty Men coat on the porch beside a door, holding a club. Marike swallowed as an empty feeling grew in the pit of her stomach.

Dirck dragged her up on the porch, knocked on the door, and opened it when someone spoke from inside. He looked down at her, said, "Brother Caspar wants to speak to you," then pushed her through the doorway. She heard it close behind her as she stood there, frozen, clutching her grandfather's Bible, eyes on Brother Caspar sitting in a chair behind a narrow table, staring at her, no expression on his face.

Marike swallowed but said nothing; did nothing except clutch the Bible even harder. Her stomach was tied in a giant knot. Long moments passed. She felt cold; her hands and feet felt like ice. Brother Caspar eventually blinked, then lifted a hand and pointed a finger. "Sit."

There was a stool half under the leading edge of the table. Marike sidled up to it, pulled the stool out and gingerly seated herself on it, placing her grandfather's Bible directly in front of her and sitting upright with her hands clasped on her lap. She stared at Brother Caspar's nose to keep from looking into his eyes, and concentrated on breathing slowly and evenly. Her stomach had started trying to climb up her throat. The back of her mouth was flooding with saliva, and she had to swallow every couple of breaths to keep it from leaking out her lips.

Brother Caspar began tapping a fingernail against the tabletop. *Tic . . . tic . . . tic . . . tic . . .* still staring at her . . . still saying nothing. Marike held her body motionless, but her hands twisted together so hard that all her knuckles were white and she could see her fingertips turning a dark red. She wanted to jump up and run away, but she knew Dirck was standing outside the door and would just push her back inside unless Brother Caspar said she could go.

Tic . . . tic . . . tic . . . tic . . . The sound was resonating in her head. She blinked. She couldn't help it. She wanted to close her eyes tight, but she was starting to get angry, and she wouldn't give him the pleasure of seeing her give way.

Tic . . . It took Marike a long moment to realize the noise had stopped. She almost melted from the relief, but Brother Caspar's expression had changed, and she didn't want to give way before him. His eyes had narrowed, and his lips, which were not exactly full to begin with, had narrowed to be not much more than a compressed line. His finger was pressing so hard on the tabletop that its first joint was white. Marike held her breath.

"I am told that you are attending a Bible study other than ours." After the long silence, Brother Caspar's voice when he spoke seemed rather louder than normal, even more so than his sermon voice. The tone didn't match his sermons either, being deeper, darker, and not as warm. It wasn't hard or cold, but it didn't thrill her in her core as his sermon voice often did. "Explain why, if you will, or can."

After a moment, Marike opened her mouth, but nothing came out. She coughed, cleared her throat, and tried again. "We—I—are

Anabaptists." Her voice was shaky. She coughed again. "Most of the girls and women in the Bible study are Anabaptists, and some of them are girls I go to school with. They invited me several times, and I decided it would be good to get to know them. The teacher is very good. I've learned quite a bit from her."

"Saint Paul says women should not teach." Vertical creases appeared between Brother Caspar's eyebrows.

Marike shook her head slowly. She had to force the words past the lump in her throat. "He said that women should not teach men, but he allowed them to teach women. And even with that he praised Priscilla for teaching Apollos." She shrugged diffidently. "My grandfather allowed women to teach other women." The mention of her *Grootpapa* gave her a bit of strength. She gave a firm nod, as if it settled the matter—which it did, for her.

The corners of Brother Caspar's mouth turned down, and his gaze grew colder. "I'm certain that your grandfather was an admirable man and pastor. But there are so many false teachers now, especially from the up-time. I feel you are simply following one of them."

The chill had returned. Marike dipped her head and looked at Brother Caspar from under her lowered eyebrows. "Frau Burroughs teaches nothing but Scripture, and she knows it well."

"Satan knows Scripture, and thereby tempted our Savior." A light appeared in Brother Caspar's eyes.

Marike's stomach churning was growing stronger. Grasping at the memory of her grandfather, recalling his teachings, she said, "All the more reason to be as a Berean, then, and diligently compare the words of teachers against the Scripture." It took every ounce of strength she had, but she raised her head to stare Brother Caspar in the eye.

"Admirable, to be sure," he retorted, "but I would say instead that it is best to follow the leadership of an anointed elder." His gaze seemed to grow a bit brighter. "One that God has chosen and placed for that purpose."

Marike wasn't sure how to respond to that, but then her grandfather's voice seemed to prompt her. "Would not the Pope say much the same thing?"

Brother Caspar's face twisted, and the snarl that appeared for just a moment made Marike flinch. "Do not equate the demonic-led heretics who populate Rome with the select of the Lord." His eyes were even brighter, and his voice had turned cold. Marike could feel a tremor in her right leg. She pressed her clasped hands down firmly to try to still it.

His face smoothed out, and a bit of warmth returned to his voice. "But this is why we are told to not fellowship with those who follow false teachers. This is why I instructed our folk to beware of false teachers and to be close only to those who follow the true teachings. Can you understand that?"

After a long moment, Marike nodded. She could understand that. She wasn't sure she agreed with it, but she could understand it.

A smile appeared on Brother Caspar's face, transforming it. "Good." His voice warmed even more, approaching the tones he used in his sermons. "Sister Marike, you are a young woman of amazing discernment, you know, despite this issue. You have impressed me greatly over the last few months. Would that more of our women could be the same."

Marike lowered her eyes. The churning in her stomach raised its pitch. "Thank you," was all she could manage in response. "If I am as you say, it is because my *Grootpapa* led me to it." She unlaced her fingers and laid a hand on the Bible where it lay on the table. "This was his Bible. It is one of the few things I was able to bring out of Holland."

The light in Brother Caspar's eyes seemed to flicker, and a muscle along his jawline tensed at the mention of Marike's grandfather. She pulled her hand back into her lap to intertwine with the other. Her leg started its tremor again, and she pressed down on it.

His face smoothed out again, and the smile became more natural. "Have you thought of marriage, Sister Marike?"

Bile rose in the back of her throat, burning and making her cough. She shook her head as she swallowed several times, trying to clear her throat and mouth.

"I find that hard to believe," he said, still smiling. "A young woman, beautiful in form and in spirit . . . surely the thought must have crossed your mind."

"I have nothing to offer," Marike said in a voice that wavered a bit. "I have no dowry, no relations but for a poor brother, no prospects or expectations. No one of worth would consider me." The bitterness of that truth burned to match the bile.

Brother Caspar uncrossed his legs and leaned forward onto the narrow table top. When he spoke, his voice attained that especially warm timbre his best sermons reached. "God will provide, Sister Marike. A man called by God would prize you for a wife just as you are. You would be a Tabitha, a Dorcas, or even a Priscilla to match such a man's Aquila."

Her heart responded to his voice even though her mind recoiled. He lifted his right hand and reached across the table to lay it on her cheek. It was the first time he had actually touched her. She closed her eyes and shuddered.

"Even I would consider such as you," he said softly. "For you are fair both in body and in soul. You would grace a lonely life, and would be a reward for a life of service and challenge. You would be a helpmeet above all others."

Marike turned her head away, and felt him draw back. She opened her eyes to see him smiling at her. Her head was pounding now, and the sour taste of bile was still in the back of her throat. She had clasped her hands so tightly that some of her fingers were going numb. And still he smiled at her, eyes alight.

She licked her lips. "Is this what you've been after all along?" she asked, her voice husky with emotion. "Is this what you've wanted from the beginning? Is this why you were giving us, me, all those things—the rich clothes, and the money?"

Brother Caspar said nothing, simply spread his hands palms up before him. She shook her head. A long silence stretched out between them. "Simply say the word," he finally said. "You know Brother Dirck would approve."

"I'm sure he would," Marike whispered. "I'm sure he would." She closed her eyes for a moment, praying for deliverance. There was no sound, no movement, no hint of salvation. Her eyes opened, and she reached out her right hand in desperation, laying it on the Bible before her. It felt warm under her hand. The warmth penetrated her, and she relaxed a bit. Then, just for a moment, she had the sensation of her grandfather's large calloused hand lying atop her petite and slender fingers, pressing it into the Bible. At that moment, she knew what to say. "My grandfather, however . . ." She caressed the Bible. ". . . would not."

The smile crawled off of Brother Caspar's face. "What do you mean?" The warm tone was gone, replaced with a voice that sounded like a grist mill stone turning.

"*Grootpapa* would not have been happy with the difference in our ages." Marike's voice was stronger now. It didn't matter what this pastor thought, her grandfather knew the truth. "He didn't mind husbands being older than wives, but only by a few years, no more than ten. He might have accepted that, though, if there were good reasons, or if we were truly mated by God. But he would never have accepted your theology. You call Gustavus Adolphus the Antichrist, but I've read the Revelation of John more than once, and I know that *Grootpapa* would agree with me that if there is one walking the earth who is the Beast or the False Prophet, it is you."

If possible, the light in Brother Caspar's eyes grew brighter. He leaned forward, not touching the table. "How dare you? Your grandfather was a deluded fool, like almost every other pastor and professor out there. They know the truth, but will not admit it." His voice had gone nasal and reedy, and drops of spittle were flying from his mouth. "It is only men like me and Matthäus and your brother who see the truth and follow it! Your brother will approve our match, and once we are married, you will be mine!"

Marike was standing now, shaking and filling with rage, hand still on the Bible. "Maybe if we were in Holland still, or most places. But we are in Grantville, in the middle of the County of West Virginia, and the laws here do not permit Dirck to make decisions that bind me just because he is my brother." She gave a sharp grin at the shock on Brother Caspar's face. "A judge would have to appoint him to be my legal guardian, and that hasn't happened, and I pray to God it never will."

Brother Caspar's jaws clenched, and a rising tide of red suffused his face. His eyes seemed to stand out even brighter in contrast. He lurched to his feet, pulling a dagger from his sleeve. He raised it, blade downward, and Marike flinched back in reaction. The dagger fell like a thunderbolt, and skewered the Bible. "That for your grandfather," he spat, "and that for the County of West Virginia!" The smile on his face was cruel.

Marike stared at her grandfather's Bible, horrified, frozen for a long instant. She was unable to believe that Caspar had done that. And the expression on his face—the smile, the light in his eyes—the moment extended on and on as she came to realize that there might just be more to Caspar than she had realized.

The moment broke, and she bent over the Bible to try to wrestle the dagger out of it. Just as her hands reached the haft of it, she felt Caspar's hand entangle itself in her hair and drag her across the table toward him. She caught a glimpse of one of his hands on the table as he leaned forward and pulled her mouth into a bruising kiss, grinding her lips back into her teeth. She lifted a hand and scratched at his face, hard. He jerked away from her hand, which broke the kiss.

"You wretched sow!" he yelled, pulling on her hair and yanking her head to one side.

"You're hurting me!" she screamed.

"You deserve it!"

At that moment the dagger came free from the Bible. She raised it, and using both hands slammed it into the hand Caspar had braced on the table top. She felt the blade punch through the skin and flesh and slide between the bones to sink into the wood of the table.

Caspar shrieked and pulled on her hair so hard that a hank of it pulled free from her scalp in his hand. He began to beat her on her head and back as she leaned on the dagger, trying to force it deeper in the wood.

Marike kept her head bowed as she kept pressing down on the dagger. The blows on her back and shoulders were hurting her, but not enough to make her stop. Then one of Caspar's wild swings landed on the back of her head. Her hair cushioned the blow from behind, but the impact drove her forehead into the table top, which stunned her. Her hands loosened, and she staggered back, vision blurring, knocking the Bible to the floor as she did so.

Landing against the wall beside the door, Marike steadied herself. She looked at Caspar and gasped. His visage was almost wrecked: mouth in a rictus, blood oozing down his cheek from the scratches, eyes almost glowing they were so bright.

"You . . . you . . ." he mouthed in a high-pitched yammer. "You sow's get, you unnatural child, you succubus! I will banish you to the fires of Gehenna. I will . . . I will . . ." He wrenched at his pinned hand and shrieked as the edges of the blade cut deeper into his palm, setting nerves afire.

Marike thought in her daze that Caspar looked to be the one who was demon-possessed. She searched for her Bible, her shield, and spotted it on the floor in front of her. She slid down the wall into a crouch to drag the Bible nearer and gather it up to cradle in front of her like a breastplate or a shield. Just as she managed that, the door burst open and slammed against the wall on the other side of the doorway.

Astrid Schaübin stepped through the door, pistol in hand, aiming first left, then right, before setting her sights on Brother Caspar. Marike watched as she aimed at the bleeding disheveled wild-eyed figure crouching over the table and said, "I suggest you stand still, unless you want to find out if your holiness is stronger than my bullets."

Caspar's mouth moved, but no words were uttered. Astrid looked down at the girl huddled at the base of the wall for an instant. "Are you all right, Marike?"

"I . . . I think so," Marike said, pushing herself up more against the wall.

"Let's get you out of here," Astrid said. She reached a hand down and braced herself as the girl grasped it and pulled herself up, but her gaze and aim remained focused on Caspar.

Just as Marike reached her feet, Caspar shouted, "No! You'll not escape me!" He took his other hand, grasped the hilt of the dagger, and wrenched it out of both the table and his hand, scattering blood droplets across the table and much of the room. Eyes aflame, he pushed at the table to get it out of the way. "You are mine, you unnatural child. I will bring judgment on you." He lifted the dagger and lurched toward them.

Astrid cocked her revolver, and fired once, twice. Even though it was a .22, a small calibre pistol, the reports were loud in the room.

Two red spots appeared on Caspar immediately, one on his left shoulder, and one just to the left of the center of his breastbone. The light bullets didn't drop Caspar, but he did stop and waver on his feet. His gaze went out the door, and he seemed to lose focus on Marike and Astrid.

"Out the door, Marike," Astrid said. "We need to be leaving now."

Marike stumbled out the door, Astrid's grip on her hand guiding her. Astrid left the door open behind them as they turned enough to take in part of the porch and yard in front of the building. The sight of several of the Mighty Men moving toward the building from multiple directions caused Marike's gut to tighten up, and her grip on Astrid's hand tightened.

"Come on, Astrid," a man in a tan uniform like Astrid's said from the yard where he stood with a pistol covering the two men on the porch. She urged Marike down the steps to the yard and stood to his left, making sure Marike was behind them. Several of the Mighty Men gathered near the porch and spoke to the man with the cudgel. After a moment, two entered the building and the rest gathered to start toward Marike and her defenders.

At that moment an up-timer pickup truck came roaring out of the alleyway and slewed to a stop with a squeal and a cloud of dust, with more men in tan uniforms leaping out of it before it stopped rolling to form a line on Astrid and her companion. Marike almost sagged to the ground in relief. Astrid holstered her pistol and turned Marike to face her. She clicked her tongue at the large lump and bruise on her forehead and the blood trickling down from her scalp.

"Talk to me, Astrid," an older man in tan said quietly from beside them.

"Mission accomplished, Neustatter—subject extracted. Victim needs to go to the hospital right now."

"What about the perpetrators?"

"The tall skinny one on the porch says he's her brother."

"He is," Marike hissed as Astrid wiped at her face with a handkerchief.

"He's not hurt," Astrid said. "Brother Caspar is inside, has a serious through and through knife wound to one hand, not from me, but I put two bullets in his chest when he approached and threatened us with a knife." She looked at Neustatter. "He was still standing when we left. No other damage that I know of. And seriously, hospital, now."

"Right. Get her in the cab with Reardon." Astrid starting urging Marike to the truck. Marike's legs felt like she was going to drop any moment, which caused Astrid some difficulty, but shortly she was loaded into the truck.

"You in the coats," Neustatter barked. "We've got what we came for. We rescued the girl. We're leaving now. If you don't follow us, there won't be any more trouble."

"You shot Brother Caspar," one of the men shouted from the doorway.

"Then he shouldn't have assaulted a girl," Neustatter snarled back. "Be glad he's still breathing. My people usually shoot to kill." Everyone in black and gray froze at that. "Mount up, guys."

Astrid squeezed onto the seat beside Marike, which made her thankful that the two of them were both slender. "Start rolling," she told Reardon, "but don't speed up until they're all aboard."

Reardon flashed a grin at her. "No worries, Miss Astrid, I've done this before." He turned the steering wheel a bit and started the truck moving slowly. Tan-clad bodies were moving in their direction. The first two swung up over the sides and held hands down to their fellows, and within moments they were all aboard and Neustatter was banging on the roof of the cab to urge Reardon to speed.

"How did you know to find me?" Marike asked.

Astrid smiled. "Barbara saw your brother take you and came back in the house to tell us. I followed you, while Kathy Sue called the police and Neustatter. Otto caught up with me before you turned off the main road, and the rest of the guys showed up . . . well, you saw them."

"Tell them thank you for me," Marike said. She leaned her head back against the seat and closed her eyes. She was suddenly incredibly weary, and seemed to just float away into darkness.

*** * ***

Dirck stood to one side and watched as the Mighty Men boiled around the little house. In a couple of minutes, they brought Brother Caspar out, blood showing on his roughly wrapped hand, his face, and his clothes. The elder was talking incoherently, something about a succubus and a judgment. He started to collapse at the bottom of the steps, but two burly Mighty Men swept him up in a chair carry with their arms and swiftly bore him away.

Most of the others dispersed at that point, leaving a couple on the porch to watch over things. In a few minutes, one of them returned with a fuel can. He went inside, and there were splashing sounds. He came back out and turned to Dirck. "If you don't want to get burned, get out of here. We'll be in touch with you." He turned to the others. "Let's go."

Dirck watched them leave, then went to the doorway and peered into the building. The fire was starting to catch along all the walls and on the table where the fuel had been spilled. He saw a patch of cloth on the floor near the door, and reached to pick it up. He realized that he was holding Marike's favorite bonnet. It crumpled in his fist as something seemed to explode in his head.

Without thought, Dirck found himself removing his Mighty Men coat. He held it up before him, that black and gray banner that had seemed so important to him. In disgust, he threw it on the nearest billow of flame.

He left the building without looking back.

❋ ❋ ❋

"Sounds like you had a busy day yesterday," Al Green said as he entered Press Richard's office. He took a seat beside Kathy Sue Burroughs.

"You could say that," Press said. "I assume you're mostly talking about the Marike Gendt matter." At the pastor's nod, he continued, "We have statements from Marike and from Astrid Schäubin that Brother Caspar assaulted both of them. Marike was hit several times and was bruised, but she was not raped. That was confirmed by the hospital staff. By the time my men got there, Brother Caspar had left the scene, and the building had been set on fire. This did not make the owner of the building happy, you understand. He's been grousing about that for the last twenty-four hours, trying to make it my fault."

"They got the fire out quickly?" That from Kathy Sue.

"Oh, yeah. Funny how, even though no one says they saw who did it, the alarm got called in pretty quickly. The fire team got it out and salvaged most of the building. Mostly just burned the paint off the inside of the building and scorched a few of the boards and timbers. They may have to replace a few of the floorboards, but yeah, it's going to be back up to snuff before long. It was enough to burn up the evidence, though. Nothing to be proved from that."

"No bodies, then?" Al asked.

"Nope. The only thing they found outside of a few pieces of burnt furniture was the remains of one of those black and gray coats those Mighty Men of Caspar's wear. Wool doesn't burn as well as people think. Looks like one of the Mighty Men resigned."

"More power to him, then," Kathy Sue said.

"So what's the status?" Brother Al again.

"We have sworn statements from two eyewitnesses and can definitely charge Brother Caspar with assault and battery, sexual assault, and assault with premeditation. I suspect he's long gone from our jurisdiction, though. He may still be in the State of Thuringia-Franconia, but he'll be hard to find. So until we're given a hint of where he's at so we can send a request for extradition, there's not much we can do. I'm more concerned about the girl. Kathy Sue?"

"Marike gave me a written request yesterday afternoon at the hospital asking that someone other than her brother be appointed her legal guardian. It was witnessed by a couple of the hospital nurses. Katharina Meisnerin's parents have said that they will serve, and I will put myself forward for that as well. It's supposed to go before Judge Cochran after lunch as a request for an emergency order, and we should have an order by the end of the afternoon."

"Where will she stay?"

"Since Katharina has left for school in Prague, the Meisners have an empty room. They have said they will take her in at least until she graduates from high school, maybe longer."

"The Meisners are *Stäbler Täufer*, are they not?" Al noticed the slight furrow in Press' forehead, and continued, "Staff, Press. Basically, the pacifist group."

Press nodded, and Kathy Sue responded with, "That's right."

"Is Marike *Stäbler Täufer* also?"

Kathy Sue shook her head. "Probably not. Her brother works for the SRG folks, after all."

"Ah. Is that going to cause any friction?"

"I doubt it," Kathy Sue said. "Katharina was the closest thing Marike had to a best friend, and since the Meisners go to Mountain Top Church, they're kind of neither fish nor fowl as far as that particular dividing line goes. I think she'll do okay with them, and it will give Katharina's mother someone to fuss over a bit. Katharina is their youngest, so I think they might be feeling a bit of empty nest syndrome."

Al smiled at that. "Yeah, I've seen that happen. Good, it's good to know she's got a safe place and good people to help her."

Grantville
Early September, 1636

Dirck entered Cora's restaurant slowly, almost diffidently. He'd been here before with some of the fellows from Struve-Reardon Gunworks, but this was for a different purpose. He looked around. He didn't know what Johann Meisner looked like, but there was only one table with an older down-timer sitting at it, so he headed that direction.

"Master Meisner?"

The older man looked up from the pamphlet he was reading. "Ja. You are . . ."

"Dirck Gendt." He gave a short bow.

Meisner waved a hand at the chair across the table from him. "Be seated, young man. Do you drink coffee?"

Dirck limited himself to, "Ja."

Meisner raised a hand to catch Cora's attention, then lifted two fingers when she looked his way. A moment later two heavy pottery mugs were set in front of them. Meisner picked up his and blew across the cup before taking his first sip.

"Ah." A smile crossed his face. "I've decided I like coffee," he said with a small smile. "Of course, I can't afford it very often, so when I do get some, that makes it seem even more special."

Dirck nodded politely, raised his own cup and took a matching sip.

Meisner set his cup down and wrapped his hands around it. "I imagine you're wondering why I asked you here. First, let me be clear that I'm not here as a messenger for your sister. Marike does not know about this, and I don't intend to tell her about it any time soon."

Dirck looked down at his own cup. "How . . . is Marike doing?"

"Mostly well," the older man said. "Her bruises have faded, and the patch of scalp where the hair was ripped out has almost finished healing." Dirck winced at that. After a moment, Meisner said evenly, "The nightmares are becoming less frequent."

Dirck closed his eyes and hung his head.

There was a long moment of silence before Meisner said quietly, "What were you thinking, boy?"

Dirck didn't move for a long time. He could feel the older man looking at him, and at length he raised his head and opened his eyes. It took everything he had to stare into Meisner's eyes, but he managed it.

"I was a fool. Probably still am a fool. We had lost so much that when we got here, I . . . was lost. I wanted something . . . someone . . . to belong to. I knew we should have looked for our own kind, but before I could get myself started, they . . . the followers of Caspar . . . they approached me. They gave us things we needed desperately, like clothing and some food and a little money, and they welcomed us warmly. I knew their teachings were a little different, but I didn't see any harm in it. And then they started giving Marike special things, and they asked me to be one of their Mighty Men, and . . ." he swallowed, "it made me feel good to think that I was special, and that they recognized that. And after that . . . I was blinded to what they were doing. I was, and am, a fool."

Dirck wanted to turn away, but made himself bear Master Meisner's gaze. It surprised him after a moment to see a small smile appear on the older man's face.

"About what I thought," Meisner said. He snorted at the expression that appeared on Dirck's face. "What, boy? Did you think you were the only young man to ever have dreams and desires and balls too big for your common sense to rein them in? Young men's arrogance is not just the domain of *Schwertler Täufer*, no." He gave a chuckle as he picked his cup up to take another sip.

Meisner was serious again as he set the cup down. "You were a fool, boy. You've got that right. And because of that, your sister got hurt physically, mentally, and in her soul. Make no mistake about that."

Dirck looked down again, unable to bear that while gazing at Meisner. "I know. I hope someday she will forgive me."

Meisner snorted again, which caused Dirck to look up again. "Forgiveness is easy, boy, and your sister is a sweet girl, and I doubt not that she loves you, despite what has happened. Trust, now . . . trust is harder. And you've broken her trust, understand? She has absolutely no reason to trust you, and every reason to not do so."

Dirck swallowed, and felt moisture gather in his eyes. He wanted to say something, to protest Meisner's statements, but he couldn't. He knew the older man was right.

Meisner saw the expression on his face, and nodded. "That's right, boy. That's what you've done. She trusted you, and you broke that trust." He let a long moment pass. "Trust can be restored, but it's not as easy as forgiveness. Trust has to be earned, boy." He took another sip of coffee. "Trust has to be earned."

"How?" Dirck felt the tears break loose and begin to trickle down his cheeks. "How do I do that? I'm a fool, and I've ruined everything already. How can I make that right?"

"I didn't say it would be easy, boy. But I also didn't say it was impossible. You're all the family she has left. It would hurt her as much to lose you as to lose her mother and father, even after what you've done. So you have that going for you. That's where you start. After that, you put her needs above your own. You see to her before you see to yourself. You live, breathe, eat, and sleep the Golden Rule where your sister is concerned. You ask nothing of her for yourself, ever."

Meisner took another sip of his coffee while Dirck considered everything that had been said. "How long?" he finally responded.

Meisner shook his head. "Months, boy. Months for sure, months if God smiles on you. But years may be the answer. Think you could handle that, boy?" Meisner cocked an eye at him over the edge of his coffee cup as he drained the last of his coffee.

Dirck took a deep breath. "I would have said yes two weeks ago, before I knew how big a fool I was. Now all I can say is I'll try . . . try my hardest."

Meisner set the cup down and nodded. "That's all anyone can ask." He paused a moment, then said, "That's also the least you can do for Marike."

They sat together in silence as Dirck drank his own coffee. When he set the empty cup down, Meisner said, "Finished?" Dirck nodded. They stood together. Meisner left a few coins on the table, waving away Dirck's attempt to pay. They walked out into the evening dusk together.

Meisner drew Dirck to one side away from the entryway to the restaurant. "One last thing, young man. I've not known Marike long, but she's a sweet girl and she's become as dear to me as my own daughter. Now, it's true that my family is *Stäbler Täufer*, but if you do anything to hurt Marike again, well, let's just say that there are those among the *Schwertler Täufer* as owe me somewhat, and it might be that I would be mentioning your name to them."

Dirck understood exactly what was being said. "Master Meisner, if I were so great a fool as to do something like that, I would deserve to have my name brought to those ears."

He gave a hard nod. Meisner gave a broader smile than he had used that evening, and clapped him on the shoulder. "Good lad."

Meisner turned and walked away, leaving Dirck feeling hollow in the middle but very determined. He would somehow earn Marike's trust again.

Angelroda, west of Grantville

Matthäus Vogel opened the door to the bedroom where Brother Caspar was resting. Anna Eckoldtin looked up from where she was reading her Bible. "Has he wakened any today?"

Anna stood. "No, Brother Matthäus. He roused a little bit when we tried to feed him this morning and again at noon, but then he dropped off again. I'm starting to get worried. We quit giving him the opium two days ago. He shouldn't be doing this."

"Sister Anna, we must trust in God. Given what Brother Caspar has been through, it's not surprising that God may be giving him more rest, so that he will be stronger when he does awaken." She nodded, but Matthäus could tell she wasn't totally convinced of that. "You go get your supper. I want to pray over Brother Caspar for the next hour. Please see to it that we are not disturbed."

Anna dipped her head. "Yes, Brother Matthäus." She slipped out the door and closed it behind her. Matthäus waited a moment, then slipped the bar into place. Then he went to the bedside and gazed down at his leader. He reached down and turned back the sleeve on his wounded arm, and saw there the red streaks that were longer than they were yesterday. Not a good sign, although the healer had not mentioned them yet.

The events of the last few weeks flashed through his mind. One of the Mighty Men running to find him and tell him what had happened. Himself running to the room where they had taken the wounded Caspar. The extent of the injuries and the effect on their leader. Sending word to burn the building, sending others to bring a wagon and their best team of horses. Putting the wounded Caspar in the wagon and leaving Grantville, driving through the night, buying replacement horses the next day and driving day and night until they arrived in Angelroda. Treating the wounded man. All the while praying that he would heal, but just as importantly, they would avoid official interference because of this.

They had to give Caspar some opium at first because he was in serious pain from his hand. Then they had to give him more opium because he would become violent if they didn't. This left him comatose most of the time. But their healer finally said they had to take him off of it. And then he didn't wake up. And now, if he died from infection, how would they handle that message?

"God, what are we to do?" Matthäus whispered.

Matthäus thought through all the plans Caspar had made, all the work that many had done, especially Matthäus himself, all the progress that had been made, all that was waiting and ready, only now this. He found himself growing angry.

"What were you doing? What were you thinking? We were almost ready to proclaim the New Jerusalem. We were almost there. Your vision was glorious, and they were following you and your vision wholeheartedly. If you wanted comfort, any of the sisters in the congregation could have given it to you, would have willingly given it to you. But no, you had to reach for a stranger, a girl newly come to us who hadn't joined us yet, not really. And because of that, everything that you've built—we've built—*I've* built—is about to fall. Fool!"

He turned from Caspar and stepped away from him. What could be done? Thoughts roiled through his brain as he stared at . . . a pillow. His thoughts continued to churn as he stared at . . . a pillow. A . . . pillow.

At length, Matthäus picked up the pillow from the table it was resting on and returned to the bed. He started down at the slack face of his leader; scarred, worn, fresh lines engraved with pain.

"You were God's anointed," he whispered, "called to the leadership of the New Jerusalem, the new chosen people. And your passion was high, as it should have been, but just like King Saul, the first king of the kingdom of Israel, you were not strong enough. And just as Saul had to be removed to make way for David, you need to be removed."

He set the pillow down for a moment, took a linen kerchief from his pocket, and spread it over Caspar's face, taking one last look at it. For a moment, it looked as if the eyes were going to open, but then they remained closed. Once the panel was covering the face, he picked up the pillow, held it for a moment, then took a deep breath and bent down.

When it was over, Matthäus smoothed out the pillow and returned it to the table, then wiped Caspar's face with the kerchief before he placed it back in his pocket. He tilted Caspar's head slightly to try to keep his chin up. He looked around the room . . . all looked as it had when he entered.

Sliding back the bar, Matthäus opened the door enough to look out. No one was near, so he stepped out, closed the door, and then slipped out of the house.

❋ ❋ ❋

Marike stepped out of the Meisners' home—her home, now, she guessed. They had certainly welcomed her as if she were their daughter, and she was so very thankful for that. But it still felt so very odd. Of course, almost everything felt odd right now. She felt numb. She felt like her body and mind were wrapped in two layers of very thick gloves, so that nothing was felt sharply, it all felt like just a vague pressure on her.

She looked up at the sky. It was not quite fall by the calendar yet, but the weather was already getting chilly, especially at dusk—like right now. As the sky began to darken in the east, and the sun settled to the horizon in the west, the warmth faded from the air. She welcomed that, because breathing cold air was one of the few things that seemed to reach her right now.

There was a tree not far from the cluster of houses that she loved. It wasn't huge, but it was full and the leaves were green—although she could see a few starting to turn color in anticipation of fall. There were usually doves near the tree. She liked the doves—small, smooth, pretty, with gentle cooing sounds. It was no wonder that a dove represented the Holy Spirit of God.

As she neared the tree, she could see a group of doves on the ground. But something was different. They didn't scatter as she approached, but stood in a circle and sang, not their usual soft coo, but a low throaty moan.

Marike stopped dead still. In the center of the ring of doves lay another dove, wings splayed, head turned to one side, one eye in the dirt and one eye staring up, motionless. She pressed her hands to her heart. That sight stripped away her insulation, the layers around her mind and soul. For the first time in days she felt something—grief.

She was transfixed by grief, felt the pain go searing right through her, much like she imagined Caspar had felt as the knife had pierced his hand.

"Oh . . ." she whispered. "Oh . . ." She sank to her knees, the doves moving out of her way. "Oh, no . . ."

The tears started as she reached out a hand to touch a finger to the head of the bird, who once flew and once sang and once preened with her fellows. Now all done, now all gone, now empty as dust lying in dust.

Marike raised her hand and bit on a knuckle. A dam broke inside, and her own grief came welling forth. She covered her eyes with her hands and wept bitterly, brokenly, piteously. Her moans blended with those of the doves who congregated around her. In her brokenness, she was another dove, crying in the way that doves cry.

AFTERWORD

Scripture quotations from The Authorized (King James) Version. Rights in the Authorized Version in the United Kingdom are vested in the Crown. Reproduced by permission of the Crown's patentee, Cambridge University Press.

By David Carrico

IF THE SHOE FITS

CHAPTER 1

Magdeburg
February 1636

Manfred Müller didn't look back as he walked up the gangplank. He and Edwulf Klein had agreed to leave the boat separately and join up later. It was Edwulf's idea, mainly. Manfred thought it a bit silly. No one in Magdeburg was going to be looking at them or for them—two nondescript country boys arriving by river boat from Halle. Especially since they arrived by boat. Anyone from the south who had serious business in Magdeburg came by train. It was faster and more reliable in schedule. But those who needed to hold onto their pfennigs and didn't need the speed would still come by the river boats. There were always a few on the way who would be willing to sell a seat on the deck to a poor traveler. But only the poorest would travel by deck passage in February. It was cold, and the water wasn't much better than liquid ice.

The gangplank flexed a little up and down as Manfred set foot on it. That combined with the narrowness made him a bit nervous. He wanted to walk faster, but at the same time he didn't want to fall off, so that made him want to slow down. When his left foot landed on the wharf, he sighed in relief and moved off.

This wharf was south of the original city—Old Magdeburg, Manfred had heard they called it—and he could see the city walls rising up just to the north of him. There were other wharves along the riverbank, of course, but most of the river freight landed at this wharf, the boat captain had told him, because that was where the industrial complex had developed. Manfred didn't understand what industry was and he didn't really care. He was here for far more important reasons.

Edwulf brushed by Manfred and moved on down the street in front of them. Manfred let a long moment go by before he shrugged and pulled his coat closed and followed, hands in pockets, bundle across one shoulder. They traded off taking the lead, until Edwulf finally spotted a tavern and went in. Manfred saw that the sign hanging out front called the tavern The Fisherhawk. He thought that was an odd name for a tavern, but shrugged and followed Edwulf in.

For a moment Manfred just enjoyed the relative warmth, edging toward the fire in the fireplace in the back wall of the room. By that time Edwulf had acquired a mug of beer and was heading for a table. Manfred strolled up to the bar. The host said nothing, just raised his eyebrows. "Beer." Manfred said. The host jerked a thumb at the sign behind him that announced that regular beer was either $1 USE or one pfennig. Manfred took the hint and dug into a pocket, pulling out a crumpled and stained one dollar bill and laying it on the bar.

The host pulled it up and held it in both hands as he looked at it against the light coming in through a nearby window. "That's the dirtiest dollar I've ever seen," he said in a matter of fact tone, "and I've seen some filthy lucre before. It looks like it's been to Moscow and back—the hard way."

"It's a real dollar," Manfred protested. "I can't help what it's been through. A storekeeper in Jena gave it to me."

The host tucked it into a vest pocket, and pulled a draft of beer from the keg behind the bar, sliding it across the counter to Manfred. "Whatever. I'll pass it on to someone else. Enjoy your beer."

Manfred took a gulp. Beer wasn't bad. "Say, I'm new to Magdeburg. Where can a fellow find work?"

The host snorted. "You a craftsman?"

"No," Manfred admitted. "Just a workman."

"Too bad. Gunsmiths make a pretty guilder these days, and masons and carpenters can find steady work with all the building going on. You might try the hospital project, though. They had a steam explosion a few weeks ago. Killed a bunch of their crew; not sure they've replaced all of them yet." He gave directions, and Manfred nodded.

"Thanks. Now, how about a place to sleep?"

"Just for tonight, or for a long stay?"

"Both," Manfred said.

The host snorted again. "There are inns and boarding houses all through Greater Magdeburg, the new part of the city. They're all going to want money up front. There are a few doss houses up in the northeast corner of the Altstadt where you can rent enough floor to curl up on for a night if you don't mind the rats chasing the mice around you, the black cavalry nesting with you, or the fact that you might not wake up. Can't say as I'd recommend that, though."

"No," Manfred muttered in agreement.

He looked around the room. The place was clean and in good repair, and brash colors aside, reasonably inviting. He turned back to the host. "What about you? You need some help in here? I've worked in taverns before."

The host pursed his lips. "Maybe. How are you at handling drunks?"

Manfred shrugged. "Country boys or mercenaries, I've dealt with them."

"How about two or three at once?"

"That might depend on whether you mind a little blood on the floor."

The host shrugged. "Floor is dark, and I've got a good cleaning woman. Been a time or three when we've had to handle three. Think you could do that?"

"Got a bung starter?"

The host reached under the bar and pulled out a long-handled bung starter which he laid on top of the counter.

Manfred picked it up and hefted it. It was solid, had some heft to it, and was fairly well balanced. He spun it through the fingers of his right hand, rolled it over the top of his hand, spun it some more, then tossed it to his left hand. It slashed through the air twice, then ended up back in his right hand, where he spun on his heel, tapping the tops of two stools behind him as he did so, and ended up facing the counter where he tapped a pattern of knocks across the top of it around and across the hands of the host without touching him. He ended by holding the bung starter in mid-air just above the host's head for a long moment before he set it back down on the counter.

The host never blinked. "Not bad," he remarked dryly. "But if you ever swing it that close to my head again I'll use it to start your teeth out the back of your head. Understand?"

"Yes. Does that mean you can use me?"

"Maybe. You got a problem lifting loads?"

Manfred snorted. "Got a cousin that's a miller. Been doing that since I was big enough to get my arms part-way around a sack."

"Right." The host turned and shouted over his shoulder. "Elsa!" An older woman appeared in a doorway, wiping her hands on her apron. "Watch the counter. You," he looked at Manfred, "'come with me."

Manfred followed him over to another door in the corner of the main room. In a moment, he was standing in a large storage area watching as the host flicked a little stick on a thumbnail to produce a flame which he in turn applied to a lamp hanging from a support column. In yet another moment, there was a small pool of golden light around them and the host threw the blackened little stick in a metal can set to one side. The host obviously caught his expression, for he grinned. "Matches," he said, "from the Grantvillers. Haven't seen them before, have you?"

"No," Manfred said slowly. I'd heard of them, but hadn't seen one pull fire out of thin air until just now."

"Not so much of a much," the host said. "Just a trick they know, like most of their stuff. Some tricks are harder than others, is all. Now," he turned to the side and pointed, "you see those barrels over there by the outside door?" Manfred nodded. "You see these barrels here by the inside door?" Manfred nodded again. "They need to change places. These are empty, those are full of beer. The brewer is going to pick up the empties in a couple of days, so they need to be by the door. Clear?"

"Clear."

The host started to open the inner door, but stopped with his hand on the latch. "Two things: first, don't mess with the cats if you see any. They keep the mice and rats down and away from the grain and roots. Second, you'll see a stack of bags with black stripes over there. That's wheat, for the baking. Leave them alone." With that, he tromped back through the door and firmly closed it behind him.

Manfred looked around, took off his bundle and coat and draped them over a peg in the wall by the door, then rolled up his sleeves.

It was hard to tell the passage of time in the lamplight. Manfred guessed he'd been working for somewhat over an hour when he moved the last empty barrels into place by the outer door. He'd been smart enough to move the full ones first, which had taken a bit longer than he'd expected. There was no handcart in the storage room, so he'd had to kind of roll the barrels around on the edge of their rims, and given that the barrels were of the size that held over forty gallons, they were quite heavy—near enough to three hundred pounds, Manfred figured. Needless to say, that had taken most of the time. Moving the empty barrels had been rather easier.

He drew his sleeve across his forehead, unsurprised that it came away damp. Even in February, strenuous indoor activity would produce a sweat. He gathered his bundle and coat and returned to the main room. The host looked around from where he stood by the counter. Elsa still stood behind it.

"Done?"

"Aye," Manfred replied as he walked over to where his beer mug still sat on the counter. By the time he finished draining it, the host returned from the back room.

"Not bad," the host admitted.

"How about another beer to pay me for it?" Manfred asked. The host waved a hand at Elsa, she took Manfred's mug, and a moment later it was back in his hand filled with beer. He took another sip, then looked at the host. "That would have been a lot easier to do with a hand cart."

The host grinned. "Ja. It's at the wheelwright's, replacing a broken wheel. Supposed to get it back tomorrow."

Manfred stared at him. "So why were you so set on swapping those barrels today?"

The host's grin got bigger. "Wanted to see how badly you wanted the job."

"Sow's bastard," Manfred muttered. The host just laughed. After another pull at his mug, Manfred asked, "So, do I have a job or not?"

"If you want it. Keep the stock room clean and ordered during the afternoons, and keep the ruffians under control during the evenings. Ten dollars a day, two free mugs of beer, and one meal a day from what we have for the patrons."

"Six days or seven days?"

"Six for sure, seven if you want it."

Manfred thought about it. "Plus ten dollars for every fight I break up."

"Five dollars."

"Seven," Manfred countered.

"Only if there's more than two in the brawl and only if you stop it before they start breaking furniture."

"Done." Manfred spit in his hand and held it out. "Manfred Müller."

The host did likewise and clasped Manfred's hand. "Jacob Schäfer."

They released the handclasp and wiped their palms on their trousers.

"Now," Jacob continued, "go see if you can clear up the stock room. The guy you're replacing slacked off."

Manfred nodded and headed back to the room he'd just left.

* * *

Three days later Manfred looked up when Jacob nudged him and muttered, "Know who that is?" He inclined his head toward a hard-faced man leading several others into the tavern. Manfred shook his head. "That's Gunther Achterhof. Be polite."

Manfred started to say something, but Jacob waved him quiet. The group settled at the biggest table the tavern boasted and ordered beer. Elsa carried six mugs of beer to the table and served them around. The men all faced inward and leaned forward a little to carry on a quiet conversation.

"So are they all Committees of Correspondence?" Manfred said, in a tone so low it was almost a whisper.

"The ones I know are," Jacob responded. "With him leading the pack, it's almost a certainty."

Manfred watched as a couple of regular patrons got up from their table and left. He caught Jacob's eye and nodded that direction. Jacob quirked his mouth. "Not everyone likes the CoC, you know."

"Politics?"

"Sometimes. And sometimes personal. The CoC has stepped on a lot of toes in the last few years."

"That's what I've heard," Manfred muttered.

"Oh, don't believe everything you hear. They're hard, but they're usually fair. I haven't heard of him," Jacob nodded toward the table, "laying a hand on anyone who didn't usually deserve it. But you know how people are."

"All I know is I heard that he showed up in Magdeburg with a big sack full of ears, noses, and foreskins from mercenaries he'd killed." Manfred frowned.

Jacob snorted, and a couple of the men with Achterhof looked their way. He waited until after they returned to their conversations before he murmured, "it was only parts from a couple of men that he thought had killed his parents. And he got rid of them a long time ago . . . I think. That said, Achterhof is a bit of an Old Testament kind of fellow. Eye for an eye, and all that. Best not to get on his bad side."

"I think I agree with that," Manfred muttered. Just then, a couple of men drinking at a side table started calling each other names in unfriendly tones, and he headed that direction.

By the time Manfred got the pair calmed down and returned to the counter, the CoC men were finishing their beers and starting to stand up. He watched as they walked out together, not looking back.

"So how often do the CoC men come by?"

"Well, first of all, there's almost as many women in the Committees as there are men," Jacob said, "in Magdeburg at least. And they're proud of that. So, unless you want some trouble with some very hard-faced, hard-handed women, be careful how you refer to the CoC members."

Manfred stared at Jacob, but the big man was not smiling, so apparently he was serious. "Uh, right."

"You have heard of Gretchen Richter, have you not?"

"I've heard the same kind of stories about her that I heard about Gunther Achterhof."

Jacob grinned. "More of hers are probably true than his." The smile disappeared. "Just remember, Achterhof takes orders from Richter. And all the women in the CoC look to her. So be warned."

Manfred swallowed. Things in Magdeburg weren't what he thought they'd be. He returned to his original question. "So how often do the CoC come by?"

"Oh, usually once or twice a week. They don't have a set patrol . . . at least, not in this part of town. Achterhof himself usually drops in once a month or so. They still keep an eye on most things in Magdeburg, both the old city and Greater Magdeburg, but they mostly work in politics now. They used to give people a hard time if they didn't clean up after their horses, mules, or oxen crapped in the streets, and that will still get you a warning."

"Seriously?"

"Ja. Time was that would get you a tête-à-tête with Achterhof, and you didn't want a second one because he'd be explaining things with a smith's hammer on your knees then. If you threw crap in the river or the Big Ditch, the moat around the Altstadt, he might have started with the hammer. 'Clean cities, clean water' is part of their official 'platform', to use an up-timer word. People in Magdeburg have learned to take it seriously."

Manfred shook his head, then looked up. "Just how old is Achterhof?"

"How old do you think he is?" Jacob grinned again.

Manfred thought about the other man's hard face, and the lines graven in it. "He looks old . . . thirty-six?"

Jacob laughed, then sobered. "Don't be guessing at people's ages if you can't do better than that. From what I've heard, he's not yet thirty." Manfred looked at him in surprise. "Truth. But he and his surviving kin had some hard times before they got to Magdeburg, after the emperor ran Wallenstein and Tilly out of the area. That kind of thing ages you before your time."

Manfred though of some of the refugees who had arrived in Jena and Grantville after the Ring of Fire, and nodded. "I can see that." He thought for a moment. "Are the CoC Lutheran or Calvinist?"

Jacob's mouth dropped open for a moment before he sputtered, "My God, boy, don't you know anything? Haven't you heard about the freedom of religion principle that's part of the USE?"

"Well, yes," Manfred responded, "but I thought in Magdeburg, they'd be Lutheran."

Jacob snorted again. "Quit thinking, boy. The CoC very much supports that idea, and they specifically disavow any one faith. I know of some Jews who are members, and I think there are even a couple of Anabaptists—or at least they claim to be Anabaptists—who are members. Can't get much freer religion than that, now can you?"

Jews? Anabaptists? Manfred's head swam for a moment. That was more than he had expected.

The door to the tavern burst open, and a rowdy group of workmen stormed in, shouting for beer. Manfred dropped all his questions and focused on the crowd.

The rest of the evening was busy. At one point, not long before closing time, Manfred saw Edwulf come in, look around, and leave.

At last the evening came to an end, and Manfred ushered the last of the loud and rowdies out the door, bringing the lantern in as he closed the door. He blew it out and carried it over to where both Jacob and Elsa were leaning on the counter, looking as tired as he felt. "Go home," Jacob said. "We'll clean up tomorrow." Elsa nodded wearily, pulled her cloak out from under the counter, wrapped herself up and left. Jacob looked at Manfred, who just held his hand out. Opening the money box, Jacob counted out dollar bills, ". . . seven, eight, nine, ten." He pushed the stack over to Manfred, then counted out a couple more. "For keeping that one drunk in his seat and out of trouble all night."

"Thanks." Manfred folded the bills and added them to the money clip he'd started carrying in his front pocket. Jacob tossed him his coat, and he pulled it on as he headed for the door.

Outside the night sky was crystal clear, and the air was not quite bitterly cold. The stars shone brightly, and the sliver of the moon showing as it moved out of new phase shone argent light brighter than should have seemed possible. Manfred took a deep breath after the fug of all the people in the tavern and felt his head clear. He was still tired, but was alert, which was why he paused at the hint of movement in a nearby doorway.

"Manfred?" he heard Edwulf's voice say.

"Ja, it's me."

"Good. It's cold out here. How is it going for you?"

"Fine. Job is good, and tonight I saw a group of the Committees of Correspondence people."

"Ah, that's good, isn't it?"

"Maybe."

"Why wouldn't it be?"

Manfred could hear Edwulf's frown in his voice. "I don't think it's going to be like Brother Caspar expected." He went on to explain what he'd learned about the CoC's membership and commitment to the 'freedom of religion.'

When he was done, Edwulf whistled. "Anabaptists *and* Jews? I can understand the Anabaptists. After all, Brother Caspar has taken some of those in. But Jews?"

"They must really mean something beyond *cuius regio eius religio*."

Edwulf moved closer. "Maybe. I always thought it was just some crazy idea of the up-timers that the emperor was spouting just to keep them happy."

"Me, too. But the CoC appears to believe it."

"Brother Caspar's not going to like that."

Manfred shook his head. "No. No, he's not. But you'd best get word to him anyway. Meanwhile, I'll keep working here and trying to connect with the CoC."

And with that, they turned and went their separate ways.

In his room, Manfred hung his coat on a wall-peg and pulled his boots off one at a time and set them beside the door. He dropped heavily onto the side of the bed, and fell backward. It had been a long day and he was exhausted, but his mind was still running like a frightened horse, unable to settle enough to sleep.

He remembered the day that Brother Caspar Bauhof and Brother Matthäus Vogel, the leaders of their congregation in Grantville, had called him and Edwulf to meet with them.

"I need you to go to Magdeburg," Brother Caspar had said. "I need reliable reports of what is happening in the capitol and what is being said on the streets. I need you to get copies of the major broadsheets and send them to me. And especially, I need to know what the Committees of Correspondence are doing. I need one of you to get familiar with them, maybe even join them, so we can know what they believe and how they think. That will be important in the future, so we need to be building that foundation now."

Manfred wasn't very familiar with Brother Caspar's plans, other than he referred to the village of Angelroda as 'The New Jerusalem' a lot. It was very odd that he and Edwulf were being sent away from the main congregation to Magdeburg. Manfred didn't understand it at all, really. But he followed Brother Caspar's teachings and leadership without question, and he was certain that Edwulf felt the same way. So if Magdeburg was where Brother Caspar thought they could serve, then Magdeburg was where they would go.

Now he was here, and Manfred was really uncertain about what he was supposed to do or what Brother Caspar expected out of him. That bothered him . . . a lot. He didn't want to fail his congregation. He didn't want to fail Brother Caspar.

Manfred threw his arm across his eyes and spent some time in prayer, reciting his evening prayers, and in particular dwelling on his unworthiness and his uncertainty. When he was done, he didn't feel more assured, but he at least felt like he'd done his best for the day. With that, he rolled over, pillowed his head on his arm, and before long was asleep.

It really had been a long day.

By David Carrico

CHAPTER 2

March 1636

It was a Friday afternoon when the door to The Fisherhawk swung open to admit Gunther Achterhof, followed by another man and a young woman—not much more than a girl, actually, for all that her eyes and face were as hard as the two men's. They came to the counter, collected mugs of beer, and retreated to a table in a corner. It was away from the fireplace, so it was a bit colder than the rest of the room, but none of it was really warm.

"Looks like a family meeting," Jacob muttered. Manfred looked at him without saying anything, waiting. "That's the survivors of the Achterhof family: Gunther, his cousin Ludwig, and his sister Hannelore."

Manfred studied them. They were obviously related—the two men shared very chiseled features, although Gunther had a bit more of a prominent nose and Ludwig's chin was stronger. Neither man was handsome by anyone's standards, but they weren't plain and didn't even approach ugly. Of the two, Gunther's face was more memorable, but Manfred judged that Ludwig wouldn't get lost in a crowd.

Hannelore's face wasn't quite as strong as her brother's—her broad cheek-bones were a difference, for example—but there was a hint that a pronounced nose was a family characteristic. For all that she couldn't be considered winsome or pretty, Manfred found his eyes turning to her again and again.

Elsa stuck her head out of the small kitchen room behind the bar. "Manfred, Martin's here with the hams."

Jacob grinned, and Manfred sighed. Jacob had been bargaining with a local farmer for weeks for some smoked hams, and the two of them had finally agreed on a price last night after drinking a prodigious amount of beer. So of course the hams had to be delivered today, when he was already tired from moving barrels around again. The Fisherhawk went through a lot of beer, he'd discovered. When he asked Jacob why he didn't brew his own, the tavern keeper had laughed before responding, "You've obviously never brewed beer. Too much time, too much mess, too much work. Better for me to buy it from Schmidt. He's good at the beer." Manfred could sort of see the point, but every time he had to roll around three-hundred-pound barrels, gurgling with beer, he wondered about it.

"All right," Manfred said as he headed for the store room. A couple of moments later he was standing in the alley behind The Fisherhawk, looking at a small cart with four rather sizable hams laying in the body. One of them was huge, and Manfred looked at Martin, the farmer. "What do you do, raise Goliaths of pigs?"

Martin just shrugged. "No, that was from my old breeding boar. He was a sport, biggest hog I ever saw. Bred big get, too, though none so big as him."

Manfred tried to heft that ham and had it slip out of his hands. He looked at it and shook his head. "From the size of that, you could have put a saddle on him and ridden him to town."

The other man snorted, then said, "I'll allow that he could have pulled this cart fully laden if I'd made a harness for him. As long as it wasn't rutting season, that is. He just had one thing on his mind, then. 'Twas how I knew it was time to butcher him, when he couldn't mount the sows last time."

"So how old was he?"

Martin pushed his hat to the back of his head and scratched his forehead, then counted on his fingers. He looked up, eyes wide. "I make it at least fifteen."

Manfred whistled. "So he was not only a Goliath among hogs, he was a Methuselah as well."

"Unless I really misremembered something, yes."

Manfred slapped a hand on the ham. "Well, then I'd best get this into storage before God sends down an angel to take him to Heaven."

Martin appreciated the joke. He didn't, however, appreciate it enough to help Manfred lug the big hams into the storage room. Manfred had to do that one at a time, and he was very thankful that Martin had tied small rope loops to the shank bones protruding from the hams. It took some effort, especially with the Goliath ham, but he was able to hoist them up to hang from hooks set into the low ceiling beams.

Once that was done, he slumped back into the common room and stood by the counter, rubbing the grease from the hams onto his trousers while he felt the burn in his shoulders from the work. "Better tell Elsa to stew those hams extra-long," he remarked.

"How so?"

"Well, the big one is from a hog that Martin admits to being almost as old as I am. I suspect that it's about as tender as old boot leather. As much as the others weigh, I doubt they're much less tender."

Jacob had a mug at his mouth and inhaled at the wrong moment, spluttering beer across the counter. Manfred smiled at that.

He looked around the common room as Jacob found a scrap of towel to wipe the counter with. He was surprised to see the Achterhofs still at their table. "Still here, then," he commented to Jacob."

"Aye." Jacob had his head down as he wiped. "Not sure why. Talk got a bit loud not long before you came back in, but it didn't last very long. Whatever it was, Ludwig wasn't very happy about it."

Manfred looked that way again. Sure enough, Gunther's cousin still had something of a sour expression on his face.

It was at that moment that Ludwig stood up, gave a short jerk of his head that was apparently supposed to be a nod, and stalked out of the tavern. "Mmm," Jacob muttered. "Wouldn't want to be around him the rest of the day."

"Me, neither," Manfred replied.

At that moment, Gunther and his sister stood and approached the counter. Both men straightened, and Manfred moved down to give them some space.

"So, Jacob…" Gunther slid his mug onto the bar and gestured for a refill. "It looks like your custom is still good."

"Good enough to keep the doors open," Jacob replied over his shoulder as he refilled the mug. He turned and delivered it to Gunther's hand, then took Hannelore's mug to do the same.

"Good enough to hire a new man, I see," Gunther replied, his eyes measuring Manfred over the rim of his mug as he took a sip. "Gunther Achterhof. Haven't seen you around Magdeburg before."

"You know everyone in Magdeburg?" Manfred tried to not sound surprised.

Hannelore laughed, and the corners of Gunther's mouth turned up a little. "Of course not." He took another pull at the contents of his mug. "But you might be surprised at how many people we do know. What's your name, and where are you from?"

"Manfred Müller. Born in Jena, most recently in Grantville."

"How old are you?"

"Twenty, if my mother told me right."

"Not much older than my sister Hannelore, here," Gunther pointed toward her.

She got a long-suffering expression on her face. "I'm nineteen. Gunther seems to think that's remarkable. I think he needs to find something else to talk about."

"I have an older brother," Manfred replied. "I understand."

"So, making the rounds, eh?" Gunther interjected

"Not so much," Manfred said with a shrug. "Got my size early. Apprenticed to a cooper for a while, but didn't have the hand or eye for it. After the second time I broke a blade on a planer, he made it clear that I had no future there, so I quit. None of the other craft-masters in Jena would talk to me after that, so I've mostly worked at jobs where a strong back is more important than deft hands." He shrugged again. "Like here."

"Grantville?"

"On the way to here. Wore out my shoes walking, so stopped there long enough to earn enough to replace them. Same story, though. Strong back work, no real hope of making something of it, so moved on afterward." Manfred paused for a moment. "Did find a preacher I liked to listen to."

"Why aren't you following him?"

That question caused Manfred to pause. "I . . . I would have liked to, but there wasn't a place for me." Manfred's evasion bothered him some, but he told himself that it wasn't a lie. There was no room for him among Brother Caspar's Mighty Men, so even if he hadn't come to Magdeburg he wouldn't have been among the leader's close associates.

Gunther nodded. "That happens sometimes when you put your trust in men." He finished his beer and set his mug on the counter. "Find something bigger to follow." He held his hand out. "Good to meet you, Manfred. He turned to his sister. "I'm off to the Fourth of July committee meeting. I'll go back to the Arches after that."

"I'll see you there," she replied. Gunther nodded, and was gone a moment later. Hannelore leaned back against the counter, holding her mug. She looked at Manfred. "So, what do you think of Magdeburg?"

"It's . . . big," he said, immediately wanting to kick himself for saying something so inane. It helped that Hannelore's returning smile was friendly rather than mocking. "I mean, my rooming house is farther from The Fisherhawk than I would walk from one end of Jena to the other the long way, and that's only a small part of Magdeburg. I haven't even walked the whole city, and I don't know where most things are. For example," he grabbed for an opportunity, "I don't know where the Freedom Arches are."

Hannelore's smile broadened. "I can show you that." She set her mug down on the counter.

"You mean now?" Manfred raised his eyebrows.

"Sure. Drink up and let's go."

Manfred looked at Jacob, who said, "Back room straight?" Manfred nodded. "Be back for the shift change crowd."

With that permission, Manfred drained his mug and set it beside Hannelore's. He looked at her. "Ready when you are."

"Let's go." She turned toward the door. Manfred grabbed his coat and followed her, matching her step for step once they were on the street.

"So where are we headed?" Manfred asked.

"There are actually several Freedom Arches in Magdeburg." Hannelore didn't look at him, just stared right ahead. But given how crowded the street was, that was probably wise. "I'll take you to the first one. It's still considered the main one, and if you hear someone say just 'the Freedom Arches' or 'the Arches' or 'the downtown Arches', that's the one they're usually talking about."

"Oh, like your brother saying he was going to the Arches after his meeting."

"Right. It's in Old Magdeburg, in the Altstadt on Gustavstrasse just north of Hans Richter Square. You can see the northwest corner of the palace from the doorway."

"Didn't I hear about that one being burned down, or something?" Manfred buttoned his coat. Despite the sunshine, the air was still very brisk.

Hannelore frowned. "No. That was the second Freedom Arches, which was also in Old Magdeburg, but was in the Neustadt, north of the wall and the Big Ditch. They used to call that one the uptown Arches."

"So what happened?"

Her frown deepened. "There was an explosion. The story is that there was a gas explosion, but the investigator who looked at it for us said that he thought it some kind of bomb, because the center of the explosion was nowhere near the gas line. He also said it probably wasn't a gunpowder bomb, as black powder would have left traces. So it almost had to have been done by someone who had access to the new explosives the up-timers have produced and who also knows how to use it."

"What happened afterward?"

"Well, we can't start rebuilding until spring, and maybe not then."

"Why not?"

"We don't own the land. No one who owns land within the walls will sell it, so we ended up leasing what we needed. We got a pretty good deal on leasing the land, because it was in a part of the Neustadt that hadn't been rebuilt after a fire that happened a long time ago."

"I thought Tilly and Pappenheim burned Magdeburg." They were crossing the bridge over the Big Ditch towards the Gustavstrasse.

"His soldiers burned a lot of it, supposedly not on purpose." Hannelore's tone indicated just how much she believed that assertion. "But there were big blocks of the Neustadt that were empty, and a lot of that came from the fire that happened in . . . 1613, I think someone said."

Manfred shook his head. "If the land is so valuable, why didn't someone build on it?"

"Partly they didn't need it, because they lost about a quarter of the city's people to plague about ten years ago. And partly because of politics." Hannelore spat that last word out with venom. "But that's a long story. The land owner is arguing that even though the Committees built the building and owned it, that by allowing it to be destroyed we have damaged the value of the property and hurt his reputation. He's trying to say the lease is broken. So until that gets straightened out, we can't start rebuilding."

"Oof. That doesn't seem fair," Manfred said. They exited Hans Richter Square and entered the main passage of the Gustavstrasse.

"It's not," Hannelore said. "At least, not to any normal person. But the Magdeburg landowners, at least in the Old City, are mostly merchants and politicians. So fairness is not something they seem to care about. And that," she concluded, "is why we joined the Committees of Correspondence. And here we are at the Freedom Arches, the first one built in Magdeburg."

Manfred stood looking at the front of the building. It was plain and utilitarian in appearance—not a fancy residence, with what appeared to be shop space on the ground floor and one or more residences in the two floors above that. It seemed a bit larger than The Fisherhawk.

"Looks solid out here," he said after a moment.

"Come see the inside, then."

Hannelore led the way through the door. Manfred ducked through the doorway and walked into a room that looked larger on the inside than the building had seemed on the outside. That might have had something to do with the fact that the walls were plastered and painted a gleaming white color, widely reflecting the light from several lamps and a couple of small windows.

"This is . . . bigger than I expected."

Hannelore grinned. "It affects most people that way the first time they see it." She waved her hand around at the several tables in the room, most of which had people occupying them. "People come to talk, to argue, to discuss, to plan. It's why we exist . . . well, that and to take a stand against the *Adel* and the patricians."

Manfred had heard enough about the Committees of Correspondence that that last statement didn't surprise him. It didn't exactly unsettle him, either, but he wasn't all that certain how he felt about it. After all, Scripture did state that there was a divine order to things, and this certainly sounded as if it contested that order. On the other hand, Brother Caspar's view of what constituted the proper divine order was probably somewhat different from that of the Lutheran clergy as well. He needed to think about that.

He noticed that several people were eating the sandwiches that the up-timers had made popular. He nodded at one table and raised his eyebrows.

"And they come to eat, also. We have our own ovens and bake our own bread. In fact, that's the first job that most of us work at when we joint the Committees—helping make the bread. We can't match one of the big bakeries, but we can bake enough each day to get us through the lunch and dinner hour."

"That might keep me from membership," Manfred said with a smile. "My mother wouldn't let me help with her cooking at all. She said I was all thumbs and had no sense of taste." He sobered. "My first work rejection, as it were."

"If you want to join, we'll find a way around that," Hannelore said. "Now come on."

She led the way back out the door and pointed just a bit east of south. "And there is the corner of the palace I told you we could see."

"That bit with the balcony?"

"Yes. So we can keep an eye on them, and vice-versa." Her tone was stern, but there was a bit of a smile on her face.

"I can see that." Manfred turned and looked north up the Gustavstrasse. "What's that building?" He pointed at a multi-story structure just north of the Freedom Arches that looked more like a fortress or gatehouse than it did a business structure. It loomed over the Arches and the other nearby buildings.

"Oh, that's the Committees of Correspondence headquarters building." Hannelore's tone was matter-of-fact, as if it was no remarkable thing to have what looked to be a frontier outpost in the middle of the capital city of the USE.

"Oh." He looked up and down the height of it, then looked over at Hannelore. "You have that much organization to Magdeburg, when you already have four Freedom Arches?"

Hannelore grinned. "No, that's the headquarters for all of the CoC groups in all of the USE."

"Oh." Manfred thought about that. It made sense that keeping all of the CoC's organized and working together would be a big job. He'd just never thought about it before. It had to be as much work as keeping an army together and moving the same direction, he supposed—not that he knew anything about that, either.

He turned his thoughts to something else that was on him mind. "How far is it to the Neustadt from here?"

"A bit over half a mile. Why?"

Manfred looked at the sun, and estimated time. "Can we go look at the Arches up there? The one that burned, I mean?"

Hannelore looked at him and shrugged. "Sure, if you really want to." She led off up the avenue, and Manfred fell into step beside her. So far he had learned more about the CoC than he'd ever known. If Hannelore was willing to keep talking, he was willing to listen.

"You said there were some other Arches in Magdeburg," he prompted.

"Yes, But they're not in Old Magdeburg. There's one in the southwest quadrant of Greater Magdeburg, out toward the airstrip, and another in the northwest quadrant not far from the mayor's office. In addition to being a regular Arches, the northern one is also where we do all our printing of broadsheets and flyers. And there are several offices scattered around various neighborhoods that aren't full-fledged Freedom Arches but still represent the Committees of Correspondence."

"Flyers?" That word was not one that Manfred associated with printing.

"Up-time word," she explained. "Like broadsheets, but smaller . . . about half the size . . . they usually only deal with one thing or one article. We use them if we want to get something out quickly to a lot of people. We mostly use the mimeograph machine for those."

"Mim . . . mim-e-o-graph?" Manfred sounded out what he thought he'd heard, although he had no clue what it was.

"Another up-timer word." Hannelore smiled as she said that. "It's the name of an up-time machine that's a special kind of printer. Or at least, that's the easiest way to think of it. It's great for small and fast jobs, but it smells when it's working and the ink comes out purple on the pages. Very strange, but it works, and we can put pages in everyone in Magdeburg's hands in half a day with it."

By David Carrico

Manfred was impressed. If true, that was a lot of paper and a lot of people. Even if they only got a lot of people, that was still a strong statement.

They talked about broadsheets and flyers for most of their walk, and it didn't take long for them to arrive at the northern wall and bridge over the Big Ditch that separated the Altstadt from the Neustadt. As soon as they crossed over the bridge and were in the Neustadt, they immediately turned right into the street that ran just south of the Royal Opera House. It was only about four blocks from there to the site of the ruins of the Freedom Arches, surrounded by buildings damaged to greater or lesser degrees.

"Wow," Manfred breathed. He'd recently picked up that almost ubiquitous up-timer word of all purpose, but for the first time he felt he might understand what the word was really trying to convey.

The Freedom Arches building was rubble. The walls had collapsed and the shattered roof had fallen into the ruins. Stone and brick and broken timbers had obviously blown in several directions including out into the streets. Someone, probably the neighbors had pushed that debris out of the street back to pile in front of the tumbled-down front wall. The building looked like it had been on the receiving end of a cannonade.

The two buildings on either side of it weren't much better. The walls that had abutted the walls of the Arches had been pretty well demolished by the explosion, although efforts to rebuild them had occurred. The resulting structures weren't as smooth and regular in appearance as the rest of the buildings, but it looked like they would keep the weather out.

The rubble of the ruined Arches building was blackened by soot, evidence of a big fire. "What did you say about a gas line?" Manfred stepped closer to the ruins.

"The investigator said that the gas line wasn't the cause of the explosion."

Manfred looked at Hannelore. "But there was a fire afterward?"

Hannelore's mouth twisted. "Oh, yes. Big fire fed by the broken gas line before they could get the gas shut down at the nearest valve. They did get it shut down, but by then the buildings were burning."

Manfred looked at the adjacent buildings. He could see signs of smoke and soot on parts of them as well as some repairs to the roofs. "I'm surprised it didn't burn down this whole part of the city."

"It could have," she replied. "It helped that we're not far from the river here, and the firefighters were able to get water from the river to hose everything down pretty quickly."

Manfred moved up to the pile of debris in front of the ruined wall. Even after so long, there was still the odor of burning and ash rising up out of the rubble. "That's really too bad," he said. "That it spread so much, I mean."

"It could have been worse." Hannelore moved up beside him. "The inspector said that because the explosion was in the basement and toward the back wall, the walls of the basement channeled a lot of the force of the explosion up instead of out. The Arches was a goner no matter what, but if the explosion had happened on the ground floor, everything around it would have probably been leveled as well."

"Wow." Manfred shook his head. "It's hard to think of there being a good side to something like this, but I guess there can be." Hannelore nodded but said nothing. After a moment, he looked at her. "How many?"

A look of sadness crossed Hannelore's face, and she sighed. "They found thirty-seven bodies in the Arches . . . they think."

"Think."

Her face twisted again. "Some of them weren't . . . intact. So, they . . . think."

Manfred swallowed. "That's a lot."

Hannelore looked back into the ruin. "It was evening, they had the usual dinner crowd plus a large special group of CoC members." She swallowed. "I lost some friends that night. No one in the Arches got out alive. The buildings on either side," she shrugged, "I don't know for sure. Some deaths, some survivors, but not a lot of either. It was evening," she repeated, "so they weren't as full as they would have been during the day."

Manfred shook his head. "And they don't know what made the explosion?"

"Not for sure. Both our inspector and the Magdeburg Polizei didn't come to a definite cause. The Polizei wouldn't guess. But our inspector said that with the center of the explosion being away from the gas line, it almost had to be some kind of 'explosive device'." She pronounced the words with a certain emphasis.

"You mean . . ." Manfred thought he knew.

Hannelore confirmed his guess. "A bomb. A big one. A petard big enough to blow up a gatehouse." The hard look had returned to her face, and at that moment Manfred was rather glad he wasn't the cause of it.

"But who . . ."

Hannelore shook her head. "Oh, the Committees have our enemies, for sure and certain, and we are on our guard against those we know of. But doing something like this caught us off-guard. Shouting, attacks on the street, rocks through windows, yes. Maybe even a torch through a window. But no one expected a bomb like that, especially not in Magdeburg. Both Gunther and Spartacus were furious, more so than ever I saw before. Gunther is still angry about it and is searching for hints of who it might have been. Whoever did this made a serious mistake. The Committees do not believe in forgive and forget."

Manfred nodded but didn't say anything. He couldn't think of anything to say, actually. After a moment he turned away from the ruins.

"Seen enough?" Hannelore asked. He nodded again, and fell in beside her when she started back down the street toward Gustavstrasse.

They didn't say anything as they retraced their steps. Manfred had a lot on his mind. He guessed that Hannelore did as well.

Once they arrived in front of the original Freedom Arches, Hannelore stopped, which perforce caused Manfred to stop as well. "I need to go in here," she said.

"Sure." Manfred turned to face her. "Thank you for showing me around." He scuffed a boot. "I enjoyed it . . . well, except for the part about the bomb."

Hannelore gave him a small smile. "My pleasure," she replied. "And the CoC work isn't usually all that dangerous and is good work to do. We look to the future, not the past. If you think you'd be interested, you know where we are now."

"I do," Manfred said. "Well . . . good-bye."

She nodded to him with a smile, then turned and entered the tavern.

Manfred stared after Hannelore, then turned and headed back toward The Fisherhawk. Somehow the temperature seemed a bit cooler on the trip back, and he pulled the collar of his coat up around his neck.

When he walked into the tavern, Jacob looked up with a grin. "Well?"

"Well what?" Manfred took his coat off and stashed it behind the counter.

"Did you join?"

Manfred lowered his eyebrows in a mock frown. "What are you talking about?"

"Did you join the CoC? You do know that she was recruiting you, don't you?"

Manfred stopped still. Recruiting? He thought through everything he'd just done. "Um, no, I didn't know that, but I guess maybe she was."

He felt sheepish, and he was sure his expression showed that. "Stupid of me, huh?"

Jacob's grin faded to sympathy. "Ah, you wouldn't necessarily know that. And I haven't seen Hannelore do that before, so either she really likes you or Gunther saw something in you."

That rocked Manfred back on his heels. "Me?"

"Sure! You're big, strong, reasonably good-looking, seem to have most of your teeth, and you seem to be well-mannered. What's not to like?"

"Umm, how about I'm not from Magdeburg, my family isn't here, I don't have a craft, and I barely make enough money to feed and shelter myself. Not much future for a man like me."

Jacob laughed. "Lad, you're in Magdeburg. You just haven't found your opportunity yet. It's here, I promise you. In five years, I'll be bragging to people I knew you when you first got here." He sobered. "Seriously. And if you decide to join the Committees, that's okay. That's an obvious opportunity. But don't play with them. Joining them is a commitment, more like a marriage than anything else you know. And you don't leave them on your own. Understand?"

Manfred thought about it. "Yes, I think so."

"Good. Now, go bring one of those hams into the kitchen for Elsa. She needs to get tomorrow's soup started."

CHAPTER 3

Over the next few days, the vision of what he had seen didn't leave Manfred. The sight of the ruined Arches and the story he had been told weighed on him. He wasn't sure why. After all, it wasn't like it was his friends who had been killed; it wasn't like it was his property that had been destroyed. But something about the ruins, squatting in the dim winter daylight all lorn and forlorn kept that image fresh in his mind, especially in the evening after he finished his evening prayers. He was lying awake each night, sleep slow to come. That bothered him, and the fact that he couldn't figure out why bothered him even more.

One morning, after making sure the stock room was stocked, straight, and that Elsa had what she needed for the day, he looked at Jacob. "I have something I need to do."

Jacob looked at him from under lowered brows. "How long?" Manfred shrugged. Jacob looked back at the page where he was trying to figure out some numbers. "Be here for shift change."

Manfred could tell he wasn't happy, but he didn't seem angry either, so he grabbed his coat from behind the counter and left. He retraced his steps to the ruined Arches, not stopping at the original this time. The sun was shining, it was a bit warmer than usual, and it wasn't long before he was standing before the ruin again, toes on the edge of the void of the cellar where the front wall of the building was gone, either fallen in or piled in the rubble along the front of the space. He spent some time eyeing the wreckage in the cellar space: bricks, stones, shattered timbers, slates from the roof, many of them broken, and debris that he couldn't identify from where he was standing. There was more there than he remembered. After a time he walked to one side where there was a bit of clear space on the cellar floor, and jumped into it. He landed heavily, but kept to his feet and didn't tumble forward.

From the cellar level, the debris was even more obtrusive. Looking to his right, he saw several stones lying in a heap close to the right rear corner of the cellar. Stepping carefully over and around other debris, he made his way in that direction until he stood over the pile. Looking at the corner, he could see that most of the debris there was small rubble—pieces of wood, some charred, small pieces of stone, and a couple of fragments of slate from one or more of the shingles. He looked around, found a piece of broken board, and scraped the debris from the corner along the rear wall. Once the corner was clear, he moved the pile of stones to the corner one by one, stacking them as neatly as possible.

That freed up a little more space in the center of the cellar. Manfred looked around, took his board, and scraped more debris out of the right front corner. Once that space was clear, he started picking up bricks and brickbats from around the cellar wherever he could reach them and carrying them to that corner. As the morning progressed, more and more stones and bricks were moved to their corners, those piles growing larger while the pile of small debris moved toward the center of cellar and slowly grew in its own right.

Manfred was wrestling with a sizable piece of timber, trying to move it toward the left side of the cellar, when he heard, "What do you think you're doing?" in a harsh tone. He gave a heave, and the timber moved a couple of feet. When he looked up, he saw Gunther standing on the street at the edge of the cellar, hands on hip, Hannelore at his side. Gunther's expression bordered on fulminating, while Hannelore just looked confused.

"Sorting," Manfred replied after he got a bit of his breath back."

"Sorting." Gunther's expression eased a bit, but his tone was still harsh. "Why?"

Manfred shrugged. "It bothers me to see all this…" he waved his hand at the cellar around him, "just lying here and no one doing anything to straighten it out, sort it out, figure out what can be used again and what can't." He shrugged again. "So I decided to do something about it. Didn't figure anyone would care."

Gunther snorted. "You don't expect anyone to pay you for this, do you? We could have done this at any time."

"Not doing it to be paid. And I'm sure you could have . . . but you didn't." One more shrug. "It bothers me."

Gunther shook his head. "Fine. Sort to your heart's delight, but you don't sell anything, give anything away, or take even one pebble or splinter out of that hole without our permission. Understood?"

"Understood."

Gunther snorted again, and turned and walked off. Hannelore looked down at Manfred and shook her head. "You know you're crazy, don't you?"

"Not the first time I've been told that," Manfred replied with a lopsided grin. "But sorting stuff out has always been something . . ." He shrugged one shoulder and gave a lopsided smile.

"You're crazy," Hannelore repeated, "but if that's what you want to do, do it." She lifted a hand and gave him a bit of a wave, then turned and followed Gunther.

Manfred turned back to the timber, lifted one end enough to get his arms around it. "Come on, then, you balky sow," he muttered as he exerted his strength. It took a while, but he got the timber over to the front left corner, then followed it with the larger pieces of wood that were laying amid the debris.

He stopped working when the sun was at an angle that indicated it was late afternoon. Shift change was going to be happening soon, and he needed to get back to The Fisherhawk. He looked around. There was still a lot of debris lying around, but he could tell a difference. It felt . . . better . . . to him.

Manfred backed up to the rear wall, then took several quick steps and jumped up to put his hands at the street level and press his body up until he could throw a knee up. A moment later he was on his feet and trotting down the street toward Gustavstrasse.

Jacob looked up as Manfred stepped through the door into The Fisherhawk. He didn't smile, but his face did lighten a bit. Manfred stripped off his coat and threw it behind the counter. He held up his hands. "I need to wash."

"I'd say you do," Jacob agreed upon seeing his grimy palms and fingers. "Go."

Manfred stepped into Elsa's kitchen area, scooped up a bit of the slushy soap out of the soap bucket, and rubbed his hands thoroughly. The slush turned dark gray almost immediately, but he worked his hands with vigor before turning to the catch basin and asking Elsa, "Rinse me?"

She dipped water out of the clean water pan and poured it over his hands. It took twice to get the soap rinsed off. Manfred wiped his now mostly clean hands on the back of his trousers, that being considerably cleaner than the front, then headed back toward the main room.

It seemed like all the shift workers in Magdeburg decided to visit The Fisherhawk that night after work. The tavern was full. Every bench and stool was occupied, and people were standing elbow to elbow around the perimeter of the room. Jacob and Elsa were kept busy serving, and even

Manfred was pressed into service at times. Fortunately, everyone seemed to be more interested in drinking their beer and having quick conversations. He only had to intervene in altercations twice. It must have been apparent that he wasn't going to put up with foolishness that evening, because both times the arguers calmed down after he dropped his hands on their shoulders and squeezed.

The evening finally came to an end. That actually caught Manfred by surprise. He'd been so busy and active that he'd lost track of time. When he looked up and realized that the last few drinkers were getting up, he had to shake his head for a moment to make himself realize what was going on. The last of them traipsed out the door, waving hands and yelling good-natured calls back over their shoulders to Jacob.

When they were gone, Manfred made his way over to the counter and leaned back against it, rubbing his hands over his face. "Oog," he mumbled.

"Tired?" That was Jacob moving around as he wiped down everything behind the counter.

"Weary," Manfred replied. "Worked hard before I came back in, and then was on the run all night."

"So what did you do all afternoon? I mean, you weren't here, after all." Jacob's voice wasn't his normal pleasant tone. It wasn't cold or hard or harsh. It was neutral—neither hot nor cold, Manfred decided.

"I was at the blown up Freedom Arches, working through the rubble and sorting stuff out."

"Really?" Manfred could tell he had surprised the tavern keeper. "Why? Did they ask you to?"

"No." Manfred didn't really want to try to explain, but he knew he was going to have to when Jacob opened his mouth. "I just . . . it bothers me to see everything just strewn around like that, all the broken pieces and stones and bricks and . . . everything." He paused for a moment, then spoke as Jacob opened his mouth again. "Gunther Achterhof knows. He saw me and talked to me about it. Told me to go ahead."

"Huh." Jacob shook his head. "Never would have guessed that. Well, since you're helping the CoC, I'll only dock you half the dollars I was going to cut from your pay. I don't run a charity here, you know."

Manfred nodded. "That's fair, I guess." He took a deep breath. "I'm too tired to care."

"You don't get to do that every day, either," Jacob said, pointing a large forefinger at Manfred's nose. "You want to work here, this job comes first, understood?"

"Understood."

"You only do the other when everything here is straight. Got it?' Manfred nodded. "Good." Jacob gave a definite nod in return. He counted out the day's pay from the cash box and pushed it across the counter to Manfred. "Here. Now go home, but be here ready to work tomorrow."

Manfred just nodded, too tired to speak any more. He added the bills to his money clip, grabbed his coat from behind the counter, and stumbled out the door, shrugging the coat on as he did so. The cold breeze outside slapped his face, and particles of unexpected snow were drifting down. A fine powder overlaid the street before him, with footprints marking the paths of the patrons who had left. The snow was beginning to fill in the prints. He shivered. He didn't mind the cold so much, but snow . . . that bothered him.

"Manfred?"

Startled, Manfred's head whipped to the right, to spot a figure approaching from another doorway. "Edwulf? Is that you?"

"Yes. I came in earlier, but you were so busy I wasn't able to catch your eye. I left right before the last bunch and waited, figuring you would be out soon. And here you are."

There was humor in Edwulf's voice, which after the day Manfred had had, he had some little bit of trouble appreciating. "Come on," he growled, following the footprints down the street. "It's cold, and I don't want to be out any more than I have to."

Edwulf fell in beside him. "Do you have anything to report to Brother Caspar? Especially about the Committees of Correspondence? His last note was really strong about wanting to know about them."

"I have talked to members of the CoC," Manfred said, staring ahead. "I visited their main Freedom Arches with one of them a few days ago." He held back on who that person was. For some reason, he wasn't comfortable sharing Hannelore with Edwulf just yet.

"Did you speak with anyone important?" Edwulf's voice contained excitement.

Manfred wanted to shake his head. Edwulf sounded like a child promised a new toy. He sighed, and said, "I've talked with Gunther Achterhof on two occasions."

"Gunther Achterhof, himself? Really?" Edwulf's voice climbed in pitch and volume.

" Yes, Gunther Achterhof himself. In the flesh. And calm down, Edwulf. He puts his boots on one at a time, just like us." Manfred did shake his head at that.

"But . . . but . . . it's Gunther Achterhof. He's famous."

"He's notorious, is what he is," Manfred replied in a quelling tone. "And for good reason. He's a very hard man, Edwulf. He's not one whose attention you want to draw, and you definitely don't want to get on his shit list. Life would get very unpleasant after that, and possibly somewhat shorter as well."

"Oh." Edwulf's voice dropped in both tone and excitement.

They walked on together for another block before Edwulf spoke again. "I'll need to tell Brother Caspar about this, though. The next courier will be through in a couple of days."

Manfred looked at the snow piling up and being blown around. "You might not count on that. The snow is getting thicker. If it keeps on like this for very long, it's going to be hard to get to Magdeburg. For that matter, it will be hard to get around in Magdeburg."

"I don't have much food in my room." Edwulf sounded worried.

"I've got a bit of cheese," Manfred said. "I can make it a day or so if I have to. But if this lasts for much longer than a day, I'm going to be in trouble as well. As for your report, just get it written up and ready for the courier. He'll get here when he gets here."

"True." Edwulf peered around as they neared the next intersection. "This is where I need to head off. We'll stay in touch, right?"

"Right. I'll keep approaching the Committees and seeing what I can learn."

"Good," Edwulf said. "Brother Caspar will be impressed with that." He waved a hand and headed off down the cross street.

"I hope so," Manfred said to himself. "I hope so indeed."

It wasn't much longer before Manfred arrived at his rooming house. He used his key to let himself in, closing the door behind him with alacrity to keep the warmth from the downstairs stove in. It was late, so he moved as quietly as possible up the two flights of stairs to the top floor. The rooms were smaller and cheaper up there. Not for the first time he wished he could have gotten a room on one of the lower floors. His legs were tired of the stairs.

Once in his room, he lit a candle with a match, and checked his food. He did have the better part of at least a pound of cheese, plus the other half of a stale roll he'd gotten yesterday. So he'd be set for food for a day or so.

He dropped onto the edge of his bed, dragged his boots off and set them to one side. He said his evening prayers, making special mention of the Achterhofs, then stripped off his coat, rolled up in his blankets and draped the coat, dirty as it was, over the top of them all. It was going to get cold tonight.

Manfred settled down, head pillowed on his arm. He sighed, and with that exhalation, was asleep.

❈ ❈ ❈

The next morning, Manfred discovered the snow storm had become a blizzard. He could hear the howling wind, and a peek through the downstairs windows revealed white drifts everywhere in view with wind-driven snow adding to them by the moment.

"No sense in going out in that," Frau Kircher said. "You'd get lost, and they wouldn't find your body until the snow melts. Happens every time we get one of these storms."

"They don't string ropes between the buildings, then?"

Frau Kircher's laugh turned into a cough, and it was a moment before she replied, "Have you seen how big Magdeburg is? There's not enough rope in the city for that. They used to do it in parts of the Altstadt, but not since after the Sack." She hawked and spat into a nearby bucket. "No, just be smart and wait it out here. Besides, even if you and the keeper could get there, your tavern will have no patrons today. Nobody wants a beer bad enough to fight this."

And that was probably God's own truth, Manfred acknowledged. He headed back for the stairs.

"Don't wait for your chamber pot to be full before you bring it down to empty it," the landlord called to him. "I don't want any slops on the stairs, mind you. Especially since it will be extra-long before the night soil wagons can get by again."

Manfred waved a hand in acknowledgment and made his way back to his room, where he rolled back up in his blankets and dropped back to sleep.

CHAPTER 4

The storm finally drew to an end about noon of the following day, although it remained overcast and a bit windy for the rest of the day. Manfred took Frau Kircher's coal shovel and cleared a path from the front door through the drifts along the front of the rooming house until they could reach the trough in the street between the buildings. He returned the shovel to the rooming house, then started slogging through the snow in the streets to see if he could get to The Fisherhawk. It took some time, but he finally made it so far as to see that a monumental drift covered the front of the building, rising above the height of the door and protruding into the street, with no signs that anyone had made an attempt to clear a path. At that point, he gave up and went back to the rooming house. Tomorrow would be enough time to think about that.

He did note that the local baker was clearing the snow away from the steps and doorway of his bakeshop. That was good. That meant he would find something to eat tomorrow morning.

Manfred was thoroughly chilled when he returned to the rooming house, enough so that Frau Kircher pressed a cup of warmed wine on him. He had to admit that it felt good going down. Once he felt somewhat warmer, he made his way back up the stairs one more time, rolled up in his blankets and draped his coat on top, before once more dropping into slumber, this time forgetting his evening prayers.

* * *

Manfred left the baker's the next morning cradling a still warm roll in his hands as he began to gnaw on one end of it. He had Frau Kircher's coal shovel tucked under one arm as he slogged up the street. There hadn't been enough traffic yet to beat the snow down into paths. For that matter, there hadn't been very many walkers at all. Scattered footprints were all he could see.

For himself, he was treading the snow down as he went, trying to leave a path so that those who followed it, whether himself or others, could make their way, hopefully without getting boots full of snow.

He popped the last of the roll in his mouth as he made his way to the drift that blocked the way to The Fisherhawk. He stood and studied the drift as he chewed, then reached down and cupped some of the fresh snow to melt in his mouth and wash the bread down. Refreshed by the cold snowmelt, he took the coal shovel in hand and addressed the drift. Snow began to fly.

When he reached the halfway point to the door, Manfred stopped for a breather, thrusting the shovel into the snowdrift in front of him, placing his hands on his back and bending backwards as far as he could go. A resounding *crack* was heard as the tightness in his back released, and he went "Oof."

A hand fell on his shoulder as he straightened, and he looked around to see what he presumed was Jacob, only his face was wrapped in a scarf and he couldn't tell for sure. The build was right, though, and the voice that spoke the next moment confirmed it.

"What are you doing here?"

Manfred shrugged. "I've been asleep for the last two days. The sun is shining, and I want to be able to get to work so I can get paid. So . . ." he picked up the shovel one-handed and pointed at the drift, "I need to move that."

Jacob hefted a shovel of his own. "Then let's get at it. Sooner we get the snow moved, the sooner I can get the fires started and start warming the building a little."

They worked side by side, shoveling snow to either side and trying to toss it away from the street as well. Manfred felt they were making good progress, and was just settling into his stride when a couple of other men showed up with shovels over their shoulders.

"Who are you?" Jacob and Manfred both straightened.

"Gunther sent us. We're to help you clear this space, then move on to The Horace and help them clear up. A few other guys were sent to The Green Horse."

Jacob chuckled. "Trust Gunther Achterhof to keep an eye on the main chance. Get the taverns open first, and everyone will be out and help clear the paths so they can get to their beer."

They all shared a laugh, then bent to the work. With four willing sets of hands, it didn't take much longer to clear the path to the door. The CoC guys also spent a little time widening the path enough so that two people could pass without knocking each other into a drift.

Once they were done, the CoC men put their shovels on their shoulders and gave a wave of their hands as they headed to their next stop. Jacob and Manfred unlocked the door and pulled it open against the snow that had lodged under the edge of it, then entered the tavern and closed it hurriedly to block the breeze. Their breaths smoked in front of their faces. It actually felt colder in the tavern than it did outside, as they were getting no warmth from the sun.

Enough light filtered through the two small windows that flanked the door that they were able to make their way to the counter. Jacob fumbled around behind it, and pulled out a couple of candle stubs, which he lit with a match.

Handing one to Manfred along with another match, he said, "Even though we banked the fires, they've certainly burned out. You go start the kitchen fire. Tinder and kindling should be in the box next to the stove. I'll get the fireplace going here."

"Right."

Manfred took the candle and match and made his way back to the small kitchen room, which had no windows and was quite a bit darker. It wasn't the first time he'd had to tend the kitchen fire, so he set the candle down atop the small cast iron stove and opened the fire box. He stuck his hand inside. Yes, there was no sense of heat at all, so Jacob was correct that the banked fire coals had indeed burned out in the course of the blizzard since no one had been here to feed the fire. He took the small brass ash shovel and cleared the dead ashes out of the firebox into the bucket they kept for that purpose. The bucket was nearly full. Hopefully the soap maker who bought their ashes would be by as soon as her cart could get through the streets again.

He laid the tinder in the firebox and struck the match to apply it. As soon as the flames caught in the tinder, he opened the flue on the smoke pipe and began feeding small pieces of kindling to it, then larger, until there was a nice blaze going, after which he placed a couple of larger pieces of wood and a couple of pieces of coal. He closed the door to the firebox, assured that the fire would last now. He could already feel heat beginning to radiate from the stove.

Manfred returned to the main room to find Jacob setting a pewter pitcher by the fireplace. "Water," the keeper said as he straightened with a grin. "Frozen solid."

"Kitchen fire is going," Manfred said. "How's the beer and wine?"

"Some of the barrels may have some ice in them, but not enough to burst the barrels," Jacob said. "The brewers around here know not to let the barrels be full in the winter, so there's room for the ice if it gets really cold. And when it warms up some, the ice melts back into water and mixes back in with the rest of the beer. The wine, eh, if it doesn't have enough alcohol in it to not freeze like this, then we'll lose a few bottles. But I don't see anything back behind the counter. You'd best go check the stock room, though."

Manfred took his candle back to the stockroom and checked around. It was equally frigid back there, but he didn't find any sign of damage from the cold other than ice around the outside door. He went back in and reported .

The two of them stood close to the fire, turning back and forth frequently to soak up the warmth as evenly as they could. The room slowly warmed to the point that Manfred unbuttoned his coat, although he left it on.

They were both surprised when the door opened and someone stomped in. "Shut the door!" they yelled in unison. The second person through the door did so, but not before a blast of cold air blew into the room.

"*Scheisse!*" Jacob snarled. "It was just starting to warm up a little bit."

"Sorry," a muffled voice replied. The two strangers reached up and unwound scarves from around their lower faces, revealing the familiar visages of Gunther and Hannelore Achterhof.

"What are you doing out here?" Jacob asked. "Not that I'm not happy to see you, mind you, but I would think you'd have more important things to be tending to than whether a tavern is open or not."

Gunther gave a grating chuckle. "You weren't at the top of our list, Jacob, never fear. No, we've been walking the main streets in the south part of the city." He shook his head.

"How bad?"

"Not as bad as I feared," Gunther replied, "but bad enough. It will be some days before the snow can be cleared away from the main streets and avenues. The smaller streets and alleys may have to wait for the sun."

"I'm more concerned about people freezing," Hannelore added.

Manfred hadn't thought about that yet, but now that thought weighed heavily on his mind.

Jacob preempted his question. "How many so far?"

"Three," Gunther said. "Two caught outside, and one oldster in a leaky shed down by the river."

"There will be others, assuredly." Jacob's voice was grim.

"Indeed." Gunther's voice had a matching tone. "If we get by with only losing a round dozen we will be more fortunate than we deserve. We'll almost certainly find more as the snow melts and the drifts go away."

Manfred swallowed. That was hard to accept. "Do you send people out to search for them?"

Hannelore nodded. "If we don't get a quick warm spell, we'll have people going out with poles to probe the drifts."

"And at that, we'll probably miss some," Gunther added. He shrugged. "It's not like it will hurt them to wait. Coroner's office gets to deal with them. They don't mind. They get a fee for just looking at each corpse and writing up a death certificate, assuming the Polizei can find out who they are."

"Is that a problem?"

"How many people do you think live in Magdeburg?" Gunther looked at Manfred from under lowered eyebrows.

Manfred had to stop and think about that. How many people were in Jena? Five thousand, he thought he'd heard. Well, surely Magdeburg, as big as it was, was close to ten times that number. "Fifty thousand," he said with some assurance.

He was surprised at the laughter that came from all three of the others. Gunther was still chuckling when he offered a correction.

"Too few, Manfred. Way too few."

"So how many, then?" Manfred was starting to feel a little peeved.

"Nobody knows for sure," Hannelore said, a smile still on her face. "But the Polizei think that there are about a hundred thousand people in Magdeburg right now, with more moving here every month."

"Really? A hundred thousand?" Manfred had trouble believing that Magdeburg was that big. Twenty times the size of Jena? Surely not. "Are there any other cities that large?"

"In the Germanies, Hamburg, Nürnberg, Augsburg, maybe Vienna, maybe not." Gunther had ticked them off on his fingers. "In Italy, Rome for sure, maybe Venice and a few of the northern cities. Who knows how many cities in France."

"London," Hannelore added.

Gunther waved a hand. "England, Spain, Greece, Russia, who cares? The point is, Magdeburg is quite large, and getting larger. Which means, getting back to the original thought, that identifying bodies found dead in the streets and alleys isn't necessarily an easy task for the Polizei or the coroner, especially if no one reports them as missing."

"Does that happen?" Manfred had trouble believing that.

"Oh, yes," Gunther said with a frown. "New people come to Magdeburg every week. If something happens to one of them, who would report it? Who would go looking for them? It's a problem for the city government. Excluding blizzards, the Polizei probably have a dozen or more a month, at least three or four a week."

"Wow." Manfred used the up-time word. It seemed appropriate.

"Wow, indeed." Gunther nodded firmly.

"It's sad that someone could die with no one missing them." That thought really troubled Manfred. Death was a part of life, but to die and have no one notice, no one care? That hurt, for some reason.

"Life happens, death happens," Gunther echoed Manfred's own thought. "And when you take chances, you take risks, sometimes things don't work out the way you plan or expect or hope."

"So many times people come to Magdeburg looking to make a new start, or find work, or to escape from something or someone," Hannelore said. "Sometimes they do." She paused for a moment. "But just as often they don't. Just as often they bring whatever they were fleeing from with them, and it ends up consuming them." She shrugged. "Sad, like you say."

"Don't you . . . can't you . . ."

"Help them?" Her mouth twisted a bit. "We're not the church. We don't minister to the poor. Our work is focused in a different arena, one that will help the poor, but not by giving them food or money. We work to give them freedom, in the hopes that that will enable them to help themselves."

"Sometimes we can help in some ways," Gunther added. "But most people, if they're willing to work, don't need help so much as they need encouragement, or opportunities, or they need something to believe in, a cause outside of themselves. Take yourself," he gestured at Manfred. "What do you believe in?" Gunther's voice wasn't harsh and wasn't particularly hard. But there was a definite tone of iron to it.

Manfred's eyes widened. He wasn't used to being questioned like that. "I . . . uh . . . I believe in the Father, the Son, and the Holy Spirit."

"Ah, the *Credo*." Martin's eyes narrowed, and he looked directly at Gunther to see if he was being mocked. After a moment, he relaxed a bit.

"Most people would recite that," Gunther continued. "But do you really understand what that means, or do you simply recite what has been drilled into you over the years? Think about that. What else to you believe in?"

"Umm, the Bible."

"Again, a common belief. And again, do you understand that belief, or are you simply reciting what you have been trained to do?" Gunther said nothing more, simply raised his eyebrows expectantly.

"I . . ." Manfred began, "believe in Brother Caspar."

"Ah." Gunther inhaled. "Now we arrive at something. I assume this is the pastor in Grantville you mentioned when we first met?" Manfred nodded. "Is he Lutheran or Calvinist?"

"Neither," Manfred said. "He was raised Calvinist, but moved to be an Arminian after he left school. However, he has since studied much in Grantville's archives, so he's very versed in the up-time theologies and doesn't really fit our down-time groups and ranks anymore."

Gunther pursed his lips. "This was the man you wanted to follow but couldn't find a place?"

Manfred was surprised at how well Gunther remembered the earlier conversation. Surely he had more important things to remember than things like that.

"Umm, yes."

Gunther nodded. "He obviously made an impression on you. I think I've heard of this man. He is becoming notorious among the clergy, both Lutheran and Catholic. I suspect he was already *persona non grata* among the Calvinists if he is as you say he is." He tapped his lips with a forefinger a couple of times, then ended with, "Be careful, Manfred. Men like that, who draw other men like moths to a candle, are often dangerous, especially to those who follow them most closely."

Manfred looked away, and swallowed. He wasn't sure how to respond to that.

After a moment, Jacob straightened up. "Enough talking," he announced. "I'm thirsty after listening to all that. Beer! We need beer!" He filled four mugs from the barrel behind the counter, and put them on the counter. "Drink up! This one's on me, to celebrate surviving the great blizzard of 1636!"

They all laughed at that and picked up their mugs.

Hannelore took a drink, and went, "Oog. Cold beer. I'll never understand why the up-timers insist that cold beer is better."

"One of the mysteries of life," Jacob said. "I had one of them offer to build me a machine to keep my beer cold. I told him I had better uses for my money." That got another laugh, and Manfred listened with an ever-broadening grin while the rest of them spent the next little while trading up-timer stories.

At length, Gunther set his empty mug back on the counter and said, "Our thanks, Jacob, but we need to move on." He shifted his focus to Manfred. "You remember what I said, Manfred, and remember this as well—it's important to know what you believe, whether it's religion, philosophy, or politics. But it's even more important to know *why* you believe it. If you can't express that, then you're not really an adult. Church-goer or CoC radical, it's equally important."

Gunther nodded and turned toward the door. Hannelore set her mug down as well, lifted a hand to the both of them but gave a smile to Manfred, and followed her brother. Manfred found himself with a lot of thoughts buzzing around in his head.

Jacob shook his head. "Remember when I said she was recruiting you?" Manfred nodded.

"They're both after you now. Good luck."

Manfred had no reply to that. He wasn't sure that he ever would.

CHAPTER 5

The weather after the storm remained bright and sunny, but the temperature remained cold. Those areas where the sunlight fell saw the snow melt, although probably not as fast as everyone wished. Those areas shaded by buildings, however, saw the drifts stubbornly remain. And given how closely together the buildings in Magdeburg were set, there were a lot of shadows. So the apprentices in town found themselves doing a lot of shovel work.

In spite of the sun and the apprentices, it was some time before the streets were clear enough that Manfred was readily able to make his way to the ruined Arches building again. He had halfway expected to find the cellar space filled with snow and was rather glad to see that was not the case. However, not full of snow was not the same thing as snow-free, and he glumly contemplated the two feet or so of snow that covered the cellar space. It presented a misleading picture, to be sure, for under that mostly smooth blanket of white he knew was all the debris and stones and splinters and brickbats that were there the last time he had seen the hole. He'd have to wait for the snow to melt, and who knew how long that would take. Then it occurred to him that after the snow melted he'd have to wait for the resulting water to evaporate and the cellar floor to dry out. He shook his head.

"Why are you here?"

Manfred looked around to see Hannelore approaching from the west. "What do you mean?"

She came to a stop beside him, only she looked at him instead of the cellar. "Why do you keep coming back here? Why did you get down in the cellar and move all that stuff around?" She had her hands in her pockets and her scarf around her chin and throat, but he could see the look of mystification on her face.

He shrugged. "It offends me. Someone built that building for a purpose. It was occupied. It was put to use. And then suddenly, *Boom*, and it's shattered. For no reason. I know the Committees couldn't do anything at first because of the investigation, and I know the mess with the landowner has prevented you trying to rebuild. But it's just not right that everything down there," he gave a sidewise nod of his head toward the cellar," should just be left in heaps. It's not right . . . it's . . . disrespectful."

Hannelore's jaw dropped for a moment, before it snapped back into place. "You do this out of respect . . . for a building?"

Manfred shrugged again. "For the builder, for the building, for the spirit of the building . . . sure. It bothers me to see the shreds of the building just laying around. I mean, what if you found me here but my legs were down there," he pointed into the cellar, "and my arms were over there," he pointed to the city wall to the east, "and my head was floating in the big ditch. Wouldn't that bother you?"

"Yes," she answered firmly and forthrightly, "but you're not a building, you're a person."

"Respect is respect," Manfred said.

She stared at him for a long moment, then shook her head. "If you say so." She paused for a moment. "Do you think buildings have spirits?"

Manfred quirked his mouth. "Haven't you ever been someplace and felt something about it—happiness or sadness or darkness?"

Hannelore frowned at him, then her mouth quirked in echo of his. "Yes, I guess I have. So what do you feel here?"

"Mostly sadness," he said, looking back into the cellar. "Mostly sadness."

They stood together in silence for a long moment, then he continued with, "I know all the people died, and I know you and your friends are affected by that. I can't do anything about that. But I can do something about the ruin and rubble down there," he pointed into the cellar, " . . . or at least, I'll be able to when the snow and water are gone."

"Actually," Hannelore replied, "I'm kind of surprised that Spartacus hasn't appointed someone to see to the clearing out of the rubble. It probably has something to do with the fact that both he and Gunther are so furious about the explosion killing so many people, and about it looking like a bomb, but there being no hint or clue as to who might have done it. What did they want, and are they going do it again someplace else?" Another pause, then, "Gunther spends a lot of time thinking about that."

"I can understand that," Manfred said. "I don't think I can help there. But I can help here."

She smiled. "Yes, you can. I'll talk to Gunther, too, and see if he can get a couple of fellows assigned to help. You are right that it shouldn't have been left this long. Even if we can't rebuild now, we can prepare for the building." She took a step closer and laid a hand on his arm. "Meanwhile, there's nothing either of us can do here and now, and I'm getting cold. Let's go back to the other Arches and get something to drink."

Manfred nodded and fell in step beside her as she started back toward the Gustavstrasse.

It wasn't until they arrived at the Altstadt Freedom Arches and collected cups of hot cider that they spoke again. As they settled onto a couple of stools by a small table, Hannelore said, "So why did you come to Magdeburg? Why really?"

Manfred inhaled a large gulp of the hot liquid, and had no choice but to swallow it. It burned all the way down his throat, which in turn triggered a bout of coughing. Once that was done, he took a cautious breath, and said, "Whew."

"Sorry. Didn't mean to choke you up like that." Hannelore's face was sober, but her voice had a lilt of laughter in it.

"It's hot," Manfred replied. He took a more cautious sip and this time swallowed it without issue. Setting the cup down on the table, he wrapped his hands around it and considered Hannelore's question. After a moment, he said, "Honestly, I came because Brother Caspar asked me—no, because he told me to. I wouldn't have thought of it otherwise."

Hannelore's brows dipped a bit. "Brother Caspar . . . he's the pastor in Grantville that you liked didn't have a place for you?" Her tone made it a question.

Manfred recited curses in his mind as he realized he'd said too much. "Umm, yes. He's the pastor I meant. His closest followers are called his Mighty Men, and there are only thirty-three of them. I was never called for one, so no, there wasn't a place for me."

"So why did he send you here?"

"He didn't tell me . . . not in so many words."

"What would be your guess?"

"I think he wants to know more about Magdeburg and its people and what happens here. More than he can get from a newspaper or a few broadsheets."

Hannelore opened her mouth to continue the conversation, then closed it and looked to one side as they heard the sound of a stool being scraped across the floor just before Gunther dropped into place beside their table. He'd obviously heard the last part of their conversation, because he immediately said, "So this Brother Caspar didn't like you well enough to take you into his inner circle, but he did like you well enough to send you out to spy for him."

"I'm not a spy!" Manfred protested. "I'm not stealing secrets or army stuff!"

Gunther's already hard face took on a bit of a sneer, which made Manfred feel a chill run down his spine. "No? Do you watch people—people like me? Do you collect information? Do you send back reports?" He stared at Manfred expectantly. Manfred bore the gaze as long as he could, but finally looked down. "Sounds like a spy to me."

As Gunther lifted his own mug, Manfred started to rise, muttering, "I'll leave now." He was slammed back onto his stool the next moment, when Gunther grabbed his arm and exerted force.

Jarred, Manfred stared at Gunther wide-eyed. "Sit down, boy. I'm not done talking to you." He finished his mug while Manfred gathered his wits. Setting the mug down, Gunther crossed his arms on the table. "What you need to understand, boy, is that probably every tenth person in Magdeburg is doing what you're doing. It's to be expected. As the capital of the USE, Magdeburg is second only to Paris in terms of being able to affect the plans of other rulers." He shrugged. "I think we're ahead of Paris, myself, but Spartacus says second, and he usually knows what he's talking about. The point is," he brought his gaze to bear on Manfred again, "we know it's going on, and most of the time the information being reported is harmless, even if it's supposed to be private. At least it was when Mike Stearns was prime minister. Don Fernando Nasi knew how to keep a secret. The people in place since Wettin took over—" his mouth moved like he was mustering spit, "I'm not sure they could keep a secret from a blind choir boy, much less someone who would work at finding things out. However," a raffish grin appeared on his face, "thankfully that is not my problem. So," the grin lost its edge and broadened, "let's turn the tables.

"Tell me about this Brother Caspar." Manfred felt his face react, which must have been a sight, because Gunther chuckled and Hannelore smiled. "You've already said you're not close to him, so you can't know any secrets to betray. Just tell me what you know. What would I see and learn if I attended his congregation for a month?"

Put that way, it wasn't so bad, and Manfred relaxed. Gunther was right . . . he couldn't betray Brother Caspar . . . he didn't know anything to betray.

"What does he look like?" Gunther prompted.

"Well," Manfred began, "he's not very tall . . . not as tall as me . . . shorter than you. He's not ugly, but he's not handsome either. Kind of regular face, nose a bit large, high forehead, hair thinning a bit, a few pox scars. Not very skinny, but not fat. My Ma would have said, 'He'll do.' "

"What about as a pastor?"

Manfred smiled. "Oh, he's great. He has the most amazing voice. It's warm and smooth and melodious—makes you want to just sink into it. I can listen to him preach for hours, and when he's done, it's like I'm waking up from a full night's sleep. I'm rested and ready for everything."

Gunther's eyebrows rose. "What does he preach about?"

"He talks a lot about this being the end times. He says that Gustavus Adolphus is the Antichrist, and that we need to prepare. He also talks a lot about building the New Jerusalem. He gets excited when he preaches about that."

"Does he?" Gunther's voice was matter of fact, and his eyebrows had lowered. He changed the topic. "How does he do as a pastor, in ministering to the congregation? Does he call you his flock?"

Manfred thought about that, then shook his head. "I don't remember him saying that. Most of the time he says we're the remnant, the few who have heard the truth and are faithful to it and will receive crowns of reward in the great judgment to come. As far as caring for the people, he insists on a three parts in ten tithe . . ."

Hannelore made a sound, and Gunther frowned as he said, "Excuse me, did you say three parts in ten? Thirty percent?"

"Yes. Once someone joins the congregation, they have to pay a full thirty percent tithe. Some feel led to give more. But from that, Brother Caspar and his assistants can help anyone in the congregation who needs help."

"Congregation? He doesn't help the community as a whole?"

Manfred shook his head again. "Not usually, no. He sometimes will help someone who's new to the community, though."

"Do they usually end up joining the congregation?"

Manfred nodded.

"Hmm." Gunther paused for a moment, then said, "You said he wasn't Lutheran or Calvinist. What is he, then? Arminian?"

"No. If I heard right, he was raised Calvinist, changed to Arminian, and then the Ring of Fire happened and Grantville came back."

"So?"

"He spent a lot of time studying the records that Grantville brought back. He says he had a new revelation, and he doesn't agree with any of our movements, as he calls them."

"Ah." Gunther sat back and thought for a moment, while Manfred took a deep breath. "So, where do his followers come from, then? He can't be growing them like trees or changing them from rocks." He had a sardonic grin that Manfred tried to ignore.

Manfred shook his head. "He takes anyone who will come and follow his leadership. He said we are called out from what we were, so we're all new. Lutherans, Calvinists, I think one Hussite. The few have been Anabaptists, though."

"Anabaptists?" Gunther's eyebrows rose again. "Are you certain?"

"Yes. Sword brethren."

Gunther nodded, but didn't comment further. After a moment, Hannelore asked, "So how many people are in the congregation?"

Manfred hesitated. "I'm not sure. There are almost always a couple of hundred in Grantville at the services, but Brother Caspar sends men out on missions frequently, or to the other location, so it's hard to tell how many there really are."

"Other location?" Gunther's face went neutral.

"The place for the New Jerusalem."

"Ah. That's a real place, not just a spiritual concept or goal?"

Manfred nodded.

"Interesting." Gunther tapped his lips with a forefinger a couple of times, then straightened. "Thank you for sharing that information with us. Now, you are still free to visit and mingle with us, and we would still encourage you to consider joining the Committees, but that's up to you. I will remind you, though, that your own Scripture says a man cannot serve two masters."

He clapped his hands on his knees, and Manfred jumped a little. "Well, I'm off. Fourth of July party meeting. I'll probably be a bit late tonight, Hannelore." He stood, waved a hand in farewell, and headed toward the exit.

"He'll be a whole lot late, probably," Hannelore muttered. She looked over at Manfred and grinned, her eyes lighting with mischief. "Well, you survived Gunther again. You did good. Not very many people can handle his inquisition."

"I felt I owed it to him," Manfred murmured, downing the last of his now-cold cider.

"You didn't owe him anything," she said. "He just made you feel guilty. For all his tough guy reputation, he's also capable of being very sneaky, and he does play that when he feels he needs to. You did good," she repeated.

They talked about innocuous things for a while, casual conversation. It wasn't long before Manfred realized he needed to get back to The Fisherhawk, so he took his leave and made his way to the tavern.

The rest of the evening his conversation with Gunther was not far from his mind, especially the comment about two masters. He wasn't sure what Gunther was referring to, and he was afraid to guess.

✳ ✳ ✳

"So what do you think this Brother Caspar is working towards?" Spartacus' face was sour, and his tone of voice wasn't much better.

"I'm hoping he's just trying to start a new denomination, something between the Anabaptists and Hussites." Gunther Achterhof's voice was dry and matter of fact. His tone darkened in his next statement, though. "What I'm afraid of is we may see a down-time version of Guyana or Waco."

Early in the life of the Committees of Correspondence, as they were organizing their efforts in Magdeburg, Spartacus heard an up-timer say, "Well, they sure drank the Kool-Aid." After hearing the explanation for the phrase, the Committees commissioned a review of twentieth century events, looking for dark, violent happenings that were connected to charismatic religious leaders. The parallels to the Anabaptist revolt in Münster in 1534 were obvious.

The report hadn't been lengthy, but its accounts of people like Jim Jones and David Koresh had been sobering, and ever since the CoC leaders had been keeping an eye on up-and-coming leaders of sects, whether new or traditional. Dietrich Fischer had attracted their attention for a time, but even though he was charismatic and undoubtedly attracted people with his personality, he'd turned out to be reasonably level-headed. But this Brother Caspar, now . . .

"So, Caspar has sent his own people to try to infiltrate us here." That wasn't a question.

Gunther shrugged. "That seems like his intent. Manfred is too painfully honest to be a good agent, though."

"But is he the only one?"

"All he knows about is himself and his friend."

"Which either Caspar is not very intelligent or he's setting up a cell structure and not telling the individuals about it."

"I'd bet the latter," Gunther said. "I think we'd best ask the Grantville CoC group to try and keep an eye on him and his Mighty Men."

"As long as he's only looking for information, I'm not too concerned." Spartacus drummed his fingers on the tabletop. "But if he wants to goad action, now I have concerns."

"If the people he sends are like Manfred, I doubt we have to worry." Gunther shrugged. "If he sends people actually capable of action, the local leaders will just have to stay on top of their people."

"Speaking of this Manfred, you say he's honest?"

"I judge him so, yes."

"Cultivate him, then. We can always use honest men."

CHAPTER 6

April 1636

It had taken just as long as Manfred had feared it would for the snow in the ruined cellar to melt and for the water to evaporate. But the weather had been mostly sunny since the blizzard, and even though it was still fairly cool, the sun finally reduced the snowmelt to just a couple of small, shallow puddles on the stone floor. Accordingly, Manfred had worked extra-hard yesterday to get the stockroom and counter area and kitchen of The Fisherhawk cleaned up, organized, and supplied so that he could take this afternoon to work in the pit, so to speak. Jacob had just sighed and nodded when he told him of his plans. The standard caution of "Be back by shift change," had been uttered, and with that, Manfred was out the door and on his way.

For all that it was starting to show signs of spring, it wasn't warm enough yet to run, but Manfred did walk at a fast pace, and the streets were clear of snow, so he arrived at the site in the southeast corner of the Neustadt in short order. He put his hands on his hips and stared down into the cellar. Obviously, with no currents involved, the rocks and stones and bricks and brickbats were all pretty much where they had been prior to the blizzard. However, the lighter weight material—the wood, charcoal, ash, and other bits of what his sailor uncle would have called flotsam—except for the big piece of broken roof-beam that had been wedged against the western wall—had obviously floated around almost like Noah's ark, subject to the breezes until they had settled upon the floor or the piles of stones or anything else as the water level reduced. It was going to be a bit more work now to introduce order to the cellar than it would have been before the blizzard.

Manfred crouched on the edge of the cellar, toes of his boots lapping over the edge. He eyed the floor with care and picked a spot to jump to that was dry and appeared to be free of pebbles and splinters. When he moved, it wasn't so much of a jump as a hop. One of his boots skidded on the cellar floor, and he teetered for a moment, arms waving, before his balance settled and he stayed on his feet. He looked down to see a smear on the floor where his foot had slipped, which told him that the ash in the cellar was more finely divided and more evenly spread than he'd realized. That meant that everything in the cellar was going to be coated with it, which was going to make the work that much more of a chore. With a sigh, he took off his coat and laid it on the edge of the street above the cellar. It would be easier and cheaper to have his shirt laundered than his coat fullered. With that, he bent to the task.

He had just finished tossing a couple of charred timber pieces toward the west wall and picked up a large stone that moving the wood had uncovered, when Manfred became aware of a couple of men standing at the edge of the cellar looking down at him. He carried the stone over and added it to the pile in the north-east corner, then looked up, dusting his hands together.

"You Manfred?" the shorter of the two asked."

"Ja."

"I'm Ernst Büsinck, he's Wilhelm Flock." The short one's thumb jabbed first at himself, then at his companion. He continued in a pleasant tenor. "Hannelore Achterhof said you were working here today, said we should help." He bent down and rested a hand on the lip of the cellar. A moment later, he was in the cellar. Wilhelm followed, and Manfred found himself meeting the gaze of two strangers at very short range. "So, what's in train here?"

Manfred straightened and set his shoulders. "I know what happened here, and I know that the Committees can't rebuild right now because of issues with the land owner. But I think it's disrespectful to the building and to the people who died here to just leave all the mess. It offends me. So I'm trying to clear everything up."

Ernst and Wilhelm looked at each other, then looked back at Manfred and nodded. "Good idea," Ernst said.

"Should have been done before now," Wilhelm added in a gravelly bass voice. "What's your plan?"

"Salvage what can be reused, clear away what can't." Manfred started pointing. "Stones big enough to be used in the northeast corner, bricks and usable brickbats in the southeast corner." He turned and pointed to the other side. "Wood and charcoal along the west side. I'm thinking the smaller pieces can be taken to one of the other Freedom Arches and used in the fireplaces and ovens. That big timber," he shrugged, "I don't think it should be used in anything even though the explosion didn't shatter it. I don't know what the answer is there."

"Axes and saws," Wilhelm said. "Cut it up and add it to the fireplace wood. You're right, it shouldn't be trusted for building. It would be like a mast that had been cracked in a windstorm."

Manfred nodded. "That would work."

"Let's get after it, then," Ernst said. So they did.

By the time Manfred had to leave for The Fisherhawk, the three of them had sorted everything of any size among the debris to the appropriate piles. They looked around. Manfred felt a definite sense of accomplishment.

"I have to leave," he said. "I probably won't be able to come back for at least two days."

Ernst nodded. "We'll be here. What do we need for the next step?"

Manfred looked around again. "A couple of big scoop shovels, a couple of brooms, buckets, rope."

"A wagon or cart," Wilhelm added. "We're going to have to haul this stuff somewhere."

"Wood goes to the nearest Arches," Ernst said. "Stone and brick stays here. All the rest of it," he shrugged, "it's just dirt and pebbles and gravel. I think we can get clearance to dump it in the river. If not, any place they're making concrete will probably let us add it to their mix. Free gravel, we'll find someone."

Wilhelm nodded. "Right. One or the other."

Manfred walked over to the front of the cellar, jumped up to place his hands flat on the surface, and threw a leg up to lever himself up to the street. A moment later he was putting his coat on, glad for the warmth in the late afternoon chill. He looked to where Ernst and Wilhelm were coming to their feet after following him out of the cellar. "Two days, then?"

"Right. Unless you send word otherwise," Ernst replied.

Manfred held a hand out, to be grasped in turn by the other men. "Thanks to you. I do appreciate your help."

Like I said, should have been done before now," Wilhelm said. "We should be thanking you."

They all nodded at each other, and Manfred turned away to head for the tavern. Traffic in the streets was thicker than he'd expected, and he arrived at The Fisherhawk bare moments before the incoming off-shift workers.

"You're late," Jacob growled.

Manfred threw his coat behind the counter, dashed to the kitchen to do a fast wash to get the grime and soot off his hands, and was back out front behind the counter in time to take the order from the third man to belly-up to it. After that, it was just a matter of keeping up with the orders.

The evening was busy, but fortunately the crowd, while rambunctious, was friendly. In his role as peacekeeper, Manfred didn't have to knock heads together at all, and he really didn't have to do much more than tell a couple of tables to calm down. Compared to the previous night, that was like the lions had been muzzled.

The evening drew to its close, and the last of the patrons wandered out the door together, caroling a bawdy drinking song at the top of their off-key and cracking voices. Manfred slumped back against the bar. Jacob gave a weary chuckle, and Manfred looked over to where the keeper was leaning with both palms flat on the countertop.

"I don't know whether to be angry or gratified," Jacob said.

"How so?"

"You took time for your project that could have been spent here, and you were late coming in." Manfred started to interrupt, but Jacob held up a hand to forestall him. "On the other hand, just like the last time you did this, we had a bumper crop of drinkers tonight. I like that kind of custom, especially when they don't break my furniture or each other."

"So?"

Jacob grinned. "So consider yourself chastised for being late, and thanked for bringing the luck."

Manfred shook his head as Jacob counted out the day's wages. "I had some help today," he said as Jacob slid the money across the counter. "Couple of guys from the CoC. We got a lot done."

Jacob's eyebrows rose. "They must be taking it seriously. How long do you think this is going to take?"

"One more afternoon, I think. We're supposed to meet again in two days."

"Hmmph. Well enough, if you do. Just remember . . ."

"I know, I know," Manfred waved a hand. "Be back for shift change. Which I was today, I'll have you know. I was here before the first worker showed up."

"By less than a minute," Jacob riposted.

"That counts." Manfred grabbed his coat from behind the counter and headed for the door. "Tomorrow."

"Good night," Elsa called to him.

The night air was chill as Manfred closed the door behind him. He toggled his coat buttons as quickly as he could, then shoved his hands into his pockets. Two steps down the street, someone moved out of a doorway and fell in at his side.

"Manfred." It was Edwulf, which didn't surprise Manfred at all. "Anything to report?"

"I continue to meet various members of the Committees of Correspondence," Manfred said, "including both Gunther and Hannelore Achterhof. They continue to tell me more about the Committees."

"Anything that Brother Caspar should know?"

Manfred thought for a moment. "They sent men out to help parts of the city dig out from the blizzard. They know that several people died as a result of the blizzard. Anyone can visit the Freedom Arches locations. The headquarters building for all of the Committees of Correspondence organization is in Magdeburg located next to the first Freedom Arches opened here. And their second Freedom Arches was destroyed by an explosion and fire a few months ago. They haven't rebuilt it yet."

"How many locations do they have?" Edwulf asked.

"Two more main ones, in the northwest and southwest parts of Greater Magdeburg. Plus, I think they have several small offices scattered around."

"Why haven't they rebuilt the one that was destroyed?"

"Trouble with the landowner is what they told me." Manfred shrugged, although Edwulf probably couldn't see the movement. "I don't know that for sure and certain, but you might could confirm that with the magistrates."

"Ah. That kind of trouble."

"Ja." Several steps with no words. "Any word from Brother Caspar?"

"Just instructions to get more information, especially about the Committees."

"You still sending him the broadsheets?"

"Yes."

They walked several steps in silence before Edwulf spoke again.

"Do they know why the explosion happened? What caused it?"

Manfred chose his words carefully. "They said the Polizei could not determine a cause."

"Ah. Too bad. Brother Caspar would probably like to know that."

Manfred could see that. He wasn't too sure he wanted to tell Brother Caspar what else had been said, though. He wasn't sure it was any of the pastor's business, and after some of the discussions with Gunther, he was starting to wonder why the pastor would want or need to know that.

"Have you seen or heard anything about the army?" Edwulf asked.

"No." And that was the honest truth. He hadn't seen anyone walking around who appeared to be members of the army, and it hadn't come up in conversation at all.

"Brother Caspar wants to know about them as well."

"Why?" Manfred felt compelled to ask.

"They don't give me explanations in the communications," Edwulf said. "They just tell me what they want. It should be enough that Brother Caspar is asking for it." The tone of his voice darkened with that last sentence, and Manfred had no trouble visualizing that his face had a frown to match the tone. "You're not questioning his decisions, are you?"

"Of course not," Manfred was quick to assure Edwulf.

"You just remember that Brother Caspar is God's anointed, and he leads us in doing God's work in these dark times."

"Amen." Manfred said the only thing he felt he could say.

It wasn't much longer before Edwulf split off for his rooms. Manfred thought that he needed to find out where that was at some point.

As he continued toward his own rooming house, Manfred reviewed the conversation he'd just had. He was almost angry, and it wasn't until he realized that he was tired off all the communication being one-way, and all of it coming through Edwulf, that he began to understand why.

Manfred's evening prayer time wasn't very comforting that night. His mind was unsettled, and the very familiar forms of his regular prayers brought him no ease. He lay awake late, well after the midnight bell had sounded from the cathedral.

CHAPTER 7

Two days later, Manfred was standing before the cellar. Other than a bit of water on the floor from a short rainstorm the previous day, it looked much as it had when he had last been there. He heard the sound of wheels on stone and looked up to see a small cart coming his way. The pony pulling it was flanked by Wilhelm and Ernst.

"Hey, Manfred," Wilhelm called out. "Think we can get this done today?"

Manfred looked into the back of the cart at several good-sized buckets, a couple each of shovels and brooms, and an assortment of other tools like wedges, saws, and a mallet. "I hope so," he replied, rubbing his hands together. "Not much left to do, actually, other than cut up that beam."

"Right," Wilhelm replied. "So let's get after it." He suited actions to words by jumping into the cellar right into a small puddle, thereby creating a splash. Manfred had to smile at that. "Here, toss me down a couple of those buckets," Wilhelm said. "The big ones," he added, as Ernst reached into the cart.

Manfred made his own jump into the cellar, landing in a dry spot. He looked up at Ernst just in time to catch a bucket which he turned over and put on the floor, open mouth down, in imitation of Wilhelm.

"Right," Wilhelm said as he moved over to the big roofing timber. "Let's get this down."

Manfred took the top end of the timber and, with Wilhelm's strength at the other end, they hoisted it and laid it across the buckets. Manfred reached up to take the saw from Ernst, and he commenced to cutting about a cubit's length off the end of the timber.

By the time they got done cutting the timber up, Ernst had joined them and taken his turns at the saw. Despite having been in the snow and rain, the timber was basically dry and the saw cut well. It also turned out that Manfred's concerns about the timber being stressed and cracked by the explosion were well-founded, as every cut had lengths of the timber split off and either fall to the floor or hang by a few fibers until one of them pulled them free. This greatly reduced the amount of time they had to spend splitting the cubit lengths into pieces small enough to put in a stove or fireplace. In fact, it was only the end that Wilhelm had hefted around that remained solid enough that they had to use the wedges and mallet to split it up.

Ernst and Wilhelm went back up to street level, and Manfred began tossing the pieces of wood up to them. It was bare moments later that all the wood pieces—both what they had cut and the smaller pieces that had been gathered from the debris—had been lofted to the street level and placed in the cart.

Ernst tossed down a couple of additional buckets, then tossed Manfred a broom before he and Wilhelm jumped back into the cellar with a couple of scoop shovels. They spent the next few minutes scooping up the loose gravel and pebbles and loading them into two of the buckets then swept and scooped up the sawdust and splinters and wood chips that remained on the floor into one of the buckets.

Manfred at length grounded the butt end of his broom staff and looked around. Other than the neat piles of stone and brick against the eastern wall of the cellar, there was no debris left in the cellar. It looked ready to begin rebuilding.

He looked at the others, and nodded. "I think we're done."

They returned his nod.

"Ja," Wilhelm said. "Looks better. Glad we got it done." He tossed his shovel up on the street and followed it. Ernst did likewise. Manfred looked around one more time, then followed them with the broom. Once the tools and buckets were back in the cart, the three of them shook hands.

"So where is this all off to?" Manfred jerked a thumb at the cart.

"Wood and sawdust to the nearest Freedom Arches, like we talked about," Ernst said. "The little bit of rock and pebbles that we have can go in the river, or so we were told. It won't hurt anything."

He gathered up the patiently waiting pony's lead. "And we're off." He started turning the pony.

"Nice working with you, Manfred," Ernst said. "Come by the Arches and we'll buy you a drink."

Manfred waved at them and watched them move off. Once they were far enough down the street that the pedestrians blocked his view of them, he turned back to the cellar. Putting his hands in his pockets, he just stared at it for he didn't know how long. Finally, he gave a big sigh. "It just feels better now," he murmured.

"You do good work."

Manfred started, and looked over to see Gunther Achterhof standing beside him.

"I had a lot of help from Ernst and Wilhelm," he said.

"Maybe so," Gunther replied. "But if you hadn't taken it upon yourself to begin the work, they wouldn't have come alongside."

Manfred shrugged, uncomfortable with the praise. He didn't see that he'd done anything remarkable.

"So," Gunther continued, "have you thought about joining the Committees? We could use someone like you, willing to shoulder responsibility and do what needs to be done, even if it's just hard drudging work."

"Thought about it," Manfred admitted.

"But haven't decided yet, eh?"

Manfred shook his head.

"Let me guess: you're concerned about how working for the Committees would work or not work with your faith."

Manfred hesitated, then nodded.

"You've heard that we're all a bunch of atheists and heretics, right?"

Manfred didn't nod to that one. He just looked at Gunther.

Gunther's mouth twisted to one side. "Heh. You have any idea how many times we hear that? It's not true . . . or at least, not for all of us. It is true that we have attracted a lot of what the up-timers call 'free spirits,' folks who have either lost their relationship with the faiths around us, or never had it and are now honest enough to admit it. At the same time, though, we take very seriously the 'freedom of religion' philosophy that the up-timers brought with them. We insist on it in the cities we operate in, which is what many of the religious leaders consider interference in their business. Everyone knows that. But what isn't as well known is that we also insist on it among our members. For the free spirits—which I admit includes my family—to have the right to abandon God, or at least not associate with Him, we have to allow everyone the right to continue to attend their churches, if they choose, or to attend all churches if they so choose."

"How many are there who do?" Manfred asked.

Gunther shrugged. "Quite a few, actually. Or rather, there are a lot who still consider themselves to be Lutheran or Arminian or Calvinist or

Catholic. There are even a few practicing Anabaptists. But . . ." he held up his hand, "you won't find very many of them in church on Sundays."

Manfred tilted his head, and after a moment, gave the obviously expected query: "Why?"

"Because, Manfred, I'm afraid that even if you want to remain in your faith and associated with your church, you may find that your church doesn't want to associate with you."

That stopped Manfred's thoughts cold. After a moment, they started rolling again, this time going down a path he had never considered. Gunther began nodding as he observed Manfred's expressions changing.

"Are you more concerned about conflicts between the CoC and the church rules or between the CoC and your faith?"

"Both, I guess."

"Were you raised Lutheran?"

"Mostly," Manfred replied.

"I would have guessed that," Gunther said. He chuckled before he continued. "This is going to sound strange, I know, given what you think you know about me and my reputation, but I suggest you go talk to a pastor."

That definitely caught Manfred by surprise, and his eyebrows shot up. His expression provoked a laugh out of Gunther, and for the first time Manfred saw his face in something other than the stern hardness of an Old Testament prophet.

"Not just any pastor," Gunther got out as the laugh died away. "Do you know where Saint Jacob's Church is in Old Magdeburg?"

Manfred shook his head.

Gunther turned and pointed south and a bit west. "You can't really see it from here, but it's in the Altstadt, about a block and a half east of Gustavstrasse. It's the northernmost church in the Altstadt, it's the smallest and poorest church in Old Magdeburg, and it has the distinction of being the only church in the Altstadt that wasn't looted or burned during the Sack of Magdeburg, which tells you how poor it was. The church lost its pastor last fall after he was arrested and charged with murdering three women and cutting the eyes out of their heads."

Manfred sucked in his breath. "I heard about that. Prostitutes, weren't they?"

"No, just working class women. Servants."

"I didn't hear what happened to him, though." Manfred could taste bile in his mouth as his stomach churned at the thought of the crimes.

"The Magdeburg Polizei had iron-clad proof that he had committed the murders. The up-timers said he was insane, caused by having had syphilis for years, and they wanted him imprisoned, but that didn't sit well with the Magdeburg authorities. The Lutheran leaders were divided between that idea and the thought that he was demon-possessed. In any event, they finally renounced him as a member of the clergy and turned him over to the secular authorities in the person of Otto Gericke, the mayor of Magdeburg. He was convicted of murder by the courts and was executed by hanging not long thereafter."

"Wow." Manfred found a new use for the up-time word.

"Ja. But because of all that, the Lutheran leaders and bishop haven't been able to get another pastor to replace this man. No one is desperate enough yet to take a pulpit last filled by what appeared to be a crazy demoniac. So the weekly services are filled either by deacons from the other churches or by a retired older pastor named Moritz Gruber. Pastor Gruber is who I think you should talk to. He's an older man, and his mind has started wandering a bit, but he still preaches. He's a good man—he cares more about the people than he does about the rules and regulations of the church. I think he can help you. If nothing else, he'll hear you out, and that alone will be a help, I think."

"Pastor Gruber, you say?" Manfred tried to inscribe that name in his memory.

"Ja. Pastor Moritz Gruber. A good man, like I said."

Gunther clapped Manfred on the shoulder. "And you're a good man, too, ja? Honest, hard-working, not too proud. I like you, Manfred. You think about what I said, right? And you go see Pastor Gruber." Another heavy-handed clap on the shoulder left Manfred listing a bit to one side as Gunther headed back down the street headed toward Gustavstrasse.

Manfred shook his head. Gunther Achterhof said he liked him. Wow.

❋ ❋ ❋

Two weeks later, on a warming Saturday evening, Manfred still hadn't come to a decision about joining the Committees of Correspondence. He was flattered that Gunther had invited him, and he could see that at least some of their work was useful. And there were increasingly insistent messages coming from Grantville that he needed to join so that he could send more information to Brother Caspar.

At the same time, he didn't want to join under false pretenses. The idea of joining for the purpose of gathering information and reporting it to Grantville bothered him. His feeling that there was an innate dishonesty to it was growing stronger. It was getting harder to not snap back at Edwulf's frequent importunings, and the fact that Brother Caspar was apparently pushing Edwulf to push him was making him increasingly unhappy. This was a side of the leader he hadn't seen before—hadn't known existed—and it was beginning to make Gunther's conversations have meaning he hadn't perceived at first.

When the evening's business began with the shift change, Manfred was still chewing on that issue. He kept an eye on the big room and circulated among the crowd so the usuals would know he was there and was watching. That was enough to keep most of them in a semi-civilized mood. He didn't say much to anyone, though.

"Smile!" Jacob ordered the third time Manfred walked by the counter.

Manfred paused and looked at him, head tilted and eyebrows raised. He said nothing, just waited.

"You look like your wife and children just died. Smile, man. Don't be dragging these folks into the pits."

Manfred snorted, and one corner of his mouth quirked up. "That might have more weight if I had a wife and children."

"Well, you certainly won't get any looking like that. Smile, and be about it." Jacob was sporting his own grin as he waved his hand for Manfred to start circulating again, so he wasn't angry. Manfred took his point nonetheless and tried to look at least pleasant as he circled the room, dropping a few comments and greetings along the way.

The room wasn't just jammed-together bodies tonight like it sometimes was after shift change, but it was reasonably full. One figure caught Manfred's eye. There was a man sitting at a small table by himself, and somehow he had kept it to himself all night. That was unusual. What was more unusual was he wasn't one of the regulars. Manfred kept him in sight as he circled the room, and the next time he came to the counter he motioned to Jacob.

"What?" the host grunted as he put four full mugs on the counter for Elsa to run to a table.

"You know that guy?" Manfred nodded his head toward the table in question. "The one in the dark green coat?"

Jacob looked over his shoulder. "Looks black from here. Face isn't familiar, definitely don't have a name for him. Why?"

"He's drinking a lot of beer but not saying anything. No one's joined him. That's . . . odd."

"Hmmph." Jacob took a couple of empty mugs from Elsa and started filling them from the barrel. He looked again when he straightened. "No, don't know him. Not part of our regular crowd, either. He's a little too well-dressed to be one of the usuals."

Manfred turned and took another look. Jacob was right. The man didn't work with his hands like most of their clientele. He looked to be maybe a senior clerk or a junior agent for a prosperous merchant. The Fisherhawk wasn't a dump. They might not be a peer to The Green Horse or The Horace, but they were several rungs above The Chain, for example. Even so, as Jacob had noted, this man was a step or two above their usual clientele.

He started moving again, but wherever he was in his circles, his gaze was never far from that table. Which turned out to be a good thing, because he was looking that way when two of their occasionally-rowdy spirits stood and moved to the table. Manfred didn't hear what their opening words were, but the conversation quickly moved to shouting and name calling, at least on their part. The table's occupant didn't seem to be saying much of anything, just sat there holding his mug in both hands.

Just as one of them was reaching for the object of Manfred's curiosity, Manfred arrived and grasped the backs of their necks in his large, hard hands. The force of those grips and the pull he exerted perforce brought them upright, even to their toes, as they were smaller than Manfred.

"You two are done for tonight. Go home and sleep it off," Manfred said over their expostulations as he began marching them toward the door, everyone in their path getting out of their way, "and don't come back until you're sober." One of the nearby patrons opened the door for Manfred, and he threw them out the door, not particularly caring that he banged their heads together as he did so. "And bring money," he called after them before closing the door with a nod to the helpful patron who had opened it.

Manfred returned to the table and bent down a little to get closer to the occupant. "Are you all right?" He kept his tone quiet. The man nodded, starting at Manfred's belt buckle. "They didn't touch you or spill your beer?" Headshake. "I'm Manfred Müller and that's Jacob Schäfer." He waved at the counter. He waited for the man to introduce himself, but only got a nod. After the pause verged on uncomfortable, he concluded with, "We're glad you came tonight. Feel free to return." All that garnered was another nod. Manfred gave up and started his rounds again.

Probably because Manfred had already dealt some strength that night, the remaining hours were relatively peaceful. Some outbursts of laughter here and there, a couple of conversations where beer-lubricated throats tried to talk over one another, but nothing very rambunctious or overly loud. Manfred continued to watch the table, but the occupant did nothing but order two more mugs of beer before closing. Manfred wondered where he was putting it, especially since he never rose to seek a chamber pot or a back alley.

At last Jacob called time, and the patrons finished off their last beers, took their empty mugs to the counter, and trooped out the door. Of course, some of them were staggering enough that they bounced back and forth between the doorposts a couple of times before making their way through them. Manfred looked around, but the table was empty, and he hadn't seen the man leave. His mug was still on the table, so he had obviously just risen and walked out the door at the front of the crowd.

Manfred shrugged. A curious-making man, for sure, but no trouble. At least, not tonight. He'd reserve judgment for another time. He just had a feeling about that guy.

He took the mug back to the counter, grabbed his coat, waved at Jacob and Elsa, and left himself. He looked around closely, praying that Edwulf wasn't there waiting on him. The prayer was answered, so Manfred was able to walk home to his rooming house by himself. His evening routine followed, culminating in his evening prayers, where he asked again for guidance and wisdom to make wise choices. He lay back on the bed, turned and pillowed his head on his arm, and was asleep in moments.

By David Carrico

CHAPTER 8

May 1636

Spartacus and Gunther ran into each other in the entry of the original Magdeburg Freedom Arches. They both stopped and chuckled, then Spartacus said, "You have a moment?" Gunther nodded, and they moved toward the far corner of the common room to a small table, conspicuously unoccupied and surrounded by clear floor space. It wasn't officially reserved for CoC usage, but they were far and away its most common occupants. They settled into the chairs, and Gunther looked at his fellow expectantly.

"We received an interesting report from the Grantville branch today," Spartacus began.

"That's not a word I like to hear," Gunther said. "Interesting how?"

"They sent us some information about this Brother Caspar. It looks like we may be correct in our concerns about him."

Gunther leaned forward, and beckoned to Spartacus to continue.

"It turns out that he has begun staging confrontations with members of other congregations. Back in September he sent out teams of men to enter other churches and argue that those churches were not interpreting scripture correctly and disrupt their services. He even sent out a few women to do likewise. The Grantvillers kind of cracked down on that, and they quieted down for a while, but started back up last month. There's been some harassing of street preachers, some shoving and pushing, and even a few fists thrown, but nothing more serious yet."

"So did they disrupt any of the up-timer churches, or were these all down-timer churches?"

Spartacus waggled a hand between them. "None of the churches that came back with Grantville from the future. All of the affected churches were started after Grantville arrived, and they are all predominantly down-timer congregations, although one of them has some up-timer members and is led by an up-timer pastor."

"So he's mainly working with and toward us down-timers. That makes some sense, if he has an agenda to accomplish. As Frank Jackson once put it, 'there's zillions of you down-timers'. If he's planning something to last, he'll have to build it with down-timers."

Spartacus nodded. "They also said he's getting a bit more strident in his proclaiming that Gustav is an, or the, Anti-christ."

"Arrant foolishness," Gunther said in a hard tone. "But there he's crossing the line into politics. We need to keep more of an eye on him."

"Indeed. We may want to have Gretchen compare notes with Nasi as well."

"Not a bad idea," Gunther agreed. "Do we have any idea yet where his 'New Jerusalem' is going to be?"

"Not yet. He seems to be keeping that vague for the moment."

"Maybe not the best schemer we know of, but he's not stupid."

"Agreed." Spartacus nodded. "We need someone inside the group, but that's hard to do with a religious group. Has your friend Manfred come around yet?"

Gunther shook his head. "I think he wants to, but he still has issues with whether being in the Committees means he can't follow his beliefs.

I've explained that more than once, but he's still got a muddled mind about it all."

"Try him again. We could use any insight he would give us. The Grantville branch would take anything he would share."

Gunther shook his head. "Don't place your wagers yet."

✼ ✼ ✼

For the first time in a long time, Manfred was in a Lutheran church on a Sunday morning. It felt very odd. He was used to the very loosely organized worship services led by Brother Caspar, and returning to the very structured Lutheran order of worship, even though he was familiar with it from his childhood experiences . . . well, it was odd. That was the only way he could think of it.

He was in Saint Jacob's church, standing in the rear of the nave against the back wall. The church was old . . . but then, all of the churches in Magdeburg were old, except for the two or three that had been totally burned and gutted during the Sack and had had to be totally rebuilt. And even those had old foundations.

Despite his location, Manfred could hear very well. Several of the hymns were familiar to him, so he joined in the singing. The Gospel reading was Matthew chapter 5 verses 17-18:

Think not that I am come to destroy the law, or the prophets: I am not come to destroy, but to fulfil. For verily I say unto you, till heaven and earth pass, one jot or one tittle shall in no wise pass from the law, till all be fulfilled.

After the following hymn, an older man in black robes made his way to the pulpit, which stood to one side of the chancel. Manfred assumed this was Pastor Gruber.

"It does us good, brothers and sisters, to think upon the foundations of our faith from time to time. Today I speak of the principle of *Sola Scriptura*—Scripture Alone being the revelation of God, God's will, God's laws and precepts, and the Gospel."

The pastor spent some little time discussing the abuses of the Catholic church in elevating tradition and the decrees of men, whether popes or councils, to be equal—if not superior—to the inspired word of God. Manfred nodded along with his points. The pastor was well-spoken, and although his voice was most likely not as robust as it was when he was younger, it still carried well enough that Manfred could understand what his was saying at the back of the small church.

But then the tenor of the sermon changed.

"But such it was at the beginning of the great work of Martin Luther. And such it was before the coming of Grantville to our time. And such it is today. But Grantville brought changes, in this as in so many other things. There are many who say that that event was a great miracle, a modern-day equivalent to the parting of the Red Sea or God stopping the passage of the sun for Moses for the length of an afternoon. A great event, surely, but a miracle I will not claim it, for like all works of men, it brought back to us both good and bad. And that includes matters of faith. Some of the teachings espoused by the up-timers are not sound, are not healthy, are not holy. So I say to you that when it comes to the new teachings found in Grantville, we should be as the Apostle Paul found the Bereans to be in Acts chapter seventeen, eager to examine the Scriptures to test the teachings of the apostle to see if they were sound. We should follow the teaching of the Apostle Paul to Saint Timothy:

"All scripture is given by inspiration of God, and is profitable for doctrine, for reproof, for correction, for instruction in righteousness: that the man of God may be perfect, thoroughly furnished unto all good works.

"And if the new teachings do not agree with Holy Scripture, then no matter how good they might be, they are not of God. Think on these things, Brothers and Sisters."

Pastor Gruber led them through the conclusion of the sermon and into the conclusion of the order of service. Manfred didn't join in the responses or the chants or singing. His mind was whirling. This old man directly contradicted the work that Brother Caspar proclaimed! Yet this was the man that Gunther Achterhof had said was a good man, was even wise.

Manfred was confused. He remained standing at the rear of the nave, wrestling with his thoughts, as the congregation filed out of the church. He was oblivious, staring straight ahead, until someone spoke right beside him.

"Do you need some help, my son?"

Manfred jerked, startled, and looked down to see the cause of his confusion staring up at him with a gentle smile. "Ah . . . umm . . . no . . . I . . ." He broke off, flustered.

"It's all right, son. When everyone else has flooded out on their way to beer and sausage but one is left looking as if he is staring into the abyss, it's not hard to deduce that he may have a problem. If it would help to talk, I'm an accomplished listener." The pastor looked at him expectantly.

Manfred squared his shoulders. "Pastor Gruber?" At the older man's nod, he continued, "He told me you might be able to help me."

"And who would 'he' be?" Gruber shifted his Bible around to hold it before him with both hands at waist level. He looked like he was settling in for a long conversation.

"Gunther Achterhof."

One of Pastor Gruber's eyebrows rose. "My. That's a surprise. He doesn't often send people my direction. So, since he did send you to me, do I assume that your problem has something to do with faith and the Committees of Correspondence?" At Manfred's surprised look, the pastor chuckled. "Come now, son—what is your name, by the way?"

"Manfred Müller."

"Come now, Manfred, surely you don't think you're the first person to deal with that conflict? So many people feel that the Committees are a way to stand against the old regimes, a way to find a new way to govern and live, but at the same time, while some of them do walk away from the church because they feel that it's a tool of the aristocracy, some of them still have enough faith to stay with the church, if not the church hierarchy. And that, as you might imagine, can sometimes make for a feeling of being torn, or at least of being bent."

"I think I can understand that feeling," Manfred said. "So what do you say to people like that?"

"That God has never wanted blind faith or blind obedience. We are to study the Word for understanding, not for rote routine. God wants willing faith, accepting faith. He wants us to know not just what we believe, but why we believe it. We Lutherans, I think, do a better job of teaching that than the Catholics do, but even we still rely too much on authority in our teaching and guidance at times. Read your Bible, but ask the hard questions. God will not be angry with you. He delights in his people seeking Him, not in our just following the ruts because that's what everyone who came before us did."

Manfred blinked. That was not what he had expected. "Um, that's not what they taught us in catechism."

The elderly pastor smiled, his eyes twinkling. "Of course not. The catechism is designed to teach you the what, to ingrain it in you. Remember, that was written to lead people out of Catholicism and into the light of Martin Luther's teaching. But to create fulfilled people, that's not enough. You—we—need to know the why, as well. And you can't learn the why without asking the hard questions."

"Are you saying that to be fulfilled people we need to know everything there is to know about God?"

"No, no, no," Gruber said with a laugh, "not at all. If we knew everything there was to know about God, we would be God. But we need to know and understand what God revealed about Himself in His word. That's what He wants us to know about Him."

"And I can work with the Committees of Correspondence while at the same time seeking God?"

"Of course you can."

"What if they tell me to do something I think is wrong?"

"Then you have a decision to make," the pastor lost his smile. "Who do you serve? Christ himself said a man cannot serve two masters. But you can face that anywhere. Martin Luther did, as a monk serving the Pope. And when he finally faced that choice, he left the Catholic Church. You think he didn't feel unprepared for that? You think he wasn't asking God questions about why? I had a young man talking to me a few months ago about how his boss was telling him to do things in the bookkeeping that he knew were wrong. He was facing the same dilemma."

Pastor Gruber smiled again. "I know the Gospels frequently compare the church to sheep, and in some respects it is a fitting image. But in others, it is a bit unfortunate, because sheep are not very smart. I know—

I watched a few flocks in my youth, and sheep are silly creatures. But so are we people, at the bottom of it, so although it's not a flattering picture, perhaps it is appropriate after all. But we should not have the flock way of thinking. We shouldn't just go everywhere that the flock goes just because the flock is going. God gifted us with minds—I submit that He expects us to use them."

He shrugged. "Or at least, that's how this old pastor sees it. I suspect you might get some different answers from other pastors in Magdeburg."

Manfred sighed. "Thank, Pastor Gruber. You've given me much to think on."

The old man gave a rheumy chuckle. "Wasn't what you expected, eh?"

"No." Manfred's syllable was long and drawn out. "No, it wasn't. But, as you say, God has given us minds, so I suppose I need to use mine."

The pastor reached up and clapped him on the shoulder. "Remember to seek God. The rest will follow, I expect."

Manfred hoped so. He even prayed so.

CHAPTER 9

June 1636

It was Saturday night, and The Fisherhawk was rather full. Most of the shift change workers had funneled into the tavern that night. Manfred kept making the rounds, greeting regulars, cautioning the rowdy, helping Elsa deliver mugs when he could. And somehow it didn't surprise him that the well-dressed patron was back, sitting at what had become his usual Saturday night table, alone. Despite the crowd, so far no one was crowding into his table . . . at least, not intentionally. As full as the room was, and as large as some of the factory workers were, a certain amount of crowding was probably to be expected. But so far, the patron was not taking offense as people moved and shouted around him—was just sitting quietly and drinking beer after beer.

The evening progressed. A number of the workers started slipping out, but there was one table of men who were on their third or fourth round of beer, and were getting louder, but were not showing any sign of leaving yet. Manfred shook his head when Elsa brought their mugs back to the counter for Jacob to fill one more time. It looked like the rest of the evening was probably going to be louder and rowdier.

As it turned out, Manfred was an astute prophet. The last hour of service was indeed a lot louder than earlier in the evening, even though the number of bodies in the room was fewer than half what it had been. And as the loudness increased, so did the pushing and shoving and thumping of fists on table.

Manfred wasn't circulating any more. He was standing with his back to the counter, arms crossed on his chest, and a stern glower on his face. No smiles now. Now he wasn't the greeter and sometime host and server; now he was the peacekeeper, and anyone who looked at him could tell what would be coming if they roused him to action. And from the glances that came his way from some of the crowd, they knew it.

Unfortunately, there were a few who either didn't see Manfred or had had enough beer that they didn't care. Manfred could feel the level of tension rising, but he couldn't do anything until something broke. So he waited.

It broke in a moment. Suddenly two burly workers were on their feet, swinging wild punches at each other as they shouted drunken insults. Manfred moved in quickly. He sucker-punched one in the kidney and stomped hard on the other one's foot. As he did that, he heard, "What are you looking at?" from the other side of the table and a big crash, so he finished the fight he was in by grabbing each one by the back of the neck and slamming their heads together.

Leaving them to drop, he shouted, "Move!" then leapt to the top of the table and hurdled the patrons on the other side who tried to duck out of his way, coming down behind the man who was swinging at the solo patron. Manfred grabbed him by the shoulder, spun him around and buried his right fist in the worker's solar plexus. Struck breathless, the worker jack-knifed forward. Manfred dropped a fist like a hammer to the back of his neck, and the worker collapsed.

Manfred caught a glimpse of motion out of the corner of his left eye, and started to duck away. Consequently, the fist that would have slammed into his temple bounced off his cheekbone instead. He turned, grabbed the fist's owner by the back of the neck, and gifted him with three rapid blows in the center of the face, feeling the man's nose crunch under his fist.

He pushed the man back and spun to face the group again, fists up and ready. "Stop!" he yelled. Everyone at the table froze. "I've been nice so far," he snarled. "Next man who crosses me gets broken bones." Someone shifted position, and Manfred reached out and grabbed him by the jacket front. "Do I start with you?" At the man's frantic headshake, Manfred pushed him away. "Jacob!" he called out. "Anything broken?"

"Not that I can see," came the response.

"All right, then," Manfred returned his focus to the crowd. "Your night is done. Go home and sober up. Now. And take the bodies with you."

As they started shuffling toward the door, helping their hammered friends along, Manfred turned back to the last one he'd handled. "You . . . out."

The man's voice was muffled by his bloody hands pressed to his face. "You broke by dose."

Manfred snorted. "Be glad that's all I did. You can still work with a broken nose. If I'd broken your arm or hand, you'd be out of work and probably starve before you healed. Get out. And keep your blood off the floor."

He turned away as the man joined the tail of the crowd moving out and went over to help the other patron up from where he was sprawled on the floor. Placing his hands under the man's armpits, he hoisted him to his feet and steadied him until he seemed to have found his balance. "You all right?"

The patron wavered a little on his feet, but Manfred wasn't sure if that was from all the beer he'd drunk, from being hit on the head—he could see the red mark on the man's cheek—or both. He stayed near, just in case.

"I'm fine," the man said with great precision, then would have collapsed in a heap if Manfred hadn't grabbed his arm and guided him to a chair. Manfred looked at him for a moment, then looked over at the counter.

"Hey, Jacob."

"Ja?"

"I think I'd best take this guy home." He motioned at the patron. "He'll end up in the river if I don't."

Jacob peered at the patron, recognized him, and nodded approval.

Manfred went and grabbed his jacket from behind the counter. "I'll get my pay tomorrow. You owe me for two fights tonight."

"Two?" Jacob put some scorn into his response.

"Two." Manfred was firm. Jacob waved a hand, and Manfred grinned as he turned away and moved to where the patron was listing to one side, about to fall out of his chair. "Come along, my friend. We need to get you home."

He hoisted the patron to his feet and started him moving toward the door. "Home . . . good . . . bed . . . home . . ."

Manfred got the man out the door, closing it behind them. The cool fresh night air with its hint of moisture off the river seemed to deliver some energy to the patron, as he straightened up and pulled on the front of his jacket. "Home," he mumbled.

"Home," Manfred agreed. "Lead the way."

It took the patron a moment, but he finally stepped out. His pace wasn't fast, but his steps were solid and deliberate, so after a while Manfred let go of his arm and just walked closely beside the man. His steps traveled ever north and west, into part of the newest neighborhoods of Greater Magdeburg. Manfred followed, assuming that sooner or later the man would find his rooming house.

After traversing a couple of blocks, Manfred asked, "Hey, man, you've been at The Fisherhawk every Saturday night for the last several weeks. Why?"

The patron swiveled his head toward Manfred and mumbled, "Like the beer." After a few more steps, he added, "Like you, too. Keep it quiet . . . most nights. Get to watch people."

Watch the people? He came to the tavern just to watch the other patrons? He shook his head at that.

"Hey, what's your name? I can't keep calling you 'man', not after tonight." The man mumbled something, but Manfred didn't catch it. "Tell me that again."

"Berthold Schenk," the man said louder, pronouncing his name with precision.

"Ah. Well, nice to meet you and finally get your name, Berthold. I'm . . ."

"Manfred," Schenk interrupted. "Know. Heard it in the . . . place."

Manfred snorted at that. Yeah, as often as Schenk had been at The Fisherhawk, he'd probably heard his name, and more. "You come to watch people," he said, "and to drink beer. Is that all?"

"No." There was a long pause for several steps, then Schenk continued with, "Come to . . . forget." His voice dropped to where Manfred could barely hear it.

"Forget what?"

Another long pause. "Mother died," he finally mumbled, "after blizzard. Pneumonia."

"Ah." Manfred wished he hadn't asked that question. "Sorry, my friend."

"No. She was old . . . was already sick . . . just . . . her time. But . . . it hurts."

Manfred had no idea what to say to that, so he just walked in silence for the next block.

"So what do you do, Berthold," Manfred finally asked as the other man led him around a corner, "when you're not drinking beer and watching people?"

"Work for USE government." A more or less complete sentence. Manfred wondered if the cold air was sobering Schenk up.

"Who do you work for?"

Schenk turned his head toward Manfred and placed a forefinger before his lips. "Shh. Can't tell you. Secret."

That took Manfred by surprised. Secret? How could a mousy clerk know anything very secret?

"Well, what do you do?"

"Read papers. File papers. Know things."

"Huh. Sounds boring to me."

"Boring. Heh." Schenk snorted several chuckles. "Boring, huh? I . . ." He took a deep breath. "I know who put the bomb in the Freedom Arches."

That brought Manfred to a dead stop. "What?"

"Truth," Schenk said with a grin that trod a line between being sappy and sly.

"So who was it?"

Schenk shook his head. "Secret." He started walking again, still shaking his head. "Can't tell you."

Manfred was still struggling with what he thought he'd heard when Schenk turned and stepped up on a porch of a rather new looking rooming house."

"Home," Schenk announced with a smile. He knocked on the door several times, and in a moment an older porter opened the door.

"It's about time you got here, Berthold." He waved Berthold in, then looked at Manfred. "You need something?"

"No, I just came to make sure he got home okay. He had an awful lot of beer tonight."

The porter got a sad expression on his face. "Ja, he's been doing that."

"Well, tonight he also got a slap or hit to the head, so you might keep an eye on him."

The porter's expression turned anxious. "Thank you, then, for bringing him here. We'll take care of him." He shut the door without another word, leaving Manfred out in the dark, alone.

Manfred knew where he was, and knew that he wasn't far from his own rooming house. So, carefully not thinking about what he'd just heard, he made his way there. In his room, he stripped off his jacket, boots, shirt, and trousers. He spent more time than usual saying his evening prayers, then rolled himself in his blanket, pillowed his head on his arm, and reached for sleep.

Two hours later, he heard the cathedral clock chime, and he was still awake, mind racing furiously.

By David Carrico

CHAPTER 10

The next day was Sunday. After a night of fitful sleep, Manfred awoke with dry burning eyes, a sour stomach, and a throbbing in his head that he wasn't sure was physical or just the pressure of what he had learned the previous night or both.

Manfred hadn't planned on attending church services that morning, but when he awoke and saw that it was still early, he decided that he really needed to talk to Pastor Gruber. So he rose, washed his face, put on the cleanest of his clothes, and headed for Saint Jacob's Church at a trot.

The service was just beginning when he arrived. The congregation was light that morning, so there was plenty of room for Manfred to slip in and along the rear wall of the nave until he found a spot where he had a clear view of the chancel and the pulpit. The music was music—Manfred didn't usually pay much attention it; he definitely didn't this day. The scripture reading didn't penetrate his preoccupation either. It wasn't until Pastor Gruber came to the pulpit to deliver the homily that Manfred looked up, more or less to confirm that it was Pastor Gruber. Then he was back in his mental maelstrom, catching bits and pieces of the homily, but not enough of it to make any real sense.

The homily this week was short, even shorter than the previous homily Manfred had heard from the pastor. So he was caught a bit by surprise when the homily ended and the service moved into the concluding chants and songs. He crossed his arms on his chest and tapped a foot impatiently, waiting. Although it felt like an age, he knew it was only a few minutes before the congregation began to file out of the main doors of the nave. He continued to wait, clutching his arms to keep them still.

It was the work of moments before he could see the last of them leaving the nave and Pastor Gruber walking toward him.

"Manfred, is it? Good to see you again. Do you need something, or did you just drop by to gossip with an old pastor?"

There was definite humor in Gruber's voice, and Manfred felt his mouth respond to it by twitching its corners up into a bit of a grin.

"I am glad to see you," Manfred said, "but I do have something I need to talk to someone about, and you may be the wisest someone I know right now."

Gruber's eyes brightened, and there was a smile of his own on his face. "Well, I'll be happy to help, but if I'm the best counsel you've got, we need to introduce you to some wiser men."

Manfred waved a hand like he was clearing a table, and began. "Last night we had a good customer who was very drunk, so I walked him home to make sure he got there safely."

"God's blessing on your compassion and charity, Manfred." Gruber's expression had softened but his smile had grown.

"No, no, that's not what I want to talk about." He paused to try and bring order to his thoughts. "Okay, it is, a little bit. Anyway, I was walking this man home, and we were talking, and he started telling me that he works for the USE government here in Magdeburg, and that he can't tell me who he works for because it's secret, and he knows secret stuff."

The pastor's face had gone solemn. He said nothing, just nodded. Manfred continued.

"I didn't ask him, I swear, but then he told me one of those secrets. It wasn't a government thing . . . I don't think." Manfred shook his head. "But it is a secret about something that happened here in Magdeburg. And some other people want to know about it. They ought to know about it. They deserve to know about it. And I know something about it now, but it's not my secret. I want to tell it, but I don't know if it's right to tell a secret that I'm not even supposed to know and learned by accident."

Manfred looked at Pastor Gruber. His mouth was almost dust dry, and it felt as if his eyes were about to bug out of his head from the stress and tension.

Pastor Gruber was silent for long moments, looking down. Finally, he sighed and raised his gaze to meet Manfred's.

"Manfred, my son, I don't have a simple answer for you. There is no easy solution to your conundrum, I'm afraid. I can frame arguments supporting both sides, and there would be good and bad either way. But, having said that, having studied scripture for most of my life, I will say that God's way is truth. If you follow the way of truth, it will almost certainly turn out for the better than if you don't."

Manfred stared at the pastor, who stared back at him. For a moment he wanted to shout at Gruber for not giving him an easy pat answer. But he knew there wasn't an easy answer to this, so he shook his head.

"Thank you for listening to me, Pastor," Manfred said. "I'll have to work this out for myself, I guess. But truth needs to be part of it."

He nodded to the pastor, then turned and walked into the sunlight of the summer day.

By David Carrico

* * *

Manfred wasn't sure how long he'd been wandering, but from the look of the sun in the sky it had been for at least a couple of hours. Part of that time he had apparently been staring down into the cellar space of what he knew now was the bombed-out Freedom Arches building, because that was what he was doing when he became aware of where he was.

Despite the warmth of the sun on his back, Manfred shivered. To know for sure that the explosion wasn't an accident—that it was intentional—that someone had purposefully placed a major bomb in this building at a time when its eruption would kill people nauseated him. He swallowed, trying to keep the contents of his stomach in place.

Who would do that? Who would willingly, willfully, with deadly intent, explode a bomb in a building that really was nothing much more than a fancy eating place?

That thought horrified Manfred's heart enough, but the next question was even more appalling to him: Why? Over and over and over that refrain ran through his mind: Why? What were the Committees doing that inspired enough hatred to lead to this result?

On the battlefield, certainly. The damage and loss of life would be regrettable, but it was a part of warfare. But in a city? In the capital, at that? In a restaurant? Why would anyone want to destroy a building and kill thirty-seven people in doing so? It made no sense to Manfred. None at all. And the thought of the bodies . . .

He swallowed again and closed his eyes.

* * *

Dusk was lowering when Manfred entered The Fisherhawk. The crowd was light. He tossed his jacket behind the counter and leaned back against it.

"Where've you been?" Jacob asked.

"Church. Thinking."

"Thinking about church?" Jacob said with a chuckle.

"No. Just thinking."

"Speaking of thinking, I think you did a good job last night. Here."

Manfred turned around to see Jacob placing his pay from the day before on the counter top. From the look of it, Jacob had given him the bonus based on two altercations, so he nodded, scraped the money off the counter, and pushed it into his pocket.

"You ought to think about taking up fighting, you know." Manfred stared at him. "I'm serious. There's a couple of guys, an up-timer and a down-timer, who arrange fights between people who are good at fighting. The fighters get paid, but the winner gets paid a lot more than the loser. Makes for exciting fights, it does."

"How much?" Manfred asked.

"Depends on how good the fighters are and how well-known they are. The fighter who was the Magdeburg champion, Hans Metzger, won fifty thousand dollars in his last fight a few months ago."

That sum of money staggered Manfred. "Really? Just for fighting?"

"Yes, but he was the city's champion, and he fought the champion from Hannover. It was a big deal. Most fights go for two or three thousand."

Manfred thought about it, then shook his head.

"Why not?" Jacob pressed. "You'd be good at it."

"Maybe I would and maybe I wouldn't. But I wouldn't enjoy it, and if I won a lot I don't think I'd like myself a lot."

Jacob had to stop talking long enough to fill a customer's mug with beer, but he started back up as soon as he passed the mug over. "So what were you thinking about?"

"Things."

"Things like Hannelore Achterhof, I bet. I keep telling you, she's trying to hook you for the Committees."

"Ha."

Before Jacob could respond, several folks came in, which had him busy pulling mugs of beer. Before he was done, Hannelore Achterhof came through the door.

"Talk of the Devil . . ." Jacob said right behind him.

Manfred stopped himself from turning around. "Shhh!" he said with some force. Jacob didn't say anything else, but he could hear the other man's chuckle as he moved to the other end of the counter.

Hannelore looked around, taking her time. She finally moved toward Manfred. Turning, she leaned back against the bar with her elbows resting on it, mimicking Manfred's pose. "So, what are you looking at here?" she said.

"An easy night tonight," he replied. "Not much in the way of a crowd."

"I see that. What would you do if The Fisherhawk closed? Would that finally make you join the Committees?"

"Jacob says I should become a fighter, like some guy named Hans . . . something with an M."

"Metzger." She shook her head. "You're not mean enough to be good at that. It takes a pretty hard man to fight like that. On the other hand, Metzger is dead because of the fights, so you might want to rethink that idea anyway."

"Dead?"

"Jacob didn't tell you about his last fight?"

"Only that he won fifty thousand dollars."

"He wasn't supposed to win. Whoever arranged the fight had brought in a beast of a man from Hannover for the purpose of demolishing Metzger. Metzger still won, and that night found himself running from a pack of killers bent on revenge. They did take him down, but not before he left dead bodies all over town the next day. And he managed to get the money to his sister before he started running, who immediately put it in the hands of one of the wealthy patricians to manage for her, so they lost that as well. It was a big stink earlier in the year, but it's all played down now."

"Wow." Manfred trotted out his favorite up-time word.

"Ja. Like I said, you may be a tough man, but I don't think you're hard enough to do well as a fighter. Some of those guys are crazy."

"No, thanks." Manfred shook his head. "I can do the fight thing. I have to, to keep peace here. But I don't really enjoy it. And you're right. I may be crazy, but I'm not that crazy."

"Good."

They stared out at the slim crowd at the tables for a long moment. Hannelore finally turned to look at Manfred. "So, have you decided about the Committees yet?"

Manfred looked at her out of the corner of his eye. "Jacob says you've been trying to recruit me since that first day. He almost couldn't believe when a slight blush tinged her cheeks.

"And what if I was?" She stood up straight and turned to face him full-on. "You're a good man, Manfred. You're the kind of man the Committees need, the kind we wish we had more of. Whether you listen to me or to Gunther or to the guys who helped clean up the cellar, it doesn't matter."

"So you're not interested in me?" Manfred was teasing a little, but it dawned on him that he would really like to know the answer to that question.

Hannelore put her hands on her hips. "What, to bundle with, or to get married?" She spat on the floor. "Although I like you, I don't know you well enough yet for the first. And I damn sure aren't looking at you for a husband. Anyone I marry has got to be someone I respect as much as I respect my brother, and so far, I've met very few who even come close to his stature, much less match it. You're a good man. You show me you have integrity to match Gunther's, you show me you care about the truth the way he does, you show me you will take a stand on what is right. You show me that, Manfred. Then we can talk."

She turned back to face into the crowd, arms crossed on her chest. She hadn't kept her tone down, so some of the patrons were giving the two of them the eye. For that matter, Manfred heard Jacob's chuckle again from behind him.

Something Hannelore had just said resonated in Manfred's mind: " . . . you show me you care about the truth . . ." And that connected with something that Pastor Gruber had said: "God's way is truth." A feeling like a shock ran through him, and he felt a sensation of a click in his mind.

Manfred pushed away from the counter and stood up straight. "Where's Gunther right now?" he asked Hannelore.

She looked a bit started, but responded with "He should be at the downtown Freedom Arches. Why?"

"Take me to him. Please," he added after a moment.

Hannelore frowned at him, but at length nodded.

Manfred looked at Jacob. "I'll be back, but this is important." He didn't wait for a nod, but turned and headed for the door.

CHAPTER 11

Manfred was six steps down the street and building up speed when he heard, "Will you wait for me?" from behind him. He turned around and kept walking, to see Hannelore stretching her legs to try and catch up with him.

"Well, come on then," he said, slowing a little and reaching a hand to grab hers and yank her up beside him. Once there, he wrapped his left hand around her upper right arm and dragged her along until she was almost trotting to keep up.

Hannelore pulled at her arm. "What are you doing?"

"You want to see integrity? You want to see truth? Then you keep up." He hustled her up the street to the bridge across the Big Ditch that fed into the Gustavstrasse. Once they crossed the bridge and were inside the Old Magdeburg walls he slowed a little bit, which made it a little less strenuous for Hannelore to match his stride.

"What are you talking about?" Hannelore panted.

"Keep up. I'm only telling this once."

Manfred slowed his pace more as they were within ten yards of the door to the Freedom Arches. Once there, he opened the door, let her enter first, then followed. Inside, he looked around. He saw Ernst and Wilhelm and gave them a nod just as Hannelore started across the floor to a small table at the far end of the room that was slightly separated from the others. He followed her, to end up facing Gunther and another man, both of whom looked a bit annoyed at their appearing at the table.

Gunther frowned at Hannelore. She just jerked a thumb at Manfred and said, "He says it's very important."

Gunther took that in, then looked up at Manfred. "Well?"

"Is there a private room?" Manfred asked in a low tone. "I don't think you're going to want to let this be public right this moment."

Gunther's frown deepened, but he stood up, as did the other man. "Right. This way."

He led the way to the back of the common area, through a door and down a short hallway, and into a small room with a half dozen chairs and a small secretary in one corner. Manfred followed everyone into the room and closed the door.

Gunther turned and faced the two of them with his arms across his chest, face hard and expression boding thunder and lightning. He looked first at Hannelore. "I'll deal with you later." He switched his gaze to Manfred. "What is so important?" Manfred looked at the other man, and Gunther snapped, "He's with me, he'll learn about it immediately, so save us all some time and get on with it."

Manfred took a deep breath. "It wasn't an accident. It was a bomb."

The others froze. The silence in the room seemed to last an age. At length, Gunther seemed to break loose. "The Freedom Arches explosion, I take you to mean?"

Manfred nodded.

Gunther's face turned to iron, his eyes closed, and his hands fisted. Manfred saw that, and saw the slight tremor in the other's hands, and realized that he was now in the presence of the Gunther of the legends, the Gunther of the retributions. That thought made him nervous.

Manfred watched as Gunther's nostrils flared as air poured in and out of them. It wasn't until that breathing slowed down and the tension in Gunther's body eased a bit that the other man spoke.

"How do you know this?"

Manfred looked at the man in silence. He had Gunther's assurance the man needed to know, but that didn't mean he wanted to be questioned by him.

"Heh." Gunther cleared his throat as he looked up. "Time for introductions. This," he pointed to Manfred, "is Manfred Müller, of whom we have spoken. Manfred," he pointed at the other man, "this is none other than Joachim von Thierbach, also known as Spartacus. Answer his questions, if you would."

"Ah, we have a good customer at The Fisherhawk who one night a couple of nights ago got really drunk—drunk enough that I decided to walk him home to make sure he got there safely."

"Must be a good customer," Spartacus murmured with a smile. Manfred paused. "Sorry," Spartacus waved a hand, "carry on."

"We got to talking about what he did. He told me he works for the USE government, but he wouldn't say what department. Said it was 'secret.' He said he read papers, filed papers, and knew things. I said it sounded boring. He said he knew who put the bomb in the Arches."

Both men stiffened.

"He said that?" Spartacus demanded.

"What exactly did he say?" came from Gunther.

Manfred closed his eyes, and thought. "His exact words were 'I know who put the bomb in the Freedom Arches.'"

"Confirmation," Gunther growled. His hands flexed.

"Of a sort," Spartacus replied in a hard tone. "Nothing we can take to a judge, though. And I'm not sure we want the Polizei involved in this yet."

Gunther's mouth worked, but he nodded.

"I think we want to take this next door," Spartacus said.

"A moment," Gunther said. He pointed a finger at his sister. "Not a word. Not to anyone. You don't say anything about this to anyone if Spartacus or I aren't there."

Hannelore, stunned expression still in place, nodded vigorously.

"Good. Let's go."

Manfred followed the others out of the room and back through the building to the outside door. He noted Ernst and Wilhelm in the common room as they passed through, both of whom had quizzical expressions on their faces, no doubt because of the company he was keeping. He nodded to them, but kept up with Hannelore, treading right behind her.

A few moments later he was entering the Committees of Correspondence headquarters building for the first time. There was a small open foyer inside the door which was faced by a desk with a young man seated behind it.

"Esaias," Spartacus said, "is the first floor meeting room available?"

The young man looked down at a large page under a sheet of glass. "Yes, it is, for the rest of the evening."

"Good. Check it out to me, if you would."

While the young man picked up a grease pencil and wrote on the glass, Spartacus turned to Gunther's sister. "Hannelore, would you go locate Ingrid and tell her I need her to bring her USE government book to the meeting room as soon as possible."

Hannelore said nothing, merely nodded and went up the nearby staircase two at a time.

"Come," Spartacus said. Manfred followed them through a door and down another short hall, entering into a largish room with a long rectangular table in it and fourteen chairs around it. It wasn't fancy furniture—no ornate carvings or embellishments—but it appeared solid and well-made.

Spartacus took the chair at the near end of the table and pointed from Manfred to the chair at his right. "Sit, if you would." Gunter took the chair to his left and sat at the same time.

"So, while we're waiting, Gunther has told me much about you."

Manfred swallowed. "Not much to tell."

"On the contrary, you came to Magdeburg from the congregation of that Brother Caspar fellow, did you not? With instructions to learn some things for him?"

Manfred felt his face pale, and he nodded spasmodically.

Spartacus smiled a little. "Relax, Manfred. We were already aware of your Brother Caspar, and all you've done is made us keep a stronger eye on him."

"He's a good man, a good pastor," Manfred managed to get out.

Spartacus pursed his lips for a moment. "I know that you believe that, as do the people in his congregation. But belief in something doesn't make it so, I'm afraid."

"I wasn't sent to spy," Manfred said. "I just tell Ed . . . my friend about things I see and hear." He was starting to get defensive.

Spartacus shrugged. "No, you don't spy. And nothing you've done is wrong. But what are we to think of a pastor who sends out teams from his congregation to enter other worship houses on the Sabbath and disrupt their worship services with accusations of heresy? What are we to think of a pastor who directs his men to harass street preachers and even push them around or hit them? Hmm?"

"He wouldn't . . . ." Manfred felt a sick feeling in the pit of his stomach.

"I can show you police reports from Grantville, if you'd like."

Before Manfred could react, the door to the meeting room opened, and a short gray-haired woman carrying a large ledger book entered, followed by Hannelore.

"Ah, Ingrid, just in time. Take a seat, both of you. Ingrid, this young man is Manfred Müller."

"Ah, the young man who felt the ruins of the uptown Arches was an insult. Good to meet you, Manfred." Ingrid took a seat beside him, while Hannelore went around to the other side and seated herself beside her brother.

"Manfred," Spartacus said, "what is the name of the man you were telling us about?"

Manfred pulled himself together and sat up straight. "Berthold . . . Berthold Schenk."

Spartacus looked to Ingrid. "This man has said he works for the USE Government. Can you tell us if he in fact does, and if so, which department or group he is in?"

Ingrid opened her ledger book on the table top and began flipping pages. "S . . . S . . . S . . . here we are." She started running her finger down the page. "Schenck . . . Schenk . . . Schenk . . . Schenck, Abraham . . . here we are, Schenck, Berthold." She ran her finger across the page, and read whatever was on the page with her brows furrowed. Looking up, she said, "According to this, he works in the Treasury Department, in the Archives group." She closed the book. "You need anything else? Because if not, I need to get my report done and signed and on your desk before I go home."

"No, thank you, Ingrid." Spartacus gave a smooth gesture toward the door.

Once the door closed behind Ingrid, Spartacus looked to Manfred. "What did this Schenck fellow say that he did for the USE government?"

"He said his work was secret, and he couldn't talk about it. But like I said earlier, when I asked him what he did, he said," Manfred closed his eyes again as he reached for the words, "'Read papers. File papers. Know things.'"

"That would describe an archivist," Spartacus said drily.

After a moment, Gunther said, in a tone like a hammer hitting steel, "So, if this guy is real, what do we do? We have thirty-seven of our own calling for justice."

"We need more information," Spartacus said, "enough that we can either confront the government or present the case to a judge."

"Can we work with the Polizei to get it?" Gunther's face was dour, as if he expected the answer.

Spartacus shook his head. "I don't think so. We want this kept confidential until we can approach the government or a judge. Talking to the Polizei will undoubtedly set the word free of what we are looking for. No, we need a copy of whatever this Schenck person has seen." He paused, then looked directly at Manfred. "He doesn't know us. We need you to talk to him."

"He doesn't know me, either," Manfred protested.

"He knows you more than he knows anyone here or in the Committees," Spartacus snapped. "We need you to talk to him and try to convince him to bring us a copy of what he saw."

Manfred looked around and saw three sets of eyes, in faces varying from stern to impassioned to pleading, all fixed on him. "I . . ." In his turmoil, he couldn't figure out what to say.

After a pause, Gunther tapped gently on the tabletop a few times, then said, "We need justice for our people. What good are we if we can't get that? If you help us with this, we will owe you. *I* will owe you. And I never forget my debts."

Manfred looked at the expression on Gunther's face. It was hard, but not enraged. That gave him a bit of comfort. The thought of Gunther being angry with him was not one that he wanted to consider.

"I'll . . . try," he finally said. "But I won't lie to him, and I won't threaten him."

Spartacus leaned forward. "Be very convincing, Manfred. We really need this."

"I said I'll try." There was a little iron in Manfred's voice now.

"That's all we can ask." Spartacus didn't look happy, but he had sat back in his chair, and seemed to be willing to accept that. "How long until you see him again?"

"He only comes on Saturday nights," Manfred said. "So it probably won't be until next Saturday."

"Today's Sunday. Almost a week before you see him again?" That was Gunther, with a bit of a frown.

Manfred shrugged. "That's when he comes. Unless you want me to try go to his rooming house . . ."

"No," Spartacus said. "There's probably no one watching him, but let's not take chances. We've gone this long, we can wait a few more days."

CHAPTER 12

Manfred had to explain to Jacob why he had left that evening. Fortunately, an explanation that Gunther needed something was enough to mollify the tavern keeper enough to not give him much grief. He did dock his pay for the time gone, however. He was a tavern keeper, after all.

The rest of the week seemed to crawl along. The evening shifts were pretty busy after shift change, though, so that helped keep Manfred occupied. But when he went to his room at nights, time slowed down again, and more than one night he spent a fair amount of time staring up in the dark, unable to sleep. His nightly prayers included pleas for the days to pass quickly and for sleep to overtake him sooner.

Neither seemed to help.

Saturday finally arrived with a rainstorm. It wasn't a thunderstorm, just a constant mild level of rain falling—enough to drop the temperatures down to borderline chilly and get his jacket pretty wet when he walked to the tavern. He hung his jacket on a hook near the fire to try dry it some.

Manfred spent part of the day bringing the stock room up to his usual level of organization, then made sure that Elsa had what she needed in the kitchen. After that, he leaned on the counter and talked to Jacob as he tended to the customers who came and went during the afternoon. As shift change approached, Manfred started to get a little nervous. Berthold never arrived until after shift change, but he had been here for every Saturday night for several months now. Manfred expected him to follow that pattern, but he was afraid that luck would change and something would keep Berthold from coming.

The door slammed open, and the first group of workers stormed in, shouting, "Beer!" at the top of their lungs. Was it going to be one of those nights?

The first group was followed by several more, and in very short order the common room was filled with workers, talking and gossiping at the tops of their voices. Elsa and Jacob were kept busy keeping mugs filled, and Manfred was walking his routine pattern around the room, going by every table every few minutes in a slow walk. He hadn't seen Berthold come in, but when he walked by his table the first time, he was sitting there, drinking his first beer.

Relief washed over Manfred. Since he knew Berthold was here now, his concern faded. He would approach Berthold in the middle of the evening, after the initial surge of customers and orders were done and before they'd had enough beer to start feeling rowdy.

As he finished his third circuit of the room, Manfred looked over to see Hannelore coming through the door. That caught him off guard, but then he realized it shouldn't have. Of course Spartacus and Gunther were going to want a witness, and of course it couldn't be either one of them. They were just too prominent. The presence of either would have changed the atmosphere in the room, and if Berthold was sensitive to that it might have scared him off. So Hannelore was the only other choice, because she was one of the few who knew what was going on, and she wasn't as publicly well known as the men.

Manfred went and stood back to the bar, as he was wont to do, and stared out over the crowd, checking the behavior and noise and activity.

Hannelore moved to the bar and ordered a mug of beer from Jacob, facing in while Manfred faced out.

"Is he here?" she murmured.

"Yes," Manfred turned slightly toward her and whispered.

"Have you talked to him yet?"

"No. I'm about to. You stay here and watch."

He did one more scan around the room, then started his next round, this time stopping at every table to clap people on the back, chaffer with them, and laugh at their jokes. At one table there was an empty chair, and he dropped down in it and told a couple of jokes of his own, leaving them laughing uproariously. By the time he got to Berthold's table, it was no surprise to anyone when he dropped down into the empty chair on the other side and leaned forward a little bit. Berthold reflexively leaned toward him.

"How are you, Berthold?"

"Good. Why do you ask?"

"Well, you were very drunk and looked a little bruised when I walked you home last Saturday."

"Huh. Was that you? The porter said someone had brought me home, but I don't really remember it."

"Ja, it was me. You're a good faithful customer, and like I said, you were very drunk, so we made sure you got home safely."

"Well, thank you." Berthold lifted his mug to Manfred, and took a sip.

"You talked while we were walking. Told me all about your job, how you're an archivist for the USE Treasury, and how you read papers, and file papers, and know things." Berthold had set his mug on the table and was looking a little uneasy by the end of that second sentence. He turned white at Manfred's next words. "Then you told me you knew who placed the bomb in the Freedom Arches."

Berthold was absolutely still. He seemed not to be breathing. Manfred held still as well, not wanting to startle him into flight.

"I . . . I . . . I was drunk," Berthold muttered. "I didn't know what I was saying. You can't take the drunken ramblings of a grieving man to mean anything."

"Well, maybe so," Manfred said softly. "But you seemed to be very certain that you knew that, and it is the kind of thing an archivist would know, isn't it? You are an archivist, aren't you?"

A long pause, then, "How much do you want?" Berthold's tone was bitter. "I don't have a lot of money, but I can probably come up with something to buy your silence."

"Oh, money isn't what's needed." Manfred had to dance his words around to avoid telling Berthold that several people knew of this secret. "I need you to make a copy of the report or document that tells about what happened."

"I can't do that!" Berthold's tone got a little louder, and Manfred held up his hand to forestall him further speech.

"The thing is, the government has kept that a secret," Manfred maintained his soft tone, "and there are people who deserve to know the truth about it."

"I don't care! I can't do this!" The last word hissed coming out of Berthold's mouth.

Manfred took a deep breath. "I need you to meet someone. Don't leave, or I will take you down."

He stood, leaving Berthold huddled behind his mug at his table. He moved to the bar long enough to whisper, "Come with me," to Hannelore, then retraced his circuit to Berthold's table, where he gestured at the empty chair. Hannelore seated herself and placed her mug on the table.

"Berthold, this is Hannelore. Hannelore, this is Berthold." Manfred was still speaking in his soft tone.

"Berthold, thirty-seven people died in the explosion in the Freedom Arches that night. Thirty. Seven. Men. And. Women. Mothers and fathers, some of them, leaving orphans behind. Sisters and brothers, some of them, leaving siblings grieving. Sons and daughters, all of them, some leaving grieving parents behind. And Hannelore knew every one of them. They were all close friends, and it is only by the grace of God that she wasn't there with them. But she is here now, and they are not. And just as you grieve for your dead mother, she grieves for her dead friends—her thirty-seven dead friends. And she doesn't know what happened, or why, or how, and that makes her grief that much stronger. Can you understand that, Berthold?"

Manfred saw tears trickling down Hannelore's face, and he saw that Berthold's own face was now covered with a stricken expression. After a moment, he asked the question again.

"Can you understand that, Berthold?"

Berthold looked down to where his white-knuckled hands were clutching his mug. He said nothing, just nodded his head. "Do you see why she wants that paper, Berthold? If it was your mother who had been blown up, wouldn't you want to know how and what and why?"

Berthold nodded again, and looked up with eyes gleaming with moisture. "All right," he said, his voice husky. "All right. I'll do it. But it's going to take me some time, because it's four pages, and I'll only be able to copy a little bit at a time, maybe not even every day. I'm not going to lose my job for this, so you'll wait until I'm done. I'll bring it here. It will take at least a week, more likely two, so don't get anxious, and stay away from me otherwise. All right?"

"Sure, Berthold," Manfred said as a feeling of relief poured into him. "Whatever you say."

"Whatever I say," Berthold said. "Now go away and leave me alone."

"I'm leaving now. Hannelore, give it a couple of minutes."

Manfred resumed his circuit, and before long Hannelore returned to the bar. No one in the common room throng seemed to be paying any attention to her. He guessed they thought she was either a casual acquaintance of Berthold or maybe was a prostitute who failed to connect with a possible client. Regardless, it seemed to have gone well, even though it had left him feeling exhausted.

The next time Manfred completed his circuit around the room, Hannelore was standing at the counter. He leaned back against the counter next to her. "You bastard," she said quietly. "Did you have to do it that way?"

Manfred shrugged. "It was the only way I could think of that might get through to him. And it worked."

"That's the only reason I didn't hit you. It worked."

After a moment, Manfred asked, "Were those real honest tears, or can you produce them when you want to?"

"What? You think I can cry at a moment's whim?" She turned a sardonic grin on him.

He shrugged again. "I knew a girl in my catechism class who could cry at a moment's notice. It was almost like turning a spigot. She could stop just as quickly. So . . ."

"So you asked." Hannelore turned to face out like he was. "Yes, I can do that, too. A surprising number of girls can. Not so many boys, but then, they probably don't get the acceptance or expectation that girls get. But to answer the question you really asked, yes, they were real. Bastard."

"I'm sorry." And he was, Manfred discovered. Sorry to have plumbed her heart and to have awakened her grief.

"Don't be. It needed to be said, and it accomplished its goal. And in the end, it was true." After a moment of silence, Hannelore continued with, "You wouldn't think it to look at you, but you have a way with words, Manfred. I think I'm a little jealous."

That caught Manfred off-guard. Him?

"Umm, I'm just a common laborer from Jena. I'm no speaker."

"Not in the statesman or preacher ranks, no. But you see people where they are, and you can speak truth to them where they are. Spartacus can do that. I can a little bit. You're already better than I am, and you might be as good as Spartacus one day." She concluded with, "You are a dangerous man, Manfred Müller. I'm glad I know you."

Manfred didn't know how to respond to that, so he pushed off on his next circuit of the room. He noted that Berthold was still there, but he didn't say anything to him.

The rest of the evening was eventless, if not exactly quiet. At its close, Manfred watched as the crowd rose and left in a short wave. He did manage to catch sight of Berthold slipping out between two groups of workers. The man was elusive, no doubt about it.

When the last of the customers walked out the door, Manfred looked at Hannelore. "You need something?"

"Just to talk to you on the way back to our rooms."

He looked at Jacob, who counted out his pay and tossed him his jacket. Gathering that up, Manfred followed her out the door.

"Talk about what?" he said after they had moved several steps down the street.

"So I tell Spartacus and Gunther that you got Berthold to agree to copy the document, and that it will be at least a week, maybe two, or possibly more before we see it. Right?"

"I believe so," Manfred said.

"Good."

They walked together in silence. After another block or so, Manfred looked at Hannelore. "Did you really mean what you said?"

She looked back at him, and he could see her smile in the moonlight. "About what?"

"That I'm a dangerous man."

She stopped, which brought him to a halt, too. "Yes, I meant it," she said

He shook his head. "I've never considered myself dangerous. I don't even like to hit people."

Hannelore laughed. "Oh, the people you've had to chastise in The Fisherhawk might have a different opinion." She laughed again, then sobered quickly. "You see things that other people don't see. You take on burdens that aren't yours, in order to see right done. You do what you say you will do. You speak truth, even when it's not to your advantage." She tilted her head, then lifted her hand and jabbed his chest with a hard forefinger. "You are the most dangerous kind of man, a man of integrity who will speak truth to anyone."

She dropped her hand and started walking again. Manfred fell in beside her.

"I'm no different from anyone else," he said. "Not special, not dangerous, not rich or powerful. Just a strong back and a pair of strong hands, trying to get by."

This time it was just a chuckle. "You can tell yourself that. But that's part of what makes you dangerous, Manfred. You don't think you're special, but you're going to do what you think is right no matter what. Every time I meet you I learn something new about you. Every time I see you, you do something that impresses me. And yes, you are a man of integrity. Which is why now, more than ever, I want you to join the Committees of Correspondence. We need men like you. We need *you*, in particular."

She stopped at a corner. "This is where I turn off for our rooms. Good night, Manfred, and thanks for everything you've done and everything you're going to do."

He lifted a hand in farewell as she turned, said nothing, but just watched as she walked away until she disappeared into the shadows.

By David Carrico

CHAPTER 13.

July 1636

The next days moved slowly, at least as far as Manfred was concerned. He got up each morning, bought a barley roll for his breakfast, spent each morning and early afternoon working at The Fisherhawk, then spent the evening watching the common room at the tavern, ending with evening prayers and bed. Each day was like the one before it. It didn't help any that he saw no one from the CoC. He didn't expect Spartacus, but both Gunther and Hannelore avoided the tavern as well.

Day followed day, with the July 4th events on Friday providing some excitement. The tavern was very full and very joyful that night, with many of the local CoC and Fourth of July party members celebrating. Manfred was really glad when the evening finally ended.

Saturday finally arrived. Manfred cautioned himself against expecting too much, but he still was expectant when the evening crowd arrived. He didn't see Berthold until after he started his first round through the tables. After he spotted Berthold sitting in his usual chair, he snorted and decided he would start calling Berthold 'Shadow' because he seemed to be able to slip in and slip away like one.

As he approached that table for the first time, Manfred raised the eyebrow that was away from the crowd. For a moment, Berthold did nothing, leaving Manfred to wonder if he hadn't been seen, but then Berthold moved his head to the left a couple of inches and back again. Manfred gave no response, just continued walking as disappointment welled up. He caustically reminded himself that Berthold had told them it would probably be at least two weeks. He finished his round, spent a few minutes by the counter as he usually did, then began again.

Nothing remarkable happened in the tavern that night. He left the tavern after collecting his pay, a bit frustrated with what hadn't happened, only to find that tonight of all nights Edwulf was waiting for him outside.

"Manfred," his friend said, pushing off from the front wall of the tavern and falling in beside him. "Any news to report? Anything noteworthy to send to Brother Caspar?"

Manfred shook his head. "I'm continuing to talk with the Committees of Correspondence folk that I've met."

"Folk? Not just men?"

"No, Edwulf. They involve their women members in everything—remember Gretchen Richter—so you have to expect to talk to women. As it happens, one of those women is the sister of Gunther Achterhof."

Edwulf sucked in his breath, apparently impressed. "You've made more and better contacts than any of the others."

"How many others?" That question suddenly intrigued Manfred.

"Umm . . . four." After the hesitation, Manfred was sure the number was larger, but he didn't challenge Edwulf. "Do you have anything else to share?"

"Not really," Manfred replied. "The broadsheets and flyers probably tell you more than I know. Even though we are friendly acquaintances, they don't talk to outsiders about their business."

"Hmmph." Edwulf sounded disappointed. "I was hoping you had something to share."

"Why? None of the others come up with anything?"

"Mmph."

Manfred took that for a "No" and smiled a little in the darkness.

Before long they parted ways, and Manfred made the rest of his way home, still a bit frustrated. Just as with all the preceding nights in the week, he said his prayers and went to bed, hoping he would sleep better than the previous nights.

Sunday was different because he went to St. Jacob's church. When he saw that the preacher was not Pastor Gruber but was a younger man, probably a deacon or an assistant pastor from one of the other churches, he slipped out of the church, glad that he had stood near the door.

That week passed the same as the previous week. If anything, it felt like it lasted longer. And no sign of Berthold during the week at all—not that Manfred expected any. But he was glad to wake up on Saturday. He felt almost like he'd had some *branntwein*, not enough to make him really drunk but enough to loosen his grip on himself. He found himself chuckling now and again during the day for no good reason.

He was standing by the bar when the workers came in off of shift change. It was a large group, if not one that filled the room and left people bumping elbows every time they lifted their mugs. That was fine with him. It made it easier to make his round.

And once again, Berthold snuck in without Manfred spotting him. It was a good thing he wasn't a pickpocket. He could steal the whole room blind.

Having ignored Berthold on his first two circuits, Manfred started his third round with his usual back-slapping, joke-swapping, laughing at other people's jokes approach. And as usual, by the time he got to Berthold's table, no one was watching him. He caught Berthold's eye as he turned the corner around the last table he had stopped at. Berthold gave him a very slight nod, and Manfred's heart began beating a little faster. He bent over Berthold and clapped him on the left shoulder with his right hand, then dropped it.

"This it?" Manfred whispered.

"Yes." The other man slipped his left hand under his jacket and pulled out a packet, hidden by the tabletop, and slid it across his lap and over to rest under Manfred's right hand.

"Good. Our thanks." Manfred took the packet, which was small enough to nestle in the palm of his hand, and carried it with him as he finished the round and went back to stand by the counter for a few minutes. He turned to face Jacob, and seeing that the tavern keeper was turned around himself reaching for a bottle on the back counter, he stuck the packet inside the left side of his vest, then brushed at his front.

Turning back around, Manfred managed not to take a big sigh, but the relief that he felt should have been pouring off of him like beer from a pitcher, which made him chuckle. He let himself relax at the bar for a couple of minutes, then pushed away for his next round.

He did two more rounds before Jacob called time, and the crowd began leaving. He watched for Berthold, but took his eye off the door for just a moment, and when he looked back Berthold's table was empty and he wasn't in sight. How did he do that?

The last of the crowd trying to leave seemed to stumble at the door, then were pushed back by none other than Gunther Achterhof, followed by Hannelore. As the last of the muttering patrons exited, Gunther walked up to Manfred.

"Well?"

Manfred took the packet from inside his vest and handed it to Gunther. Gunther looked down at it for a moment, then closed his hand on it. He turned and headed for the door. Hannelore paused to throw a smile at Manfred.

"Hey! You coming?"

Manfred looked up to see Gunther staring at him from the open doorway. He pointed at his chest. "Me?"

"Yes, you. You want to see what this is all about or not?"

Manfred looked to Jacob, who waved a hand. "Go on, I'll hold your pay until tomorrow."

Manfred hustled himself over to the doorway, which was clear by the time he got through it. Three more fast steps and he had caught up and fell in beside Gunther, with Hannelore on the other side.

"I owe you for this," Gunther said, repeating his words from their discussion a couple of weeks earlier. "Regardless of what it says, I owe you. And I remember my debts."

Manfred said nothing. The rest of their walk passed in silence. Gunther had set a fast pace, and they arrived at the CoC headquarters building before long. They passed through the outer door, and Gunther led the way to the same meeting room they had used previously, where they found Spartacus waiting, tapping his fingers on the tabletop. They took the same chairs they had used the previous time.

Spartacus looked at each of them in turn. "Well?"

Gunther pulled the packet out of his pocket and handed it over. Spartacus turned it around in his hands several times. "I'm surprised you didn't open it and read it right away," he said, a bit of humor sounding in his voice.

In the daylight, the packet was revealed to be a smallish envelope, thick with pages. Gunther pulled a knife out of his other pocket which he flicked with his wrist to pop a long slender blade out. He passed that to Spartacus to use for opening the letter, then looked to Manfred, whose expression of interest had caught his attention.

"It's called a gravity knife," Gunther explained as Spartacus slit open the envelope and returned the knife to Gunther. "An up-time design. Have you heard of switchblades?"

"I think so," Manfred replied. "Push a button and a spring forces the knife out of the handle?"

"Yes. Like that, only without the spring." He showed Manfred the button to hold down, then flicked his wrist to open it up again.

By that time, Spartacus had unfolded the papers and finished reading the first page. He gave a dry chuckle. "Your friend is actually very smart," he said to Manfred. "Listen to this:

"To whoever receives this: I copied this using standard Magdeburg merchant hand, so I strongly doubt anyone will be able to identify me from it. Still, I ask you to keep my name from your mouths, so that I will be able to keep my job."

"Smart man," Gunther said. "It's just the four of us and Ingrid who know the name." He looked around. "We will keep silent." His voice was hard. Manfred had no trouble at all resolving to lock Berthold's name behind his teeth.

Spartacus was reading through the first page. As he finished each page, he passed it to Gunther, who passed them to Hannelore, who passed them to Manfred. It took some time for everyone to read them, particularly Manfred, who wasn't the most skilled reader around.

"So," Spartacus said, "the good news, if there is any in this whole affair, is that the attack was not against the Committees as a whole. It wasn't against us as an organization. It was a targeted revenge attack against Christoph Brockmann for a battle he led a company in during the Krystallnacht campaigns. Not the only attempt at revenge we've seen, but the only one that succeeded to that extent, and so bloodily."

"We'll have no revenge of our own," Gunther said in a controlled tone. Manfred could see his hands clasped together tightly on the table before him. "The man who ordered the bombing is already dead."

"Klaus von Bülow," Spartacus said. "Pity, that. As are all of his officers. The only one from that side who seems to still be breathing is this . . . Mads Bendtsen."

"But according to this, he's the one who actually built the bomb," Manfred offered, a bit tentatively. He wasn't sure he had a voice in the discussion. He wasn't really a member of the CoC.

"True," Spartacus said. "That makes him a tool."

"A tool that killed thirty-seven of our brothers and sisters and customers," Gunther grated, his hands twisting.

"Also true. Reading this," Spartacus replied, "this is now a governmental matter. I think we need to have a discussion with a wider group."

Manfred shifted positions uncomfortably. Spartacus looked at him and lifted his eyebrows. "Umm . . ." Manfred said, "just remember . . ."

"Not to mention the name Berthold Schenck," Spartacus said with a slight smile. "No, Manfred, that remains with the three of us . . . four, counting Ingrid."

He gathered the papers before him, and looked around. "I'll keep these for tonight. Hannelore, have they taught you how to use the new typewriter yet?"

"No." She shook her head.

"You should learn, but no time for that now. How good is your handwriting?"

"Not as good as that," she pointed at the papers, "but pretty good."

"So you could make some clean copies of this?"

"I think so."

"Good. We need to keep this among ourselves for a little while, so tomorrow tell whoever you would have been working with that you're working on something for me and meet me here. I've already blocked the whole day out. We'll sit in here together and make three or four copies. And you," he said, looking at Manfred, "thank you for your help with this. We will keep you involved as things go along, but I think it's going to take a little time to pull this next bit together, so don't be surprised if you don't hear about anything for a while."

CHAPTER 14

Late July 1636

It was a Friday morning when Hannelore burst into The Fisherhawk without warning.

"Manfred! Spartacus sent me to get you. He wants you at the headquarters as soon as you can get there!"

Fortunately, no customers were there at the moment. The last of the early morning patrons were gone, and the mid-morning crowd hadn't started showing up yet. Manfred looked at Jacob, who waved a hand.

"I don't want to know. Go. Just be here for shift change." Manfred grabbed his jacket and headed out the door with Hannelore on his heels.

"What is so urgent?" Manfred asked as they trotted up the street.

"I don't know," Hannelore panted. "He just called me down and sent me out with the message."

Manfred saved his breath and stepped up the pace a little bit, making sure that Hannelore was keeping up. It wasn't long before he pulled up before the headquarters building. He was starting to pant a bit himself by then, so he waited until Hannelore's breathing slowed down some before he pulled the door open and ushered her in.

"He's to see Spartacus," Hannelore told the young man at the desk, who nodded and pointed to the meeting room they had used before. A moment later, they were in that room, looking at Spartacus and Gunther.

"Good," Spartacus said, "you're here. Thank you for coming so quickly. Now, we're waiting on one more person. Once he's here, we can start." He gestured at the table. "Please, be seated. Hannelore, you sit beside me, Manfred, beside her."

Spartacus took the end seat, as usual. Hannelore sat to his left, with Manfred perforce to her left. The chair to Spartacus' right was left empty, and Gunther sat beyond it. That took Manfred aback. Who was coming that Gunther would give that precedence to?

It seemed longer than it actually was, Manfred was sure, but before too long the door opened and admitted a man who was an obvious up-timer. Manfred wasn't sure exactly why he knew that. Oh, part of it was the clothes and the so-called baseball cap he swept off his head as he came in the door. But part of it was probably just the way he carried himself. He was about the same height as Spartacus, maybe a bit taller. His thick hair was cut short in one of the common up-time styles, mostly gray with some brownish threads. Wrinkles around his eyes and the fact that his hairline had obviously receded a bit showed that he was older than Manfred might have otherwise expected. He'd heard that the up-timers usually looked younger than their real ages. It looked like it was true.

Spartacus stood as soon as the open door revealed the up-timer. Manfred and Hannelore took their cue from that. Gunther was a little bit slower in rising, but even he was standing by the time the up-timer turned from shutting the door.

"Spartacus! Gunther!" the up-timer said jovially. By that time he was at the table, so he shook hands with both of them, then tossed his cap on the table and sat down, followed by the others. "Who are these two young folks?"

That surprised Manfred. He'd expected to be ignored in this meeting.

"My sister Hannelore," Gunther made the introductions, "and our young friend Manfred Müller. Hannelore, Manfred, this is Ed Piazza."

That revelation took Manfred's breath away. It was exciting to be in the same room as a real up-timer, but to be sitting across the table from the President of the State of Thuringia-Franconia, who also happened to be the man who would probably be elected the next Prime Minister of the USE. He had to sit on his hands to keep from squirming.

"Hannelore, Manfred," Ed said with a nod. "Nice to meet you."

"They've both been involved in the circumstances of developing the information we're going to share with you now," Spartacus said smoothly. "Manfred, in fact, was instrumental in acquiring it."

"You called this meeting," Ed looked at Spartacus. "What's up?"

"This is." Spartacus passed a copy of the document Berthold had given them to Ed. His eyebrows rose, but he picked up the document and began reading.

Ed's eyebrows lowered to a frown very quickly. By the end of the first page his eyes had tightened and his lips were drawn into a very thin line. He read through the four pages once, then started at the beginning and read them through again. When he finished reading it, he laid it on the tabletop before him. The eyes of the others were all fixed on him as he took a deep breath.

"Well." Ed tapped a finger on the document. "I won't ask how you got this, but I assume you are satisfied with the truthfulness of it."

"Everything we've been able to check out agrees with it," Gunther said.

"I'm not surprised." There was a short pause. "This explains a lot. I never bought the idea that it was a gas leak explosion. It just didn't make much sense, given the circumstances. So this is more logical."

He looked around at them. "Have you talked to an attorney about this?"

"No," Spartacus replied. "We wanted to talk to you first."

"And you've kept it quiet otherwise?"

Spartacus nodded.

"Good." Ed steepled his hands before his face and tapped his index fingers against his lips a couple of times, then lowered them to rest on top of the document. "This is a real can of worms, make no mistake."

Manfred frowned a little. Can of worms? What was that? The up-timer was making no sense.

Ed saw his expression, and smiled a bit. "That means it's a real mess, Manfred. Like worms tied into a ball."

Manfred's frown cleared, and he nodded.

"So," Ed began, "I think part of the problem is going to be that the crimes were committed in Magdeburg and should be—should have been—judged under the laws of either Magdeburg the city or the laws of the Imperial City of Magdeburg in its status as a province. But the federal government of the USE got involved because the perpetrator of the crime, this Klaus von Bülow, was also involved in the federal crime of counterfeiting. So you've got multiple crimes and multiple jurisdictions. Problem number one.

"Problem number two is that Bülow, his main ally, and most of his supporters were killed in the action that concluded the counterfeiting investigation. So you have no recourse there, and no way to get justice. Most courts won't prosecute a dead man."

"But the bomber is still alive." Gunther's tone was grating.

"And that's problem number three: this . . ." Ed turned the document over and leafed through the pages, "Mads Bendtsen, the guy who made the bomb, was pardoned by the USE government for his role in the whole affair because he provided knowledge and evidence that helped close down the counterfeiters."

"So the man who blew up thirty-seven of our fellows and customers is still breathing and walking around in the sunlight," Gunther grated. "That's not right."

"No, it's not. But you've lived long enough to know that sometimes what's right and what's legal isn't the same thing."

The expression that was on Gunther's face was hard and cold. Manfred was glad he was across the table.

Ed sighed. "Look, believe me, I do understand what you're feeling. And with a good lawyer—this new guy Wulff, maybe—you might be able to bring a case to the Supreme Court that argues that the USE government overstepped its bounds with that pardon. But that's the legalities of it, and that's probably iffy at best.

"I'm more pissed off that they didn't tell anyone. They didn't tell you, they didn't tell the families of those that died, and they didn't bother to inform the members of Parliament who should have been informed out of courtesy, if nothing else. I get they were concerned about the Danish connection, but they could have downplayed that and still told everyone what happened."

Ed picked the pages back up. "Before we do anything else, I'm going to get in this Balthasar von Brunne's face about why Parliament wasn't informed and why you were not informed. If I can get a face-to-face with him, are you available?"

"For this, any time, any place." Spartacus' face was almost as hard as Gunther's. Almost.

"Good." He lifted up the pages. "Can I take this with me?"

"If you'll keep them confidential. We haven't broken the news yet to our people. We want as much resolution as we can get before then."

"Understood." Ed stood and picked up his cap and put it on his head. "Well, I need to go call in some favors and yank some chains. I'll let you know when I get something scheduled."

"Send word here." Spartacus stood to shake hands, followed by Gunther.

Manfred stood uncertainly, followed by Hannelore. Ed waved a hand at them. "Nice to meet you." A moment later he was out the door, and they all sat again.

Manfred felt exhausted. "Are all the up-timers like that?" he asked.

"Not all."

"I hoped for more," Spartacus admitted, "but as he says, it is a real can of worms. We'll just have to see what he can pull from the government, if anything."

"This will not go well with our people if Bendtsen continues to walk free." Gunther's face was still hard. "Not well at all."

"I know."

They all sat there and contemplated that thought.

CHAPTER 15

August 1636

"**M**anfred!"

Hannelore was developing a habit of loudly bursting in the door of The Fisherhawk, Manfred thought as he turned to face her after placing several mugs on the counter. "Let me guess," he said. "Spartacus wants to see me now."

"No, not right now," Hannelore replied with a smile. "But he does want you at the main doors to the palace when the Dom clock strikes one chime after noon. Ed has got the meeting together."

"Understood," Manfred said. "I'll be there."

"Good. See you there." She spun and was back out the door in an instant.

"Do I want to know what this is about?" Jacob asked dryly.

"Not at the moment, but it will probably be common knowledge soon."

"And will that mean you'll stop leaving the tavern at odd hours?"

"I think so." Manfred grinned. "No promises, though."

"Good. Elsa needs a ham in the kitchen. See to it."

"Done." And Manfred headed for the stock room to put actions to words.

❋ ❋ ❋

The Dom clock sounded its chime as Manfred trotted up the steps to the palace to join Spartacus, Gunther, Hannelore, and Ed Piazza.

"Good, you're all here." Ed nodded to the nearest guard, who opened the door for them. "Let's go."

They gathered inside the door as a footman approached Ed. "May I be of service?"

"Ed Piazza and associates. We have an appointment with Balthasar von Brunne."

"This way, if you please." The footman led them down the hall, up some stairs to the second floor, and down that hall to an open doorway. "Herr Brunne," he announced as he entered the doorway, "here are Herr Ed Piazza and his associates." He didn't quite sniff as Manfred brought up the tail end of the procession, withdrawing and closing the door behind him.

"Ed! Good to see you." Brunne stood and held his hand out over his desk.

Ed reached across to shake it. "Good to see you, too, Balthasar."

"Please, all of you, be seated. There are enough chairs."

Ed took the center chair facing the desk flanked by Spartacus and Gunther. Hannelore took a side chair against the wall near the desk. Manfred took a chair that was against the back wall. He didn't want to attract attention, and hoped he could avoid notice if he sat away from the others.

The smile left Brunne's face. "All right, Ed, I recognize Spartacus, so I assume the others are with the Committees."

"Correct. This is Gunther Achterhof." he nodded that direction.

"Ah, the formidable Gunther Achterhof," Brunne said. "I am glad to finally get to meet you. And the others?"

"The young woman is Gunther's sister Hannelore Achterhof," a gesture toward her, "and the young man is Manfred Müller from Jena." Manfred started. He didn't remember telling Ed where he was from. He must have gotten it from one of the others.

"They are all involved in one way or another with what I need to talk to you about, so I wanted them here to hear what was said," Ed concluded.

"Pleased to meet you as well," Brunne said. "Now, what is on your mind, Ed?"

Ed reached inside his jacket, and drew a couple of very white pages folded lengthwise from his pocket. "We recently got a copy of this. And we have some concerns, needless to say." He rose enough to hand it across the desk, then resumed his seat.

Brunne was obviously a well-educated man, for he read much faster than Manfred. He reached the bottom of the pages well before Manfred would have.

The official laid the pages down on his desk, closed his eyes, and pinched the bridge of his nose with his right hand. "Congratulations," he said. "I think you may have managed the leak of a government secret in record time. I had hoped we would make it a couple of years before this leaked out. Oh, and well done," he said, dropping his hand and opening his eyes, "to have it typed up so I have no clue as to who copied it out. Very sneaky, Ed."

"Thank you." Ed grinned at him.

Brunne straightened in his chair. "Very well. I'll not attempt to deny it. What do you want?"

Ed sobered. "There are at least three issues. First, why was this not made known to the opposition in Parliament? This is a big enough deal that we should have been told about it."

"Ed, the political ramifications were too sensitive. We had to hush the Danish angle to keep King Christian from becoming more of a problem than he is."

"You still should have told the leadership."

"Oh, come now, Ed. Your own people use the expression 'Three can keep a secret if two are dead.' We needed to keep this quiet for as long as possible. Not that we appear to have managed that very well," Brunne concluded, with a sour look on his face.

"You should have told the leadership," Ed said, leaning forward. "Your turn is coming to be the opposition. If you want to be informed then, you have to play the game by the same rules."

Brunne sat still for several moments, then nodded with some reluctance. "All right, Ed, I understand your point. It's too late to fix that, obviously. Sorry. So what else are you concerned about?"

"Second issue: your whole handling of this and not sharing information with the Magdeburg authorities means you preempted their entire justice system."

Brunne snorted. "What justice? Brunne and his allies and most of his soldiers were killed. There's no one to hold accountable there. And the counterfeiting had nothing to do with the city."

"I'll grant you the counterfeiting was a federal crime," Ed said, leaning forward again, "but the bombing was a major crime of property destruction and manslaughter, at least, if not murder. The mayor and Polizei should have been informed about what you found out about who did the crime and that the main perpetrator was dead. Mayor Gericke is not going to be happy when he hears about this, and he's on a first name basis with the emperor."

Brunne sighed. "Ed, I can't argue with that. But the emperor wasn't here and the decision was made above me to try and keep the whole thing secret to protect the Danish exposure. In hindsight, we probably should have told them as soon as we knew. But we didn't. I'm sorry. If something like this happens again, I'll try to get it done right."

Ed nodded. "You'd better. It won't do you any good if you get the reputation for withholding information."

Brunne simply nodded in return.

"Third issue." Ed made a palm up gesture toward Spartacus. Manfred could see Brunne stiffen a bit.

"Herr Brunne," there was a bit of a bite in Spartacus' use of the title, "that bomb killed thirty-seven people in that Freedom Arches, most of whom were members of the Committees of Correspondence. By what right did the government pardon their murderer, the man who made and placed the bomb, and allow him to go free?"

Sitting behind everyone, Manfred could see everyone stiffen, including Brunne. Both Spartacus and Gunther were leaning forward slightly. They almost looked like mastiffs about to pounce.

Brunne folded his hands together on his desk and looked down for a moment. When he looked up, his face was drawn.

"Whether you believe it or not, that thought has cost me sleep at night. That decision was not made by me, and to some extent the government's hand was forced by then-Colonel Lillie. He promised Bendtsen his freedom if Bendtsen would give him all the information he had about Bülow and his operations. That information was critical to Lillie in his efforts to track, trap, and ultimately capture Bülow, although Bülow died in the capture attempt. Given the success of the operation, the government felt it had no choice but to honor the colonel's promise and let him go."

"Thereby denying our dead the justice they deserve, to see their murderer hang," Gunther growled.

"I understand how you feel . . ."

"Don't patronize us, Herr Brunne," Gunther interrupted. "Unless and until you've been on the sharp end of the stick, until it's been your family and friends lying broken and bleeding, until you've had to go into a ruin and pick up the pieces of their bodies and seen smashed heads and ruined faces, you don't know. You don't understand. You can't. So spare us your mealy-mouthed platitudes. You and your government have disrespected and ignored and trod upon the rights of our dead, the very people you're supposed to be representing. You're no better than the *Hochadel*. And you wonder why we resent you and don't trust you."

Gunther's voice had been like a hammer clanging on iron, and after he finished, there was a long silence, finally broken by Brunne.

"What do you want from me?" His face was sad, his voice was tired and low.

"We want you to make this knowledge public," Spartacus said evenly, "and we want you to revoke the pardon given to Mads Bendtsen."

"As to the first," Brunne said, "if you will release the news, I think the government will not deny it. If you will keep the Danish angle out of the story, I think I can get them to confirm it.

"As to the second, after the story is published, I will raise the issue with the government. I cannot guarantee that they will do that. Actually, I'm not sure they legally can, and if you think about it, I'm not sure you want that precedent being established. I'm sorry, but that's the best I can do."

Ed looked at Spartacus and Gunther. After a moment, Spartacus nodded. It was a much longer moment before Gunther gave an infinitesimal nod. "Deal. But if you're going to let the Committees break the news, you'd best brief the opposition and Mayor Gericke tomorrow. You really don't want them finding out from the newspapers and broadsheets."

Brunne grimaced. "You are right." He looked at Spartacus. "Can you wait until the day after tomorrow to release it?"

Spartacus nodded. "It will take us that long to get it printed up anyway."

Brunne nodded in return.

Ed stood, which brought the others to their feet as well. "Sorry to ruin your afternoon, Balthasar, but you know how it is. Thanks for listening to us and working with us." He held his hand out across the desk, and Brunne shook it again.

"I do," the official said. "I do, indeed. Goodbye, Ed."

And with that, they were done. Manfred found himself following the others through the door and retracing their steps until they were outside. Ed led them down the steps and out into Hans Richter Plaza, where they could stand together but not have anyone close.

Ed looked at Manfred and grinned for a moment. "How does it feel to have been a fly on the wall of a secret meeting? That's something to tell your grandchildren."

"I'll have to have some first," Manfred muttered, which sparked chuckles from everyone else, even Hannelore.

Ed sobered and continued, "We got what I hoped to get. We really didn't have a chance at the pardon, unless you want to spend a lot of money in the courts. But that's okay, really. Here's what you're going to do instead."

He lowered his voice and spent several moments explaining. By the time he was done, there were identical evil grins on everyone's faces, even Manfred's.

By David Carrico

CHAPTER 16

August 1636
General Axel Gustafsson Lillie's headquarters

General Lillie looked up from the report he'd been reading as the door to his office opened to admit his bodyguard, Sergeant Jon Joakimsson, who had a sour look on his face. Lillie pushed back in his chair. The sergeant's expression did not bode well.

"These came in the mail pouch from Magdeburg," the sergeant said, holding out a couple of pages.

Lillie took the pages with his one hand and set them down on the desk. There was one broadsheet and one poster of broadsheet size. He read the broadsheet first. By the time he got done he was swearing under his breath. He looked up.

"Obviously written by the Committees of Correspondence."

"Ja. Other than their digs at the government, they seem to have told it pretty straight."

"Reasonably so," Lillie agreed. "I suspect they somehow got their hands on the government report. Interesting that they left out the counterfeiting problem and the Danish involvement, though."

By David Carrico

Joakimsson shook his head. "They wouldn't be concerned about that so much."

Lillie put the broadsheet down and picked up the poster. In bold letters it said:

WANTED
MADS BENDTSEN
FOR MURDER, ATTEMPTED MURDER, AND
ARSON
IN MAGDEBURG
REWARD of $10,000
DEAD OR ALIVE
CONTACT YOUR LOCAL
COMMITTEES OF CORRESPONDENCE OFFICE
IF YOU HAVE INFORMATION
LAST SEEEN IN THE VICINITY OF STRALSUND

Lillie whistled. "Ten thousand dollars. I believe the Committees are serious about this."

Joakimsson nodded. "I believe they're seriously pissed."

"I do believe you're right."

Lillie gathered the two pages in his hand and handed them to the sergeant.

"Send these to our friend with a note that we didn't tell them."

Joakimsson nodded again. "And it might be a good idea to tell the men to walk wary around the CoC for a while."

"Wouldn't hurt," Lillie agreed.

The sergeant turned and left the room. Lillie returned to his report, muttering, "I wish Sergeant Falkenhayn would learn to spell."

Magdeburg

Manfred looked up as the door to The Fisherhawk opened. He smiled when he saw it was Hannelore.

"Spartacus hasn't called another meeting, has he?" he asked.

Hannelore shook her head. "No. I'm not here on his business. I'm here on yours."

Manfred tilted his head at that, puzzled. He didn't think he had any business with Hannelore.

"Can we go sit down?" she asked.

"Sure." Manfred led the way to Berthold's small table, which was away from the few table occupied by the early afternoon patrons. They settled into the chairs facing each other, and he looked at her. "What business of mine are you concerned about?"

She obviously hesitated, then said, "I overheard Gunther and Spartacus talking. They've gotten a report from Grantville. Apparently your Brother Caspar caused a sixteen year-old girl to be kidnapped, and he beat her when she wouldn't agree to marry him."

Manfred was stunned. He couldn't believe what he was hearing. But Hannelore continued speaking.

"Some folks from Neustatter's European Security Service rescued her, and Caspar was apparently shot. He's alive," Hannelore hurried to say as Manfred jerked in shock, "but the report says he's disappeared from Grantville."

Manfred shook his head, unable at first to gather all that in. He looked up. "Are . . . are you sure?"

Hannelore nodded. "They sent copies of the police reports, apparently. It's official and documented."

"Wow." Manfred was shocked. For all that he had begun to have some doubts about Brother Caspar, he had never expected this. Wow, indeed.

The door opened again, this time to admit Gunther. He looked around, and when he spotted Hannelore he headed their way. He hooked a chair out from under another table with his foot and sat down between them, making the small table feel very crowded.

"Well, I came here to tell you something," Gunther said, "but I suspect you already know."

"Brother Caspar?" Manfred said. Gunther nodded. "Yes, I know." He shook his head.

"Not news you wanted to hear, I'm sure," Gunther said. "And no offense, but I believe I told you when we first met something about being careful about putting your trust in men."

"That's no consolation," Manfred muttered, looking away.

"Sorry." Gunther didn't sound sorry at all; just rather matter-of-fact.

As his whirling thoughts began to slow and coalesce, Manfred found himself facing a choice he'd been putting off for some time. Now it was in his face, and this news forced him to decide. He looked up.

"You also told me some time ago you wanted me to join the Committees. Were you serious?"

Gunther nodded.

Manfred sighed. "All right. I'll do it. And I'm going to stop reporting to Brother Caspar. I've been feeling like I belonged already, anyway."

Smiles broke out on the Achterhof faces across the table. Gunther clapped him on the shoulder, and said, "We've been thinking of you as one of our own after everything you've done in the last few months." He chuckled. "There's an up-time expression, Manfred . . . 'If the shoe fits, wear it.' You're just admitting what everyone around you has already known. Welcome."

DRAMATIS PERSONAE

Achterhof, Gunther   Down-timer, Committees of Correspondence Magdeburg leader, hardcase
Achterhof, Hannelore   Down-timer, Gunther's sister
Achterhof, Ludwig   Down-timer, Gunther's cousin
Achterhof, Ludwig   Down-timer, Gunther's cousin
Bauhof, Caspar   Down-timer, pastor creating a cult
Beierschmitt, Fritz   Down-timer, CoC associate of Gunther, brother of Heinz
Beierschmitt, Heinz   Down-timer, CoC associate of Gunther, brother of Fritz
Brenner, Otto   Down-timer, operative for NESS
Brunne, Balthasar von   Down-timer, deputy secretary of the USE Treasury
Burroughs, Kathy Sue   Up-timer, homemaker, and women's Bible study teacher
Büsinck, Ernst   Down-timer, CoC member
Chieske, Byron   Up-timer, Polizei detective, Marla's brother-in-law
Eckoldtin, Anna   Down-timer, Casparite
Engelsbergin, Marta   Down-timer, Anabaptist who befriends Marike
Eschbach, Johann   Down-timer, Casparite who befriends Dirck and later spies on Marike
Flock, Wilhelm   Down-timer, CoC member

By David Carrico

Gendt, Dirck	Down-timer, Anabaptist refugee from Holland, Marike's half-brother
Gendt, Marike	Down-timer, Anabaptist refugee from Holland, Dirck's half-sister
Green, Al	Up-timer, Baptist pastor and teacher
Gruber, Moritz	Down-timer, retired Lutheran pastor, serving as part-time pastor at St. Jacob's Church
Haan, Elsa	Down-timer, server/cook at The Fisherhawk
Hoch, Gotthilf	Down-timer, Polizei inspector
Honister, Karl	Down-timer, Polizei sergeant
Ingenfrits, Anna Maria	Down-timer, Catholic, Bible study attendee
Joakimsson, Jon	Down-timer, sergeant, Lillie's bodyguard
Kellarmännin, Barbara	Down-timer, Anabaptist who befriends Marike
Kircher, Elizabet	Down-timer, Manfred's landlady
Klein, Edwulf	Down-timer, Casparite
Kuhlmann, Ingrid	Down-timer, CoC member
Lillie, Axel Gustafsson	Down-timer, Swedish general
Linder, Marla	Up-timer, musician, wife of Franz Sylwester
Meisner, Johann	Down-timer, father of Katharina Meisnerin
Meisnerin, Katharina	Down-timer, Anabaptist who befriends Marike
Müller, Manfred	Down-timer, from Jena, Casparite
Neustatter, Edgar	Down-timer, owner/operator for NESS
Peltzer, Kaspar	Down-timer, Polizei sergeant
Piazza, Ed	Up-timer, President of the State of Thuringia-Franconia, leader among the Fourth of July Party
Ramsenthalerin, Amalia	Down-timer, Lutheran who befriends Marike
Rice, Alicia	Up-timer, Methodist, Bible study attendee
Richards, Press	Up-timer, Grantville police chief
Rimpler, Magdalena	Down-timer, Catholic, Bible study attendee

Rusche, Anna	Down-timer, server at Walcha's Coffee House, married to Georg Walcha
Schäfer, Jacob	Down-timer, owner/host of The Fisherhawk
Schäubin, Astrid	Down-timer, team leader for NESS
Schenk, Berthold	Down-timer, clerk in the USE Department of the Treasury
Schlotheim, Rosina	Down-timer, Lutheran, Bible study attendee
Schneider, Wilhelm	Down-timer, pawnbroker and fence of stolen goods
Sylwester, Franz	Down-timer, musician, husband of Marla Linder
Thierbach, Joachim von	Down-timer, a/k/a Spartacus, CoC leader
Tralles, Karl	Down-timer, musician/guitarist from Hamburg, befriended by Franz and Marla
Vogel, Matthäus	Down-timer, Brother Caspar's chief assistant

Printed in Great Britain
by Amazon